TAKING ON LUCINDA

A Kent Stephenson Thriller

FRANK MARTORANA

$\mathcal{V}_\mathcal{V}$

VinChaRo Ventures

Taking On Lucinda
Copyright 2018 by Francis S. Martorana

VinChaRo Ventures
3300 Judd Road
Cazenovia, NY 13035

vincharo.ventures@gmail.com

*This book is a work of fiction. Names, characters, places, and inci-
dents either are the products of the author's imagination or are used
fictitiously, and any resemblance to actual events or persons, living or
dead, is entirely coincidental.*

ISBN: 978-0-99893-260-6 (print)
ISBN: 978-0-99893-261-3
Library of Congress Control Number: 2017914877

Cover designed and illustrated by Amanda and
Sebastian Martorana
Sebastianworks.com

Author photo by Rosemary C. Martorana

Printed in the United States of America

Dedicated to the memory of

Fredrick M. Holmes, DVM
1932–1994

Fred was the essence of all things good
in veterinary medicine.
He was my friend, teacher, mentor, and partner
for seventeen years.

ACKNOWLEDGMENTS

Over the years that it took to write this series, countless clients, friends, and acquaintances, close and casual, have contributed when, often unbeknownst to them, I picked their brains. I can't possibly name them all without embarrassing errors of omission, so I won't try, but I do thank them all deeply.

There are some I just have to give special acknowledgment because they contributed so much and in ways that, if they had not, this book would never have been written, much less published. Thanks to Garda Parker, Rhoda Lerman, and S. V. Martorana, all three world-class authors, for neither laughing nor rolling their eyes when they first read my manuscripts. Thanks to Alicia Bazan-Jemenez, Sylvia Bakker-Moss, Deborah Fallon, Mark Andrews, Felicia Lalomia, Andy Olson, and Jeannine Gallo for assorted advice and technical support. Marlene Westcott, you are truly the Word Wizard. Sebastian and Amanda Martorana, what you did with the covers is amazing. Rosemary Martorana, you get special thanks for always smiling and showing great patience while solving my many logistics issues.

Last, but never least, there is my wife, Ann Marie. I don't know how you put up with me through it all, honey, but I'm sure glad you do.

CHAPTER 1

Fall 1982

CHIEF MERRILL STEPHENSON SNATCHED HIS police report out of the typewriter, studied it, and realized with a grin that this was something he should show to the kids around town. They were always complaining that nothing ever happened in Jefferson. Their little upstate burg was totally boring. *Why do we even have policemen anyway?* Probably most of their parents agreed too.

Well, here you go, folks. BIG-CITY ANIMAL RIGHTS ACTIVISTS INVADE JEFFERSON. That wouldn't make a bad headline.

He scanned the document, admiring his deceptively neutral tone:

> *At 0900 hours today, a complaint was received from Stephanie Copithorn, CEO, Copithorn Research, Re: Trespassers. Upon arrival, investigation, and discussion with Ms. Copithorn, the trespassers were identified as twenty-three members of FOAM (Freedom of Animals Movement), an animal rights group based in Hollywood, CA (see attached list of names and addresses). Their purpose: To protest Copithorn Research's use of animals to test cosmetics. Since they were not interfering with operations at Copithorn, CEO Copithorn agreed to allow the*

protest to continue if they remained peaceful and agreed to restrict their presence to a designated area of lawn and parking area.

Merrill tossed the paper on his desk, stretched back, and then sank low in his chair, using the mountain of paperwork to shield himself from other members of the force strolling past his window. He closed his eyes and let his mind drift. Life was good…just enough agitation in town to keep things interesting.

His report sounded neutral, but Stef Copithorn sure as hell hadn't been. A faint smile of admiration for the savvy corporate boss played on his lips. She wanted the sons of bitches out of there just as fast as it could happen, but she was too clever to let them know that. She had been blindsided. She wasn't going to let a gut reaction limit her options.

"Let the bastards stand in the rain for a day or two, Merrill," she'd told him when they'd met in her office. "We'll see what that does for their self-righteousness."

The two of them came up with a quick strategy to corral the demonstration and agreed to let Merrill do the talking. The protesters never got a glimpse of Stef.

His eyes drifted then fixed in a dreamy stare through the window out into the main room of the station house. Two uniformed officers, one male and one female, chatted and joked. Sipped coffee. They half studied a memo he had posted describing new firearms recertification requirements. A protest rally? It would be a nice change for his little force, a break from the humdrum DWIs, domestics, vandalism, and traffic stuff.

He hadn't been back at the station for more than an hour when Stef called again. This time, the voice of Jefferson's foremost employer didn't have its usual self-assuredness. Merrill released a soft groan. A powerful citizen on edge was never a good thing for the head cop. So much for a nice change in Jefferson.

"I made a few phone calls," she said. "I underestimated this FOAM group. It's no two-bit bunch of college kids. They've got a ton of Hollywood celebrity backing. Major bucks. Professional PR. And lately, they've decided to move away from their usual attacks on meat producers." Her next words came out as more of a curse than a statement. "Their new plan is to focus on lab animal use. Especially cosmetics."

"Any history of violence?"

"Depends on what you call violence. They're definitely disruptive. That's violence, isn't it? From what I've been able to find out real quick, they are wizards with the media. They can turn public sentiment against us, pressure suppliers to refuse to sell to us. That sort of thing."

"For how long?"

"Who knows? But even a few days of bad press could cripple my company for a long time."

Merrill absorbed the new twist. Jefferson could not afford to let anybody or anything endanger its number one job source.

"You want me to head back over and boot them out?"

"No." There was a thought-filled pause. "At least not yet. I want you to get Kent involved."

The resentment needle rose in Merrill's head to the *almost angry* mark. "Meaning?"

"Meaning we need somebody on our side who the public holds as a champion of animals, like your brother."

"I'd wait for the dust to settle a little."

"It may turn out to be ashes, not dust that settles. We need him."

They batted that around for a while. Finally, he agreed to see what his brother thought of the whole thing. After all, Kent was the veterinarian, the animal expert, wasn't he? He should know about humaniacs. Hell, they'd probably fall for his humble keeper-of-God's-beasts routine just like most everyone else.

Merrill reached onto his desk and pulled the incident report back off the stack of files. Scanned it again. Suddenly, it seemed to carry more weight.

Back in high school, he had hated all the peace and quiet in Jefferson and its boring congeniality toward all, just like the town kids did these days. It was the reason he had left. But a stint in Vietnam firebases and a cop tour in that hellhole known as the Big Apple had woken him up just before the last drop of human dignity was bled from his veins. Now it was what he liked about Jefferson. He liked unlocked doors, grocery boys who carried out bags with a smile, and boredom.

He ran his fingers over the chief insignia on his dark-blue uniform. He'd been the top guy for eight years now. Really, as chief in Jefferson, he was just another patrolman, except he got the paperwork. He didn't mind. He got his own office, even if it was barely big enough for his desk, a file cabinet, and one chair.

He brushed a hand over his midsection. The buttons of his uniform shirt were pulled tight. Somehow his once impressive upper body had settled to pillowy softness around his waist. That was a drawback of the slow pace—at least that was his excuse. He was still in his forties, he could turn that around.

He pushed himself to his feet. He'd kill two birds with one stone. He needed a chance to think about Stef Copithorn and the protesters. And Kent.

He marched through the lobby of the station and made a broad display of tossing the keys to his cruiser on the duty officer's desk. "Janet, I'm taking a walk to see what's cooking around town. I'll be back in a couple of hours."

She nodded as if playing make-believe with a child. "Uh-huh." She'd worked with Merrill a dozen years. She knew how long the walking would last.

He ignored her. Tapped his belt radio. "Any problems, you know how to get me."

The gusting fall wind made him push hard to open the heavy door of the station's entrance. For two breaths, he reconsidered the wisdom of walking. Then he felt Janet's eyes on his back and pushed even harder. At least last night's rain had stopped. Besides, this was the first, but it wouldn't be the last storm of the season. Was he going to do this weight-loss thing or not?

The wind hissed in the leafless trees. He flipped up the collar of his blue flight jacket.

Out of habit, he turned and admired the circa-1940 station house that he loved as if it were his home. Limestone, Greek revival. Police headquarters downstairs, town clerk and village court on the second floor, and a wing off the east side with three large bays for the volunteer fire company. It had been erected just before he was born, but it would be there long after he died.

He turned back to his walk, dodging a skateboarder who breezed by. Shoulders back, knees relaxed, a young Mick Jagger. Mad cool. Iridescent blue wheels sent a rooster tail off the wet sidewalk.

The boy drawled a mix of humor and sarcasm. "Mornin', Officer Stephenson."

"Nathan, I'm swinging by the school in ten minutes. I swear, if I don't see you there, I'm kicking your butt."

Nathan waved over his shoulder. No reply.

Merrill watched him glide away. Blew a short laugh out his nose. No way would the kid be there.

He hadn't taken a dozen steps when his radio sounded.

"Damn. I can't even get to the street."

He keyed the receiver's button.

"Chief, you better get back in here. Lalomia, from County, is on the line. He says it's urgent."

He trudged back into the station and hung up his jacket before taking the phone.

"Mike. What's up?"

He expected the Dewitt county sheriff's usual upbeat voice—loud, clipped, like the winning quarterback during a postgame interview. But today, Merrill couldn't decide if the voice at the other end sounded more like his old high school principal or a priest. His policeman's sense of dread kicked in.

"Merrill, a call came in this morning for a body in a car out at Cuyler Lake. We just confirmed the ID. It's Aaron Whitmore. I figured I'd give you a call because he was a friend—"

Merrill didn't let him finish. "Aaron Whitmore?"

He threw a glance out his window to see if his shocked reply had made it through his open office door. Janet spoke into her phone and jotted notes, as usual.

"It's definitely Whitmore."

"How? When? Wait. Never mind. Where are you now?"

"At my office, but I'm about to head back over."

"I'll be there in fifteen minutes."

"No need for lights. Take your time."

"Fifteen minutes. Or less."

Merrill patted his pocket and headed out the door, retrieving his keys from Janet.

It started to rain again as Merrill headed for Cuyler Lake. Nervous little rivulets trickled down his windows. He rubbed them with the back of his hand, smearing the condensation into streaks. He peered through it at the landscape. In town, he passed Copithorn Research. If he hadn't been driving, he might have genuflected before the altar of the town's prosperity. Then he was out into the mix of hardwood forests and small farms that made up the vast landscape of upstate New York. Cuyler Lake was only ten miles from the village, but it might as well have been in a thousand square mile tract of wilderness. That's why Aaron Whitmore had chosen to build his cabin there, three quarters of a mile from the boat launch around the unblemished shoreline. Aaron liked to hunt and fish. And he liked solitude.

The boat launch's design was a credit to the new Jimmy Carter environmentalism wave. It was a buildingless patch of macadam, totally incongruous with the rest of the primitive lakeshore. There were half a dozen parking spots designed to accommodate vehicles with boat trailers. A concrete ramp with deep grooves molded into it for traction descended into the water. A bumper-high, single-rail fence made of used telephone poles ran the perimeter. Aaron's Land Rover was parked so that its back bumper was almost against the heavy rail.

The lot was jammed with official vehicles parked at all angles, the way cops like to do. Merrill pulled over on the shoulder of the road and walked in. A skinny boy Merrill guessed to be about six raced up to him. Tugged at his hand. His flyaway yellow hair whipped in the wind. Large brown eyes above his pinched nose radiated his excitement. He reminded Merrill of a Pekingese he'd seen at Kent's animal hospital.

"The body's over there!" the boy said, all pride, not the least distraught. He pointed with both hands like six-shooters toward the throng of men swarming inside the yellow crime scene tape. "He's in the Jeep. I found him."

Merrill halted his march toward the activity. He turned to the Pekingese. "Land Rover."

"What?"

"It's a Land Rover. Not a Jeep."

"Who cares about that?"

"Cops like to have the facts straight."

An old man who was with the boy swung a protective arm around him. His pointed gray beard made him look like a schnauzer. "Ted, you hush up. Let the policeman do his job."

"But I found him, Grandpa."

"They get a statement from you?" Merrill asked the schnauzer.

"Not yet. That's what we're waiting around for. Close to an hour ago they said they'd get to us as soon as they could. Not much to tell, really." He nodded at the Pekingese. "Ted and I come by here to see if the perch was biting. Ted wandered over to the Land Rover, or whatever you call that Jeep, and all hell broke loose. Wish we'd tried Oneida Lake instead."

"Wouldn't have made as good a fishing story. Would it?" Merrill's eyebrows did a devious roll. He tipped the bill of his police cap, John Wayne style. "Thanks. Hang in there a few more minutes, and you'll be able to get back to your fishing. I'll see if I can speed things up." He strode off toward the other officers.

It was a Land Rover, all right. He'd know that vehicle anywhere.

He ducked under the tape and immediately caught the eye of a crew-cut, barrel-chested, plainclothes police officer who was fighting the same glacier as Merrill. "What you got, Mike?"

Dewitt county sheriff Mike Lalomia worked a hardcover notebook from his raincoat pocket. "Like I told you on the phone, the guy's name was Aaron Whitmore, white male, age—"

Merrill cut him off. "I know *who* you got. I want to know *what* you got."

Mike flipped his notebook shut. "I figure the old guy put himself out of his misery."

"Suicide? Not likely."

"You knew him well enough to make that kind of judgment?"

"Absolutely."

Merrill squinted up at the raindrops then scuffed his toe through a puddle. "Rained last night. Hard."

Mike squeezed the lapels of his overcoat at the thought of it. "Washed away about everything. Fall is here, and winter ain't far behind." He gestured toward the Land Rover. "Window was down. The victim is soaked too."

"Cause of death?"

"Gunshot to the neck. Close range."

"Got a weapon?"

"A Smith and Wesson .38 revolver. Haven't checked it out yet."

Merrill kept his eyes on the puddle. "It'll be Aaron's. It's his old service weapon."

Mike nodded slowly, thinking. "When we ran the plates on the vehicle and got Aaron Whitmore, I called you. I figured you'd want to be involved, even though you're village and this is county stuff at this point. But I didn't figure you knew him *that* well."

"He was chief of police in Jefferson for fifteen years. My boss a lot of that time."

Merrill stepped over to the Land Rover, shouldering his way through a bevy of evidence hounds decked out in latex gloves. One was using tweezers to fill small plastic bags. Another was wielding a camera. They discussed their findings in low, detached voices.

He wanted to remind them that the body they poked and prodded was a person—a *real person,* his friend and mentor, not just the *victim.* But he knew it wouldn't do any good. So he bit his tongue, rare for Merrill, and ignored them.

He peered through the open driver's door and into the front seat. Aaron's body was still where they had found it. In life, Aaron had been a big man, even at seventy. Not quite as muscled-up as in his prime, but still a rugged woodsman. He lay right side down on the front seat, rump still behind the wheel, head on the passenger seat. His silver hair looped onto the collar of the dark green chamois shirt Kent had given him last Christmas. He was wearing his hunting boots. His once blue eyes, now chalky, stared blankly at the dashboard. A massive rent in Aaron's throat loomed at Merrill like swollen lips around a slobbering mouth. A pool of blood half as big as Cuyler Lake had congealed on the floor. The .38 hung from his right hand.

A half cough rolled up the back of Merrill's throat.

"They're never pretty, but it's worse when you know them," Mike said from behind him.

Merrill kept his eyes on the carnage. "I'd like a copy of the complete report when you've got it."

"I'll make sure."

"No witnesses. Right?"

"Nope. Only ones we have to question so far are the old man and boy who found him this morning. I saw you talking to them."

"Yeah." Merrill stood straight, thumbs in his thick uniform belt. He shifted his eyes to the two fishermen, still waiting to be interviewed. "You think they did it?"

Lalomia's lips pulled into a thin smile. He blew a quick laugh through his nose. "Yeah. They look the type." He let the humor dissipate. "You don't think it's a suicide?"

Merrill shrugged. "Just keep an open mind. I know you will without me telling you to. Aaron was a real good friend."

"Didn't he write for the *Dispatch*?"

"Yeah. He's been their outdoors writer for six or eight years."

"Hunting and fishing articles mostly, as I remember."

"Uh-huh. Pretty low-key stuff. It was something to occupy his time."

"Nothing controversial. Right?"

Merrill let his eyes drift out onto Cuyler Lake, its surface choppy from the wind. "Nothing that would make someone want to kill him, if that's what you mean. As far as I know, he didn't have an enemy in the world."

"Brings us back to suicide."

Merrill stared at the churning water. There'd be a few more nice days, but before long, arctic air tumbling down from Canada would turn the green, undulating surface into rock-rigid, white desolation. He looked forward to winter. Cold, clear days. Frigid, hushed nights. Deer season. Wood smoke. The holidays. Winter brought out the warmth in Jefferson.

"They tell me his place is around on the other side of the lake."

Merrill pointed north. "It's a little log cabin he and his wife built."

"She's dead. Isn't she?"

"She died in seventy-seven."

Lalomia spoke thoughtfully. Not pushy. "So. He was old. His wife's been gone what, five years? Maybe he just got tired of the hassle."

"He had a ton of friends."

"Maybe he was sick—you know, cancer or something."

"I'd have heard if he was. Aaron visited my mother at the nursing home at least once a week. He couldn't keep a secret from her, and she wouldn't have been able to keep it from me or my brother."

Mike nodded. "Okay. We'll follow up on it. I'll get you the report."

"Thanks. Keep in touch."

"You'll be the first to know."

As Merrill climbed back into his black-and-white, he noticed the Pekingese and schnauzer still standing by the telephone-pole rail where he'd seen them before. They were treading and dipping at the knees to stay warm.

He eased his car down into the lot so that the yellow crime scene tape was within inches of his window.

Lalomia noticed his return and gave him a questioning look.

"Can you have one of your men take care of those two who found the body before they freeze to death?"

Mike glanced at the pair. Signaled back an *okay*.

Merrill nodded thanks and gunned his cruiser up onto the highway back toward Jefferson. Protesters at Copithorn, Aaron Whitmore dead—all before lunch. Maybe it wasn't such a boring little burg after all.

CHAPTER 2

KENT STEPHENSON'S FORD PICKUP WAS AS familiar around town as the mail carrier. The veterinarian making his rounds, a comforting fixture of small-town living. He braked it to the end of a line of idling cars. One or two drivers cast him a smile and a wave. He returned their greetings. He was a lifelong resident of Jefferson and the only veterinarian anyone could ever remember in the tiny village. He knew everything there was to know about the town, its people, and their animals. Right now he knew something was fishy. Jefferson had no rush hour. Traffic backups just never happened.

He reached over and stroked the soft fur of his best friend, Lucinda. The massive redbone coonhound relaxed on the seat next to him.

"Now what?"

He could see other drivers craning their necks for a better view of whatever was causing the delay.

Lucinda wagged her tail and smiled back at her master through keen eyes that reflected endless devotion.

Kent leaned out the window and squinted into the morning sun. Several car lengths ahead, he could make out people milling around like cattle. They brandished placards that were too far away to read. The entrance to Copithorn Research seemed to be their target, but the congestion spilled out into the street and slackened traffic to the pace of an overweight basset hound on a hot summer day.

He pushed a hand through his hair. *Must be a strike. A bunch of picketers holding up the show.*

Slowly he inched the truck toward the commotion until they were within earshot.

A dark-haired woman in her thirties moved toward them, wielding her placard like a battle-ax.

"Would you burn out *your* eyes for a rabbit's vanity? Kill computers, not puppies!"

"What the hell?" Kent said, leaning toward the windshield to read her sign: A RAT IS A PIG, IS A DOG, IS A BOY.

A deep growl rolled up Lucinda's throat. Kent grabbed a handful of her russet coat. "Take it easy, girl." Then it hit him. This wasn't a strike. It was an animal rights protest! He almost laughed.

"Hey, girl. That woman is on *your* side!"

Lucinda growled again.

Loose curls, so black they diffused the sun's highlights into a splendor of iridescent blue, fell onto the woman's shoulders. She wore no makeup and didn't need it. Her skin was smooth, maybe Native American, Kent thought. Behind her she-wolf glare was a glint of conviction.

"Uh-oh," slipped from his lips and caused Lucinda to glance his way.

"Mister, let that dog go! It's not natural for one animal to own another!" the she-wolf shouted.

Kent's mouth tightened. He hated it when people tried to bully their opinions onto others. Lord knew he faced that enough from his family nowadays. He sure as hell did not need it from these nuts.

"I take that back, Lucinda. They are not looking out for you. Ignore the misguided screw-ups. Hopefully they'll go away." But as he said it, an irritating little warning rose out of his subconscious. *That's wishful thinking.*

They continued past the melee and traffic speed began to pick up. Kent saw his brother's police cruiser pull up to the demonstration.

"There we go, Lucinda," he said. "Merrill's on the scene. He'll get things straightened out."

● ● ●

Kent peered into an incision in the belly wall of a golden retriever and groped with two fingers for her uterus. "Anyway, Sally, you listening?" he said loud enough to be sure his voice made it from the surgery room to her office.

"I hear you," Kent's one and only receptionist, bookkeeper, surgical assistant, and kennel cleaner answered from her desk around the corner.

Her auburn hair cut short and with freckles across the bridge of her nose, Sally had a round face, round fingertips, and a round rump. She was hefty enough to be a good assistant yet graceful enough to move easily around the tiny hospital. She loved the animals, and they loved her. In contrast to Kent, her mood was always upbeat.

"Getting back to Mrs. Crane. Like I said, they called me from the vet school in Ithaca about her gray cat I referred down to them."

"Cinder?"

"Right. The oncologist agreed it's lymphosarcoma. So here's old Cinder, fourteen years old, he can hardly breathe, he's got screaming diarrhea, and they recommend that she get chemo for him. Does that make sense to you?"

"She can afford it."

"That's not the point!" Kent's tone dropped to a mechanical drone. "I need you in here for a second to open a packet of suture material." Then it heated up again. "The point is we shouldn't let Cinder suffer. You know? To my mind it's just not right to keep that cat going for, at tops, six more months if he's vomiting all the time, his hair is falling out, and he's generally too miserable to move. Even if the owner *can* afford it."

"I know, but maybe she doesn't want to put him to sleep."

"Of course not. No owner *wants* to, but it's part of being a responsible owner to—"

The phone rang, and Sally grabbed it so fast Kent could tell she was relieved to be spared his opinion.

He heard the initial exchange from Sally's end and knew it was Merrill.

"Kent, your brother's on line one," she said, as if they had a line two.

"Tell him I'm in surgery."

"I did. He wants you to meet him for lunch."

Kent released a long breath as he daubed the blood from his surgical field. Was he going to have to put up with another of Merrill's *get-your-life-together* lectures? "I'll call him back in a couple of minutes."

Sally said something into the phone and then hung up.

Kent turned back to his patient. What did Merrill want now? Irritation transmitted through his hands. He closed the incision, suturing as if he were in a MASH unit. Why was Merrill constantly pushing him to be what he wasn't anymore? Because he was his brother? Because he was a cop? Kent didn't care if he didn't meet Merrill's expectations. He knew he had done better, but that was when Mary was still around.

Kent snipped the last suture on the retriever's abdomen and pulled off the drape. He paused at the photo of his ex-wife and their daughter that hung even with his diploma on the surgery room wall, stared at it, then picked a clean gauze from the counter and wiped its glass. It had been taken six years back, when they were a family. Emily was all smiles sitting in a shiny new Radio Flyer wagon, Mary pulling. It was her third birthday. Thinking about Emily made his heart ache. She was growing up so fast, and he wasn't there to be a part of her life. His constant absence had been too much for Mary.

That damned divorce had nearly killed him. His intestines knotted even now as he recalled Mary's bitterness. He had conceded everything to her, for Emily's sake, but she kept sic'ing her lawyers on him. They bled him more and more until all he had left was his clinic. He had sacrificed too much for his profession. He shook off his funk and glanced at his watch.

"Sally, bring out the Dobie pup. Let's get him done."

By the time Kent had cleaned the table, Sally was easing into the operating room with a black-and-tan pup nestled in her arms. "Don't be nervous," she cooed, as she stroked his back and set him on the table. "A few minutes and it'll be all over, no more hernia." She held his ears out playfully. "You look more like an old hound dog than a Doberman pinscher."

"Don't insult Lucinda with your hound-dog remarks," Kent said, gesturing at his dog, who was lying on a rug in the corner. The sleepy-eyed canine raised her head.

Sally gave an apologetic look. "Sorry, Lucy. Nothing personal."

Lucinda thumped her tail on the linoleum a time or two and then rested her chin back on her forefeet.

A short time later, Sally carried the limp patient back to his cage, complete with a white belly wrap that he'd be able to play up for all kinds of sympathy when he got home.

Kent snapped off his gloves.

He punched the Jefferson police station number into the phone. "Hello, Janet? This is Kent. Is the chief in?"

"No. He had to take off, but hold on one moment."

He could hear papers shuffling in the background.

"He did leave a note for you. All it says is he'll meet you for lunch at the diner. Quarter to one."

Typical, always a big mystery, Kent thought as he replaced the phone. Then he remembered the animal rights protest he and Lucinda had seen earlier. Maybe Merrill wanted to talk about that.

A professional matter? That would be a nice change from the usual commentary on how he was letting life pass him by.

CHAPTER 3

KENT LOVED TO WATCH LUCINDA SITTING UP straight in the passenger seat. Riding in the truck was her favorite thing in the world—next to coon hunting. She pushed her nose through a crack in the glass, analyzing long whiffs of the olfactory smorgasbord as it breezed past.

Beyond Lucinda, the village passed—tidy storefronts with quaint names, a tiny college, several pristine churches, a shady green with a statue for the pigeons. Two decades ago, Jefferson's sylvan seclusion had been discovered by developers struggling to accommodate the swell of urbanites retreating from Syracuse. Land prices were pushed beyond the reach of farmers, inflated by speculators who converted alfalfa meadows into housing tracts. Jefferson's sower-reaper heritage had begun to fade away like its farm fields until the Chamber of Commerce took Stef Copithorn up on her offer to keep her thriving, triple-A-rated enterprise in the community. Copithorn Research was Jefferson's savior. It, too, encroached on farmland, but it replaced that land with *jobs*, not houses.

Kent cruised down Albany Street, found a parking spot no problem, right in front of the Village Diner.

It was a utilitarian restaurant, brightly lit, with curt service. One-page plasticized menus that no one bothered to read. Customers were locals: farmers, merchants, mechanics, and the village cops, of course. More interested in the quantity than the quality of their meal, they ordered the daily special off a blackboard behind the counter.

Kent stepped inside and scanned the lunch crowd. Merrill's was not among the faces. Figured. He wove his way between tables, exchanging quick greetings with half a dozen diners. Most were former schoolmates. All were his clients. He slid into a booth where he could see the door and waited.

After twenty minutes of drumming his fingers to Dolly Parton and a string of other country chart toppers, Kent saw Merrill crossed in front of the cash register.

He eyed his brother and figured Merrill had been indulging in greasy diner food too often lately. The only physical resemblance they shared was the sharp angle of their jaws, an inherited trait from their mother's side of the family, and Merrill's appeared more blurred than ever, hidden by his fleshy jowls. That was where the brotherly similarity ended, unless food might be a common denominator. Neither one of them could boast of healthful eating habits, a fact that had made their mother crazy all their lives. Merrill had always been the short, robust one and Kent the tall, skinny one. Even though they were both in their forties, that had not changed.

Today, Merrill's face looked too puffy to be blamed on his diet.

"What's the matter with you?" Kent asked as Merrill slid in across from him.

Merrill stared directly at his brother and then let his eyes settle toward the napkin dispenser. "Aaron Whitmore is dead."

Kent's arm was resting on the table. When he jumped, it rattled the ketchup bottle. He stared back at Merrill, searching his face for some sign that this was a black joke. There was none.

"If this is some of your sick humor, it's not funny," he said, longing for it to be a joke but having enough experience reading his brother to know it was not.

"Last night. Out at the boat launch on Cuyler Lake. They think he shot himself."

Kent leaned toward his brother, gripped the table with both hands. "Shot himself? No!"

Merrill shrugged. "Maybe he was lonely, Claire gone and all. No kids."

"That's bullshit!"

Kent took a deep breath to continue the volley when a gray-uniformed waitress appeared at his elbow.

Merrill spoke first, without looking at the menu. "Hi, Tammy. I'll have the special. But don't give me any coleslaw. Coffee."

Tammy turned to Kent, gum snapping.

He ordered quickly, anxious to get back to Aaron's death. "I'll have a BLT on white, a cup of soup, and iced tea. Then I also want two plain hamburgers to go."

Merrill looked at Kent quizzically as Tammy headed to the counter.

"Lucinda's in the truck."

"Oh, Jesus. You and that dog."

"No way Aaron committed suicide. He was happy. Busy. Too involved. I ran into him at the nursing home just last week. He stopped in to see Mom."

"He thought a lot of Mom."

Kent rocked back, stared at the ceiling. Aaron Whitmore dead. "He was telling me all the things he had going on." Suddenly Kent felt as though someone had stuffed a dry rag in his throat. "He is—was—real busy with the Scouts. Just like he was when we were young. Remember?"

"Sure I do. If ever there was a guy who should have had kids, it was Aaron."

They pondered that until Tammy returned. She slid their meals in front of them.

Kent directed a finger at his brother, who had begun sawing his meatloaf. "He was saying how great things were going at the newspaper."

Merrill nodded, loaded his mouth, and kept right on talking. "The other day, here in this diner, he told me he had a big story in the works, but he wouldn't give me the details. Said something about how he was feeling guilty about it and that some people would suffer because of it."

"Leave it to Aaron to be the world's only sensitive newsman. You've got an investigation going, right?"

"Minimal. It looks pretty cut and dry. Shot himself with his service revolver. Lalomia promised me a copy of the report."

"At the boat launch? Why there?"

Merrill scooped another forkful of meatloaf. Didn't reply.

"Did you see…the body?"

"Yes. It was Aaron. Lying across the front seat of his Land Rover."

"Did anything look suspicious?"

Merrill stopped chewing. Looked straight at his brother. "I'm a cop. I'm suspicious by design."

"That's good. What bothered you?"

"I want to see Lalomia's report before I say anything."

"Jesus!" Kent panned an unfocused stare out over the other patrons and then leaned at his brother. "Merrill, I'm telling you, it couldn't be. I know Aaron better than that. Hell, so do you."

"And I'm telling you we've got an old man with virtually no family, out in the boondocks with no witnesses, sitting in his own vehicle, shot with his own service revolver." Merrill held up his palms. "Come on, Kent, Dewitt County has a small force—under-manned and underfunded. They can't mount a large-scale investigation on a case like that."

Kent pushed himself to his feet, tossing his napkin onto his plate. "Forget that crap! I'll figure it out myself." His face reddened. He glanced left then right, not knowing what to do, but knowing he needed to do something. "Think about it. Things don't fit! Why would he do it at a public boat launch? Come on, Merrill! You knew him. Privacy was his thing. Where would Aaron Whitmore, the woodsman, choose to end his life? Where did we find him when Claire died?"

Merrill's jaw slacked as his brother's prodding struck home. "Big Rock."

"Exactly!" Both brothers' mental eyes formed an image of the beaver meadow on Metcalf Mountain. Along its southern edge, a granite boulder the size of a country church warmed in the sun all day long, all year long. It overlooked some of the best whitetail ground in New York State and was known among the locals to be Aaron Whitmore's personal deer stand. Kent and Merrill knew it was his thinking place.

"Big Rock, where he shot the twelve point. Where he talked about wanting to have his ashes scattered!"

Kent watched his brother assimilate the new information until his frustration boiled over. "Hell, if you can't do it…"

He took a step to leave and felt Merrill grip his arm.

"Hold on, Kent. Man, that's the hottest I've seen you get about anything in a long time." Merrill's voice rang with approval. He signaled Kent to take his seat again. "All right. I'll dig into it some more."

"As a favor to Mom."

"And you."

Kent slid back into the booth and gave his brother a defiant look. "Did you invite me to lunch to tell me about Aaron or was this another attempt to advise me about my lifestyle?"

"Did you see those picketers at Copithorn this morning?"

"As a matter of fact I did. Some of the local do-gooders up in arms? They better be careful. If Stef Copithorn gets pissed off and moves her business to Timbuktu, Jefferson goes down the toilet. You better remind folks around here who butters their bread. Tell them to stop reading all the animal abuse propaganda."

Merrill swallowed a dry mouthful with great effort as he shook his head. "This is serious. They aren't our people."

Except for the pretty one who had harassed him, Kent hadn't paid much attention to the crowd. "Who are they?"

"A group from California. Well organized. Seems they've targeted Copithorn—cosmetics, you know?"

Kent bobbed an ice cube in his tea with a fingertip. "That's a little bigger problem," he admitted and then added, "but they won't last long either. Some new cause will crop up, and they'll move on."

The chief shrugged but said nothing.

Kent knew he was being baited but decided to bite anyway. "So. How are you figuring me in this?"

An irritating little smile of satisfaction crossed Merrill's lips. "Stef is thinking like you. I spoke with her this morning. For the time being, we've decided to keep a low profile. See if the thing burns itself out like you say. They're peaceful enough for now. They're not damaging any property or obstructing business."

"That's what will happen. You can bet on it. They'll leave all right. There's nothing at Copithorn Research for them to sink their teeth into. Stef plays by the rules."

"Well, if they do, great. But while we're keeping an eye on them, we decided we'd better start getting ready for a fight. Just in case."

Kent's eyes narrowed. "You still haven't explained my role."

"Stef wants to be able to go on record as having an animal health care inspector or supervisor—call it what you want—some outside person who insures that Copithorn is treating their animals humanely."

"And you figure I'm the man for the job."

Merrill's hands shot up, pleading innocence. "It was Stef's idea, but sure, you come to mind. Why not? What's wrong with it anyway? I know you're bored to death working in that little shoebox of an animal hospital. Besides, you and I both know Stef Copithorn does everything top shelf. She'll pay great, for sure. You could use the money, couldn't you? Be honest."

God, he hated it when Merrill was right. Merrill had a habit of being right, which was probably why he had become a cop. Kent shook his head. "Remind me never to accept another lunch invite from you. First you tell me about Aaron, then you try to drag me into a hornet's nest."

Merrill just sipped his coffee.

"Listen, they don't have any animal welfare problems over at Copithorn. I've never been through the plant, but I know Stef. She wouldn't allow it. Besides, this is a small town. Word would have gotten out. Jesus. I don't need this." Kent blew a breath out his nose. "I'd have to check out the place for myself before I can agree to anything."

"Does that mean you'd consider the job?"

"Maybe." Kent gave his brother a *don't-push-me* look. "Only because it's Stef."

Merrill pulled a napkin from the dispenser, wiped his face vigorously, and tossed the crumpled wad onto his plate. "Good. I figured that was the best I'd get out of you. You'll do a great job."

"Don't assume anything. I said I'd consider it. That's all."

"Right." The chief brushed aside his brother's caveat. "This will be a good project for you. Help you out of your doldrums, maybe. Get you back on top like the old days."

"I don't know what you're talking about."

"Hell, Kent, you can handle this job with your eyes shut. I figured you'd give us the go-ahead, so Stef and I arranged a meeting at two o'clock tomorrow so you can see their setup firsthand."

At his truck, Kent opened a white paper bag and took out the two burgers for Lucinda. She gobbled them. He watched her and provided dinner conversation.

"Girl, what am I getting us into? This Copithorn thing is going to be a huge headache. I want to focus on what happened to Aaron." He wadded the bag and tossed it behind the seat. "Come on, Lucinda. We need to take a ride over to Mid-York, see what Mom knows about all this."

CHAPTER 4

KENT TURNED INTO THE MID-YORK EXTENDED
Care facility and followed its smooth macadam through lush lawn
and fat maples. The main residence building was modern, with lots
of glass and an angular sprawling profile that fit surprisingly pleasantly into the rural landscape. It cost a mint, far more than his mother's retirement benefit provided, but he and Merrill had agreed it was
the best around. They made the monthly payment willingly—not
easily, but willingly.

He proceeded down B-wing, stopping here and there to nod
hello or pat the fleshless shoulder of long-retired schoolteachers,
pastors, and local businesspeople who had been part of his life at one
time or another. He squatted in front of a special few of the wheel-
chairs parked along the hall and smiled into the cloudy eyes that had
sculpted his youth.

A young woman at the nurses' station greeted him. "Hey,
Dr. Stephenson."

"How's my mother today?" Shortness of breath had plagued
her for the last six months.

"Better. The doctor checked her yesterday and changed her
medication. That seems to have helped."

"Excellent." He pushed through a door into room 135.

June Stephenson Mays was propped in her wheelchair with a
cloud of pillows. The chair seemed like a massive amount of metal
to hold her tiny body. She wore a crisp pink housecoat. Matchstick

legs descended into fluffy blue slippers. Her kittenish white hair was neatly brushed, and Kent noticed the aides had even applied a touch of lipstick. It helped to distract one's eye from the tiny oxygen hose that ascended to just below her nostrils.

He bent down and kissed June's cheek. It was like the muzzle of a new foal. "Hi, Mom."

"Did you hear about Aaron?" she asked in a soft voice.

He nodded, surprised at how fast she brought up the subject.

"I don't believe it was suicide," she said with as much conviction as she could muster. She watched Kent's face for a reaction.

"Neither do I."

She patted his hand. "Good."

"Merrill is looking into it."

"You be sure he does." She hesitated for a moment. "Aaron had been here a lot lately. He said he just felt like visiting, but I know there was more to it than that." She toyed with the oxygen hose. "He was worried about something. He kept saying how he had this big story, but he didn't want to hurt me."

"Hurt you? How?"

"He wouldn't say. Only that he wasn't sure how to handle it."

"Did he say what the story was about?"

"I asked, but he wouldn't tell."

Kent considered his mother's words. "You don't think he was upset enough to kill himself?"

"Never."

He let his eyes drift around to the various pieces of medical paraphernalia in the room. "What sort of a story could Aaron Whitmore have that would hurt you, Mom?"

"I don't know. His articles were just about hunting and fishing stuff, as far as I know."

"What exactly did he say?" Kent asked in a stronger voice.

June's eyes filled with tears. "I can't remember."

Instantly he was sorry. He squeezed her hand. "That's all right, Mom. You've still got the best brain in the family."

He steered the conversation to her new breathing medication, then over to who she had heard from lately and what activities the center had planned. He managed to make it last an hour. He promised to stop by later in the week and left.

● ● ●

All the way to Copithorn, Kent pondered what sort of a "big story" Aaron Whitmore could have been working on. What could he have known that might have hurt his mother?

Stef had told him how to bypass the protesters by following a service drive to a secluded parking lot behind Copithorn Research's main office building.

He pulled into a space next to Merrill's black-and-white, twisted the rearview mirror to see his face, and ran his hand over his clean-shaven cheeks. It felt good. Lately he'd gotten lax about going through the motions every morning. It just didn't seem to matter much.

He glanced down at the tie he had bought yesterday. The clerk had assured him it was "the style." He held the tip out toward Lucinda, gave her a dubious look. "At least it makes this old sport coat look a little more presentable."

Lucinda slapped her tail in agreement.

"Keep an eye on the truck till I get back."

Lucinda's tail went again.

Kent stepped up onto a concrete loading dock and knocked loudly on a green steel door marked Employees Only. As he was waiting for a response, he turned back to the truck. He could see Lucinda's nose pressed to the windshield. "Don't even *think* of joining any animal rights groups while I'm gone," he actually said out loud.

As the door opened, Kent was greeted by a security guard and politely steered toward Copithorn's main lobby.

Classic modern architecture of the eighties, it was actually more of an atrium than a lobby, with its forty-foot skylighted ceiling and three floors opening onto balconies above. The air was made tropical by a jungle of lush hanging greenery and exotic trees with twisting hairy trunks the size of a man's leg. The centerpiece was a fountain that babbled into a crystalline pool.

He noticed Merrill seated on a bench. Beyond him, through giant sepia-toned windows, a throng of protesters churned on the lawn. Merrill was watching them.

"Look pretty nasty, don't they?"

Merrill turned quickly and rose. He looked uncomfortable, out of place in his police uniform. "Yeah. I'd say so. What took you so long? I was beginning to think you chickened out."

"I might still. Stef didn't call and cancel our meeting or anything, did she?"

"We're on in about five minutes."

The woman who had harassed Kent stood on a stone retaining wall. She spoke to her disciples with a bullhorn that carried her rhetoric through the glass.

"Every generation prior to our present leaders has strived to leave the world in better condition than they found it," she blasted. "But the generation of Huns that reign today has disgraced tradition. Like some insatiable monster, they claw the products of nature into their maws without thought to any other creature on earth. And what is the cost of this rapacious appetite? Animal pain, suffering, and death! That's what. It's time to change! It's time to stop indulging in selfish behavior at any price. Do we really need eyeliner? Mascara? Lipstick?"

"Does this bunch have a name?" Kent asked his brother.

"Freedom of Animals Movement. FOAM for short."

"As in foaming at the mouth?"

"It would fit."

Kent stared at the group with a disdainful expression he had unwittingly learned from Lucinda. "There is nothing so boring as a zealot."

"They may be boring, but they're also disruptive," came Stef Copithorn's commanding voice from behind them. Both men spun on their heels.

Stef was the same age as Kent but looked years younger. As the highly visible owner of a cosmetics company, she was very much aware of her appearance. Tall and willowy, she had auburn hair cut short and gelled smooth, a chestnut show horse on a sunny day. Her skin reminded Kent of French vanilla ice cream that was just starting to soften. She wore an above-the-knee black silk dress that clung perfectly. Heels, diamonds, uptown all the way.

She was single and always would be. Kent had learned that secret long ago when they were in high school. The night she told him, they had been parked where the kids hung out behind the airport. Just the two of them. It had been such an epiphany for her. She had bubbled with relief as she confided in him about her sexuality.

Stef extended a firm hand to both men and looked straight at each with penetrating hazel eyes. "Thank you for coming."

"Our pleasure," Kent said, and it was not totally a lie.

Stef gave Kent a questioning gaze. "A pleasure, huh? Merrill told me he thought he might have to put a bullring in your nose and lead you here."

"The business part doesn't thrill me, but it's nice to see you again."

She smiled warmly. "Me too."

Their exchange was interrupted by a commotion at the front entrance. All three turned to see a flood of protesters stream in past startled security guards. The bullhorn woman was in front. She marched directly up to Copithorn's chief executive and gave her a surly look.

Kent straightened his back, readying himself for battle. But he felt something strange about this woman who was here to devour them. Her conviction! That was it. Twice he had seen her, and both times he had been struck by how she glowed with the vehemence he had enjoyed during his early years as a veterinarian…and had lost. It had made his life worthwhile back then. He was envious of her passion.

She held out her hand to Stef. "Aubrey Fairbanks, field representative for the Freedom of Animals Movement. We saw you through the window and decided to come in and have a word with you."

"You are on private property," Merrill interrupted. "On behalf of Ms. Copithorn, I'm asking you all to leave immediately and peacefully."

Without breaking eye contact with her adversary, Stef held up her hand to signal Merrill. "That's all right, Chief. If Ms. Fairbanks can keep her people under control, I have no objection to them being here. In the lobby only. For now."

Merrill took a breath to argue then shrugged his shoulders in a whatever-you-say gesture and settled back to see what developed.

Both women bristled, exuding dominance like two dogs meeting for the first time.

"Thank you."

"You're welcome."

"I'm sure you know by now why we're here."

"Well, Aubrey…may I call you Aubrey? Why don't you tell us anyway?"

"First names are fine with me and, in a nutshell, we are against any exploitation of animals—no wearing, eating, using, or owning animals." Aubrey leveled a venomous gaze. "Your company exploits animals for research. In *cosmetics,* of all things."

"It is necessary," Stef said evenly. "And all of our testing is done humanely."

"Most cosmetics are not necessary, and no animal testing is humane. There are alternatives. We believe animals should not suffer for humans' vanity."

"There are no reliable or legal alternatives."

"Computer models? Time-tested substances? Humans?"

"Sorry," Stef said without missing a beat. "Computers don't have a sense of smell. They don't have allergies. They can't get cancer. Humans are out—our insurance premiums are outrageous already."

"Some companies do it. You can buy cosmetics from companies that don't do animal testing. We can provide you with a list of the ethical ones."

Stef rolled her eyes and then let them drift over the growing crowd as employees came out of their workstations to watch the showdown. She'd heard the rhetoric a hundred times before—pure bullshit. She struggled to maintain the even temper that was control. "I've seen your lists, and I know the industry. They *all* use animal testing at some stage of production or have a subsidiary that does the testing under another name."

Aubrey jabbed a finger at Stef. "So you do admit to testing your products on animals. Right here in this building maybe."

Stef didn't back down. "Damn right I do!"

A shout came from the FOAM contingency that had encircled Aubrey and Stef. "Let's go take a look! Right now!" They began cheering and jeering, waving their placards, milling like cattle in a lightning storm, each one waiting for the first one to stampede. There was a volley of sharp returns from the Copithorn troops. Police Chief Stephenson began to fidget.

Suddenly, both factions were hushed by a loud voice behind them. All heads turned in unison. It was Kent, standing on the edge of the fountain.

"Wait just a minute here, folks. I'm the Copithorn animal-care supervisor. I oversee the testing and husbandry of all animals owned by Copithorn Research, and I can attest that nowhere, now or ever, has a single animal been mistreated in any way at this facility."

He hopped down and pushed his way through the placard bearers until he was standing with Aubrey and Stef. "Sorry I interrupted," he said to the CEO. "I hope I didn't overstep my bounds."

Stef gave him the soul-mate look she used to give him in high school. "Not at all, Dr. Stephenson." Turning to the FOAM leader, she said curtly, "Aubrey Fairbanks, I'd like to introduce Dr. Kent Stephenson, our animal-care supervisor."

Aubrey's eyebrows shot up. "Doctor?"

"Yes. I'm a veterinarian. I'm in private practice—"

"A veterinarian?" Aubrey burst out, her voice dripping with sarcasm. "As an animal-care supervisor? You must be kidding!"

"Do you have a problem with that?" Stef asked.

"Yeah, I do. It's like letting the fox guard the henhouse!"

Stef squared her shoulders, struggled for self-control. "Are you implying that a veterinarian would have a conflict of interest here?"

"That's exactly what I'm implying. Veterinarians make their living dealing with sick animals. Right? If there is no animal suffering, there are no veterinarians."

"I'd say that position is a little extreme. No person is better trained to recognize whether or not animals are healthy and being cared for properly."

"Cared for properly? You jest. Let me ask Dr. Stephenson a question or two." Her tone was thick with disdain.

Stef glanced at Kent questioningly. He shrugged.

"Be my guest," she said.

Aubrey waited, letting the room settle into an uneasy courtroom silence. "Dr. Stephenson, do you work on big animals or pets?"

"Both."

"Have you docked any puppies' tails in the last few days?"

Kent winced internally. At least he hoped it was internally. "Yes. At the request of the owner, of course."

"When they were only three days old? Away from their mother and without any anesthesia? Just chop, chop. Right?"

"Actually, you make it sound worse than it is."

"That's easy for you to say. Too bad we can't ask the pups. Do you ever perform services for your clients to help them get their dogs and cats pregnant? Vaginal smears. Artificial insemination. That sort of thing."

"If the owner requests my help."

Aubrey's voice rose. "Who dictates morals in your practice, you or your clients?"

"I do."

She turned back to Stef. "I rest my case."

For a split second, Stef's jaw set hard and her eyes shot fire, but then she drew a long breath, exhaled, and countered, "I'm sorry you feel that way, but I disagree. I know I need animals in my business. And I am strongly committed to seeing that they are not allowed to suffer or be treated poorly. A veterinarian has the training to recognize problems and offer solutions." Stef held up her hands before Aubrey could reply. "Having said that, I think it's time to end this discussion until a more formal meeting can be arranged."

The animal rightists began to clamor again.

Stef gestured toward Merrill. "May I remind you of what the police chief told you earlier? You are on private property. I'll thank you to leave quietly."

For a moment, Aubrey held her ground. Glared at Stef. Then she wheeled, signaled to her lieutenants, and led their retreat.

Kent watched them disappear. He felt disheartened. He had made his decision as a gut reaction to help Stef. He had stood by while the two women discussed him like neighbors arguing over a misbehaving dog. Now he was the Copithorn animal-care supervisor. He was entangled in the web. It was going to be a huge time commitment, in spite of what Merrill and Stef had promised. He had stuck his neck out, put his reputation on the line. And for what? He did not have an answer…if there was one at all. Both sides were so adamant, so polarized, so unyielding. Besides, he wanted to concentrate on finding out what had happened to Aaron Whitmore. This was a mistake.

He turned 180 degrees and was taking the first step back in the direction of his truck when Stef's arm slid around his and held tight. She might as well have snapped a leash on him.

CHAPTER 5

AS STEF ESCORTED KENT OUT OF THE ATRIUM
and toward her office, she gave a sigh of relief so deep her
knees buckled.

"Kent, I could kiss you."

He brushed off the offer. "Yeah, well, I didn't like the way that
mess was headed."

"Thank you for not letting the situation get out of hand."

Merrill caught up with them. "That'll take care of them for a
while." He said it confidently, but Kent read his eyes differently.

Stef's office was a symphony of glass, jump-out-and-grab-you
modern paintings, and tropical plants so lush they could hide an
Amazon aboriginal. A massive desk of clear-and-pink glass stood in
the middle like an iceberg.

Kent crossed the room and stared out a huge window. "You
managed to get them back outside?"

Merrill fell onto a leather sofa. "No problem. But they'll be
back, you can bet on it."

Stef eased into her desk chair. "That's what worries me."

Kent turned to face them. "When they do, we'll just have to be
ready for them."

"Weird bunch," Merrill said.

"Like a pack of dogs after a deer in deep snow." Kent moved
from the window to a chair across from Stef. "From what I've read,

the animal welfare extremists put cosmetic manufacturers on the top of their list."

Merrill made a pistol with his fingers and held it to his temple. "Second only to the army's gunshot-wound-to-the-head testing on cats and Detroit's car-crashing monkeys."

"They're after the cosmetic industry because they consider our products to be frivolous." She dropped her chin and stared at Kent from under perfectly waxed eyebrows. "Not that I want to be compared to some helpless deer floundering in the snow."

Kent flashed her a quick smile.

Stef went on. "Cosmetics are not just perfume and makeup. We've got to have soap. Deodorant? Shampoo? There's only one way to make them safe: animal testing."

Neither man replied.

Stef waved a hand toward the atrium. "I just want to satisfy those maniacs that we adhere to all the animal welfare codes and get them the hell out of here."

"Okay. A tour of the plant, right? That's what you asked Merrill and me to come over for in the first place. So let's have our tour. Show us firsthand that Copithorn has no animal welfare violations."

Stef pushed herself to her feet, accepting the challenge. "Okay, I can do that. Let's go."

The first part of the tour went fast. Stef gave a cursory overview as they stepped lively through manufacturing, packaging, and shipping. But when they approached a heavy steel double door marked RESEARCH AND DEVELOPMENT, she slowed. Her tone sought understanding. She pushed open the door.

"Here is where it all happens. At least as far as animal testing is concerned."

They entered a long hallway. Recessed ceiling lights sent fluorescence reflecting off shiny floor tiles. Doors, evenly spaced, flanked both walls. Men and women clad in technician white crisscrossed the hallway. They jotted on clipboards or pushed lab carts clinking with vials. It rendered a surrealistic strobe effect.

Kent peered into several rooms as they passed— countertops laden with odd-colored liquids percolating through twisted glass tubing, centrifuges whirring, timers buzzing, computer monitors flickering. "Pretty high-tech, Stef."

"Got to be to compete. You can bet our competitors are high-tech too.

"Now we're coming to the testing area. Remember what I told Ms. Fairbanks out there? Some cosmetic companies *claim* their products are 'nonanimal tested' to appease the weirdos." She thumbed over her shoulder. "Or to capture the market of consumers sympathetic to animals—but those claims are simply not true. Every company in the United States animal tests at some point.

"Even if we were crazy enough to risk it, the FDA says 'no way.' They are on us like mud plaster on a fifty-year-old beauty queen. They *require* us to test, and they tell us just how they want us to do it. Sure we can use some computer models. And in the final stages, we can field test on people. But the brunt of the testing is conducted on live animals."

Kent lagged behind, studying Stef, admiring her self-assured body language. She was in control. Since high school, her confidence had grown as much as his had diminished.

They passed through a door marked WARD 7, LIVE TESTING, NO ADMITTANCE.

"In here are rabbits. That's what we use, mostly. And, to be honest, they get the stuff rubbed in, brushed in, injected in, and fed to them. You name it. And, you know what else? Ninety-nine point nine percent never miss a beat. When one of those point zero one percent of samples does react, we are as surprised as anyone else."

They strolled past banks of stainless steel, alternately bend-ing at the knees and standing on tiptoes to peer in cages containing white rabbits that looked like any backyard pet, except for an occasional area of clipped fur.

"Here is a problem area," Stef said. She paused so they could watch a young technician move down the row of rabbits. She lifted each furry creature from its cage, cradled it gently under one arm, and shone a penlight into each eye. She returned them carefully and then jotted on her clipboard. All the while, she spoke to them with a soothing line of chatter the way Sally talked to patients at Kent's hospital.

Stef explained, "She's reading a Draize eye irritancy test. Solutions are dropped in the eyes of these bunnies for a given period of time to test for reactions." She shrugged and flashed an apologetic look. "Eyes are sensitive."

Kent recalled the question Aubrey Fairbanks had shouted into his truck window yesterday. *Would you burn out your eyes for a rabbit's vanity?*

"I can see why someone would be put off by that."

Merrill blinked hard. "It makes my eyes water just watching."

"In reality, it looks worse than it is, and unfortunately, it is one of the most reliable of our tests. It's also a test *required* by the FDA."

"I assume these guys get euthanized at some point," Kent stated, but it was more of a question.

Stef nodded. "Eventually. Humanely and before any suffering. It has to happen so our histologists can study the effects of the test materials on tissues at the microscopic level."

"Uh-huh," Kent said. "I can see FOAM having a field day with that. What other types of animals do you use?"

"We use a lot of white rats and mice, especially if we need to see if a chemical will affect a fetus. They reproduce quickly, so we can get our data in a reasonable time frame. We use ferrets. And we use quite a few dogs. Let me take you into the next ward. I'll show you."

The trio moved down the corridor to another room. Opening the door triggered a din that squelched their conversation.

"They are glad to see us," Stef shouted to the brothers and smiled as they made painful faces and covered their ears against the barking.

As in the rabbit ward, stainless steel cages lined the walls of the room, two high. Inside each, one or a few tricolored beagles stood on hind legs pressing against the cage door. Bright-eyed, jiggling with energy, they bugled at the top of their lungs, hot on the trail of some imaginary rabbit.

Stef pointed her guests through an exit. When the door closed behind them, they were once more in relative silence.

"Sorry. Those are the young adult dogs. They get noisy when someone first enters. You know, any excuse to blow off steam. They quiet down after you're in there a few minutes. Where we are now is for mothers with young pups. It's much quieter."

Kent scanned the ward. "All I see are beagles in either room. Do you use other breeds or mutts?"

"No," Stef said. "Just beagles. We buy them from a large producer of beagle research dogs near Rochester. We have to have very healthy, defect-free dogs. If our test dogs were to break with some disease in the middle of a trial, it would cause all kinds of problems. What we would like those FOAM people and the rest of the world to know is that we do not use house pets, dogs off the street, or from the pound—period. Ever."

"And that they are given the best care and they never suffer. Don't forget those points," Kent said.

The tour completed a circle, ending back at Stef's office. "So that's the cosmetic industry in a nutshell."

"Interesting," Merrill said.

Kent had gone back to staring out at the panorama through the office window.

"No offense, Merrill, but I was more interested in Kent's opinion. He's the one we need in our corner right now." She directed her voice toward Kent's back. "I take it by the way you went to bat for me in the lobby that the chief already talked to you about what we have in mind."

Kent turned enough to look over his shoulder at the statuesque entrepreneur. "Yeah. I've got a pretty good idea."

"Officially, Copithorn's animal-care supervisor. And as far as I'm concerned, you can take the position to any level you want. Truthfully, right now I'm interested in a figurehead. Someone to hold out to these animal rights weirdos. Let them know that we are sensitive to animals. In spite of what Aubrey Fairbanks says, I believe a veterinarian is perfect for the role. But, beyond that, I am always open to advice—yours included—on how to improve my company."

Kent turned back, leaned both hands against the plate glass, and scanned the vast tract of land behind Copithorn Research. "Remember when this was a little airport? Before the research park, I mean."

He recalled when he and Stef had experienced adolescent love one muggy summer night. Sipping beer they had a friend buy. Feeling grown-up. The insecurities. He remembered being intoxicated with cheap booze and pubescent hormones. Holding Stef, wondering desperately how far she would go…and then having the moment demolished by her revelation of her sexuality. She had needed someone to talk to. Someone brotherly. They had talked to near dawn.

"Like it was yesterday." Stef gestured to one end. "We used to park beyond the fence at the end of the runway."

"And watch the stars in my dad's old convertible."

"Seemed like the planes went over low enough to touch."

"God. That was a long time ago."

"Great memories."

He let the nostalgia hang for a moment.

"I'll be honest with you, Stef. I'll do what I can." His voice trailed off.

"But—" Stef filled the void.

"But I've got no, and I mean zero, experience with this kind of stuff." He hesitated, then added, "Plus, I've got something else going on now. You heard about Aaron Whitmore."

"Yes. I'm sorry. I know how close you were."

"He was like a second father to me. And," Kent cast an accusatory look toward his brother, "Merrill and his guys don't have the time or money to figure out what really happened."

Stef considered a moment, and then in her nonjudgmental tone that Kent loved, she asked, "Do you have reason to suspect otherwise?"

He shrugged. "Yes, as a matter of fact I do. I know Aaron would not kill himself."

"Like I said, just a figurehead."

"Figurehead or not, these things get crazy. I'm no good at arguing with people." He nodded toward his brother. "You need someone more like the chief."

"People trust veterinarians." Stef gave Merrill a sidelong glance. "I'm not sure the same can be said for policemen. Kent, you're perfect for the job."

"They didn't look ready to give up out there today."

"Believe me, I'm aware of that. That's why I'm asking for your help."

Kent shifted back to the chair across the desk from Stef and sat in broody silence.

Stef turned to Merrill. "Chief, I'd like to discuss something alone with Kent. Would you mind? There's a coffee machine down the hall to the left."

She waited till the door closed behind Merrill. "If you don't mind my asking, what was your net income last year?"

"Around fifty thousand." Kent knew that to her, the amount was pocket money, but he was long beyond embarrassment in that regard and was silently grateful when she showed no reaction.

"So it's true vets don't make as much as MDs."

"Most do better than I do, but no, not even close to MDs."

"The worm has sure turned since our old school days. You were from a respected family, destined to be a professional. I was the tramp from a nothing family. Strange, huh?"

"I never considered you a tramp, Stef."

"No. I guess not." There was a tone of appreciation in her voice. "Mary? She was a different story."

"Mary was competitive."

Stef shot him a cool look. "And when you couldn't provide everything she wanted, she took up the game with someone else."

Her assessment stung Kent, even though he knew Stef didn't mean it to. Kent watched the ghostly shadows of Stef's legs as she crossed them behind a deep pink modesty panel.

"That's between her and me."

"Right. I'm sorry I brought it up. Anyway, if you agree to make one inspection here per week, be on call for any emergency, and act as public liaison, I'll pay you one hundred thousand dollars. Your income triples. That's for a one-year contract."

The offer jolted Kent. How could he refuse? Of course, Stef knew that. She knew about his alimony payments and nursing home bills. He hated being manipulated. He had long ago promised himself he would keep out of other people's affairs. People were selfish, unpredictable, and disloyal. He had buried himself in his work because animals were all the good things people were not. Now he was about to change all that—for money.

"No sense lying to you. I could use the money. You know that." He listened to himself as if someone else was talking. "You'll stand by me on this public thing? I don't want to get left out on a limb."

"We'll work together on public policy and statements."

Kent swallowed hard. "I'll take the job. One year. You can call Merrill back in."

"Perfect. So I can line up a formal meeting—you, me, and Ms. FOAM?"

"Yep, what the hell."

As he left Copithorn, picketers were still slowing traffic passing out of the industrial park. The afternoon bunch seemed even more fervent, more rowdy, than the morning group.

"Just great," he said to Lucinda. "I'm supposed to talk sense into these idiots."

Lucinda sprang from her seat and forced her muzzle through the crack at the top of the window. She whimpered softly and wagged her tail. Kent followed her gaze and was instantly transfixed. Aubrey Fairbanks was glowering at him.

Kent glanced from Lucinda to Aubrey and back. The big hound's rear end did the canine rumba she usually reserved for old friends. Aubrey continued to knife him with her eyes.

He turned out onto the highway, gave Lucinda's tail a gentle tug. "Are you trying to tell me something?"

CHAPTER 6

SALLY CLOSED THE ACCOUNTING LEDGER SHE
was working on with more force than necessary and slid it to the
back of her desk. "Jeez. You're such a grouch today."

Kent looked up from the anesthetized English pointer whose
fight wound he was suturing. "Me?"

"What did you do, stay out all night hunting?"

"Lucinda and I went out and chased a couple of coons around
the woods for a while, but we got back pretty early." Sally could read
him like an old mama cat reads her kittens.

"So what's your problem?"

"I don't know," he said. Then, after a pause, "I keep thinking
about Aaron."

Sally came around the corner, took her usual place against the
operating room wall, and said nothing.

"He was Dad's hunting buddy for all those years." Kent laced
the jagged gash on the dog's hock with a few more stitches. He
paused again, looked up, gave a short, embarrassed laugh. "It was
odd. Lucinda and I went out coon hunting all right, but we didn't
bag a single one. The trip turned into kind of a memorial service for
Aaron. Just me, Lucy, and Mother Nature."

He gave Sally a confused look. She returned a sympathetic one
but remained silent.

"We spent most of the night up at Big Rock, just sitting there thinking. Trying to figure out what really happened. The way they say he died is so contrary to anything about his life!"

Sally had heard a lifetime of Big Rock stories. Huge bucks, missed shots, getting lost in the woods—male bonding stuff. She knew it had been Aaron's favorite place in the world. It was easy for her to envision her boss going there to mourn.

They worked through another long break in the conversation. Finally, Kent said, "And there's another reason I'm grouchy."

"What's that?"

"Aubrey Fairbanks."

"That FOAM bitch is still under your skin? I'd be grouchy, too, if I couldn't get her off my mind."

"Actually, she isn't such a bitch." Kent was surprised to hear himself defending the woman.

"She ripped everything you stand for, and she's not a bitch?"

"She is...very self-confident, I'll admit, but she's not mean. She's just absolutely positive of her position. I doubt anyone's going to alter her stance on animal rights one bit."

"Whatever." Sally returned to her office, dropped a folder into the metal file cabinet, and slammed the drawer shut. "Sounds like a brassbound bitch to me."

"It would be nice to be that confident about things. She makes me question myself." Kent daubed a trickle of blood. "And my profession. I never considered veterinary medicine to be anything but honorable."

"Forget her, Kent. You're all right. They swoop down on our town and start messing up everyone's life. What gives them the right? Why don't they just leave us alone?"

He wrapped a bandage around the pointer's repaired leg. "My whole life has been veterinary medicine. Fairbanks makes me doubt all that."

"Kent, she's crazier than a waltzing mule. Forget her."

"Then…why do we dock tails and crop ears, anyway?"

"To put food on the table, for starters. But since that sounds kind of selfish, how about because owners of purebred dogs want them to look like the breed is supposed to look. If vets quit doing it, they'll do it themselves. Then you really do have a cruelty problem." She snapped up a copy of the morning paper and waved it at Kent. "You read today's yet?" She began reading aloud from an article she'd obviously noted earlier:

Police Cage Copithorn Animal Activists

Jefferson, NY—The Freedom of Animals Movement (FOAM), a California-based pro–animal rights group, met yesterday with officials of Copithorn Research to discuss animal abuse at the cosmetic company. Copithorn has recently been the target of FOAM demonstrations.

"Some meeting. Ambush would be a better word for it."

"Let me finish."

"Copithorn has patently refused to alter its R&D policy to eliminate animal testing. We object to their methods whereby innocent animals, rabbits, puppies, and even pregnant dogs are subjected to repeated and prolonged exposure to chemicals with unknown effects," FOAM spokesperson Aubrey Fairbanks said. Stef Copithorn, CEO of the firm, countered, "We, like most cosmetics manufacturers, are committed to and progressing toward implementation of the three Rs—reduction, replacement, and refinement of the use of animals.

"'Unknown effects,'" Kent said under his breath.

Sally ignored him. "Oh, looky here. You get a quote!"

Copithorn's animal-care supervisor, Dr. Kent Stephenson, a Jefferson veterinarian, said FOAM's charges are totally unfounded. "I personally monitor the company's colony of research animals and can attest to their care and housing. It far exceeds state and federal requirements. Animal testing is kept to the bare minimum that allows for a safe product that meets the FDA's requirements."

"And this is a tasteful picture they've included—courtesy of FOAM, no doubt." Sally held the paper so Kent could see the photo of a would-be scientist stretching a wild-eyed rabbit across a stainless steel table as a second scientist dripped liquid from a beaker onto an area of freshly shaved skin. "Nice touch. Too bad the stuff in the beaker isn't smoking."

Sally rolled the newspaper into a tight tube. "Maybe you should tell the bitch you like coon hunting and that you own a coon dog. That ought to make some points with her."

"Lucy already met her." He stared at his dog as if looking at Benedict Arnold. "I think Lucinda likes her. At least she wagged her tail."

"Lucinda likes everyone."

He poured himself a cup of coffee, sank into a chair, and unfurled the newspaper. He flipped to the one article he had read and reread that morning:

Aaron James Whitmore, 70, died Tuesday. A native and lifelong resident of Jefferson, Mr. Whitmore graduated from the New York State Police Academy in 1939 before serving in the army in World War II. Under the command of General Eisenhower, he fought in the Normandy invasion at Omaha Beach. After the war, Mr. Whitmore returned to the Jefferson police department and was made chief in 1952. He retired in 1972.

An avid outdoorsman, Whitmore was active in the Boy Scouts of America throughout his life. For many years, he was a freelance outdoors writer for the Jefferson Dispatch. *His wife and love of his life, Claire, predeceased Aaron in 1977. They had no children. Surviving are sister Eunice M. Robinson of Old Forge and several nieces and nephews. A private family burial is planned. Contributions can be made to the Jefferson Police Youth Program or BSA Troop 18 in Jefferson.*

He turned from the obit when Sally thumped her forehead with the heel of her hand and moaned. "Damn!"

"What?"

"I was supposed to tell you Mrs. Philips called this morning. Her Maltese, Bear, is missing."

"He'll turn up."

"Right. I guess." Sally studied her fingernails, picked at a cuticle. "Have you noticed what I have? I think."

"Noticed what?"

"We've had more than the usual number of missing pets. You notice that? Not just the everyday idiots who let their animals run loose. I mean people who watch their animals carefully. A lot of them."

"Put them on the lost and found bulletin board. I'll start paying better attention."

"Usually people call back in a day or so, all apologetic, saying they found the escapee. Seems like I usually take down about as many missing posters as I put up. But lately, the pets aren't getting found."

Kent rolled Sally's observations over in his mind. "Let's keep track of it for a while." He tapped the newspaper. "Anyway, back to this FOAM thing. I should wring Merrill's neck for getting me into this. I should wring *my* neck for letting him get me into this. 'You're just going to be a figurehead.' Right."

"I think you should meet with her one-on-one."

Kent rolled his eyes toward the ceiling. "Yeah. Ms. FOAM and me, one-on-one. I can see it now."

"Why not?"

"If I want to get chewed up, I'll try to give a shot to some junk-yard dog. Besides, what could I gain from a one-on-one meeting?"

"You'd be able to argue your side. You do better without a crowd. You know what I mean? You're most convincing when you just talk to someone. Like you were just talking to me."

Kent considered Sally's idea while she redid the operating room for their next patient. After a few minutes, he set his coffee cup aside and leaned forward, elbows on knees.

"You know, the more I think about it, the more I like your idea."

"Oh, shit. Now I've done it."

"If I get this Fairbanks woman away from her comrades, she might loosen up. You never know."

"Like I said, it's your style." She let that thought hang for a perfectly timed moment, and then under her breath but loud enough that Kent would hear, she said, "Of course, sometimes your style ends up getting your ass kicked too."

He didn't have to see her tongue to know it was in her cheek. The thought of firing her flitted wistfully through his head.

Kent sat with the phone against his ear, listening to the emptiness of being on hold. He watched the thin red hand of the clock on his office wall ticking off seconds. This animal-care supervisor thing was taking up way too much time. Sally had rescheduled several

49

appointments. He had rushed through surgery and treatments. He hated slighting his clients and patients for this stuff. Eventually, a voice came back over the line, and by midafternoon he had confirmed a slot on Ms. FOAM's calendar. He set the phone down as Sally entered the office.

"We're on for tomorrow, Aubrey Fairbanks and me. Alone. Lunch, then maybe a tour of Jefferson."

Sally didn't respond. He looked up at her. She was starting back at him with blank eyes, her face ashen.

"What?"

She mouthed something, but no sound came out.

"Sally?"

She slumped into a chair, swallowed hard, and gave him the crushed look of an owner who had just witnessed her dog being run down by a car. "I went to get the mail."

"So?"

She held out a sheet of paper with a photo collage on it. "They want me to quit. They say they'll burn down our hospital."

Kent snatched the paper from her. It was a letter addressed to Sally.

"For Chrissake. This is like something in a TV movie." He studied the cinematic cliché. Odd-sized words and letters cut out of magazines to disguise the author's handwriting. It would have been funny if it weren't so frightening:

NO ANIMAL KILLERS IN JEFFERSON.
QUIT THE TORTURE CHAMBER SALLY
IT COULD GO UP IN SMOKE

Kent grabbed the phone and punched in the chief's number.

Kent waved the letter in his brother's face the second Merrill stepped into the clinic. "This your idea of a *figurehead*?" He tossed it on the desk.

Merrill scanned it quickly without touching it. "It's probably nothing."

"Nothing? It scared the hell out of Sally. You call a threat to burn my hospital nothing?"

"Take it easy. I didn't mean it that way. We'll check it out."

Merrill placed it carefully between a couple of paper towels and secured it to a stack of tattered papers on his clipboard.

"This stuff happens when there's an emotional issue. Odds are it's a prank. Some lowlife wants to jump on the bandwagon. It wouldn't make sense for FOAM to send this. They'd have to know you would bring a threat letter right to the police, and they'd be the number-one suspects. They have nothing to gain—they're too smart for that."

Sally arose out of her daze. "Kent, you better make a big hit at your meeting with Aubrey Fairbanks tomorrow."

"I'll make a hit, all right!"

Merrill's eyebrows lifted. "What meeting?"

When Kent ignored the question, Merrill shifted his eyes to Sally.

"He's going one-on-one with Ms. FOAM."

"When?"

"Tomorrow. Lunch."

Merrill's lips pursed into a satisfied expression. "That might work. Yeah. Animal-care supervisor meets FOAM field rep." He paused for the same perfect second Sally had. "Course, it could get you killed too."

Sally couldn't help but chuckle.

"How do you go about firing a police chief?" Kent said to her.

She was trying to think of a reply when Merrill held up his clipboard. "Before you get me fired, let me tell you about Lalomia's report. He faxed it to me this morning." Merrill teased several pages out and flipped through them in a way that told Kent he'd spent some time studying them already. "A couple of interesting points." He tapped with his finger as he hit key items. "No witnesses. Autopsy put the time of death at about ten at night. Lividity and all that stuff indicated the body was not moved. Rain washed away most of the little things forensic guys collect."

He paused, eyes still on the report.

Kent and Sally waited.

Finally, Merrill let them breathe. "But." He moved his gaze to Kent.

"Come on, Chief. But what?"

Merrill held up a pair of fingers. "There were *two* rounds fired from Aaron's revolver. Both casings were recovered still in the cylinder. One bullet was recovered alongside the handle of the passenger door." He paused again.

Kent took the bait. "What happened to the other one?"

Merrill shrugged, and let his brother run with it.

"Cause of death was the throat wound. Right?"

"It took out both carotid arteries and his trachea."

Kent grimaced. "Okay. He was lying across the front seat, right side down, gun in his right hand. You said that before. Correct?"

"Yep."

"Bullet was fairly low in the passenger door."

Kent formed his left hand into a revolver, held it to his neck, elbow held high. "Wouldn't this be kind of an awkward way to shoot yourself and then switch hands with the gun? I mean, it's the only way the bullet could end up in the passenger door from where Aaron was sitting."

Merrill kept his poker face. "People get weird at the moment they're going to do it. They wince and jerk. Their hands shake like hell won't have it. He may have been trying to put the muzzle under his chin and just twitched on the trigger before he got it up there."

"With his left hand? You ever see Aaron do anything with his left hand?"

"No."

"Me either. And I've seen him shoot too. He hit what he wanted to hit."

Merrill didn't respond.

"So what's up with the other shot? Do they figure he missed altogether with one shot?"

"They have no explanation for that. Yet."

"Yet? Meaning the investigation continues."

"Kent, like I said, it's a small force. No money. And a lot of odd, unexplained things happen in a suicide."

"So they're still calling it a suicide? Aaron was a cop, your boss, for a long time. What are *you* calling it?"

Merrill's eyes narrowed, he looked straight at Kent. "I'm calling it *open*."

Sally cast an uncomfortable look back and forth between the brothers. "The sixty-four thousand dollar question is what he was doing on the launch at ten o'clock at night."

CHAPTER 7

KENT FELT THE OLD DETERMINATION COMING
back. It was exhilarating. It was the attitude that had drawn people to
him. When the passion disappeared, so had everything else. He was
ready to get his meeting with Fairbanks under way. Was she behind
the anonymous note to Sally?

He had agreed to pick her up where she was staying, the Red
Horse Inn, and then find someplace for lunch where they could talk.

The inn was one of Jefferson's oldest establishments, with his-
torical society documents dating it back to before the French and
Indian War. Three stories of colonial red brick, even rows of windows flanked with black shutters, it was a massive building for its
day. Over the years, the thoroughfare had been widened and rewid-
ened to accommodate larger, more modern vehicles, until now, the
elegant structure sat almost on the curb with barely enough room for
its signpost and seven stone steps.

In the lobby, the desk clerk greeted him. "Hi, Doc." He didn't
bother to inquire Kent's business. "It'll be a minute. Ms. Fairbanks
asked that I buzz her when you arrived."

The lobby smelled faintly of oil soap and polish. Wood floorboards creaked under Kent's feet through rich oriental carpets. On
high, plastered walls, between twelve-over-twelve windows, hung
larger than life portraits of a half-dozen of Jefferson's forefathers. He
was squinting to read the brass plate beneath one when he heard soft
steps on the center stairs that descended from the rooms above.

Aubrey Fairbanks paused on the landing and scanned below her like a hunting panther. She wore an oversized sea-green sweatshirt that was fronted with the Greenpeace logo. A whale breached in the rolling surf created by her breasts. Her eyes had softened some since the Copithorn rally but still showed a glint that said *all business.* Her presence filled the room. She padded catlike down the stairs.

"Nice to see you again," he said, and he sort of meant it. He extended his hand, and she shook it. Her grip was firm.

Movement behind Aubrey drew Kent's eyes to a dark-haired, middle-school-aged boy, gangly now but destined to be tall and athletic. He was wearing baggy jeans and a T-shirt that commemorated Pink Floyd's *The Wall* tour, Los Angeles Memorial Sports Arena, February 8, 1980. Kent studied the gray-blue eyes that dominated the boy's face and knew before Aubrey could say so that they were of the same bloodline. She encircled the boy in an arm and drew him around in front of her.

"Dr. Stephenson, this is my son, Barry. Do you mind if he joins us today? I know you mentioned a one-on-one meeting, but I'd like to have him along. His allergies are acting up."

Barry twisted from under his mother's wing, uncomfortable at the betrayal of his frailty. "Mom!" His expression was a mix of youthful intelligence and boredom at having to endure yet another meeting with adults.

Kent smiled. Saw himself in the boy. "No problem at all. There's plenty of room." Barry's hand had his mother's soft warmth and firmness.

Kent led them toward the door. "Any preference where we eat? Of course, you don't know the area, but what do you like?"

Aubrey glanced at her son. Her eyes again flashed maternal concern.

"That's part of the reason I asked if Barry could join us. His diet has been off for the last few days. I know that's contributing to his allergy flare-up."

Kent's medically trained eye detected nothing about the boy that suggested allergies or any other infirmity.

"We're vegans," Aubrey said.

"Vegans?"

"Absolute vegetarians. It's hard to eat right on the road."

"No problem." Kent said for the second time and mentally scrapped the list of possible restaurants he'd compiled. "There's a place you might like a town over called the Wheat Sepal. It's a pretty drive."

At his truck, Kent asked, "You mind hopping in the back, Barry?"

"Nope." The boy pulled open the door as Lucinda sat up. "Holy crap!" Barry jumped and slammed the door. "I didn't expect to see that dog!" he said, trying to disguise his shock.

"Her name is Lucinda," Kent said. "She wouldn't hurt a flea. I should have warned you, sorry. I guess I just think of her as another person."

Barry gave his mother a questioning glance.

Aubrey fired a look at Kent. "That's right. You *own* a dog. I remember seeing her at the Copithorn rally."

"She's totally friendly. Loves everyone."

"That's not the point."

"She's clean. Gets a bath every few weeks."

"That is not the point either!"

"All right, I'll bite. What is the point?"

"Like I said at Copithorn. We condemn pet ownership in any form."

"If I'd thought about it, I would have left her at home. It's just that she goes everywhere with me."

"That dog will make Barry's allergies worse."

Kent was struggling for a way to break the deadlock when Barry opened the truck door again and pushed Lucinda back.

"Mom, I'm okay," he said with a *let-it-rest* tone. "I don't mind riding with a dog. She just surprised me. That's all."

"Thanks, Barry. Lucinda, get over on your own side." Kent pushed the delighted canine over to make room.

Aubrey made a show of opening her window. "Keep your window cracked, Barry. I want you to get plenty of fresh air."

"Mom!"

They drove through the rural upstate New York countryside—rolling hills rife with the fall smells of lakes and leaves, fresh-spread manure from dairy farms, and unpicked apples fermenting in the orchards.

"Pretty country," Aubrey said. "Southern California is dust dry this time of year."

Kent scanned the terrain. "Sort of a harmony we have here—dairy farms using animals to give us milk and cheese, intermingled with orchards giving us the fruit we need." The second he said it he wished he hadn't. He sounded like a rep for the department of tourism.

But Aubrey looked at him with raised eyebrows, as if she had not expected such insight from this man. Her expression softened a little. "Interesting observation."

They rounded a bend that was like a dozen others they had traveled. But this time Kent lifted his foot off the accelerator. The decrease in speed caused Aubrey and Barry to perk up. They looked ahead for some obstacle in the road, saw nothing unusual, and turned to Kent for an explanation. He was staring at a simple log cabin half-hidden by spruce trees, a hundred yards off the road. Beyond was Cuyler Lake.

"What's that place?" Aubrey asked.

Kent turned his head to hold his view of the cabin as the truck eased past. "An old friend lived there."

She scanned the cabin's meager landscaping. "Lawn needs mowing."

"He died recently."

"Oh. I'm sorry."

"The lawn usually needed mowing even when he was alive."

"Let me guess. He spent all his time hunting and fishing?"

"Exactly," Kent said with satisfaction.

"How did he die?"

"We don't know yet." There was an edge on his voice that signaled the subject was not for discussion.

Aubrey caught it, stared at him a moment, and then let the subject drop.

● ● ●

"The Wheat Sepal," Barry read from his menu as the trio squeezed around a tiny table in the little restaurant. "Now, *that* sounds like LA."

It made Kent chuckle.

Decor was sixties—the furnishings were clean but second-hand—attic and auction stuff. Nothing matched. Surprising to Kent, almost every table was occupied. "I've never eaten here, but they've got a pretty good reputation."

Aubrey spoke without looking up from her menu. "Lots of good choices. Finally. I'm starving. Barry, this should suit you too."

"That's a relief," Kent said into his napkin.

Aubrey and Barry ordered things foreign to Kent and seemed satisfied with their choices. Kent ordered spanakopita at Aubrey's suggestion and a takeout order of tabbouleh. The vegetables in filo were better than he expected. He let the tabbouleh sit next to his plate in its cardboard carton.

When he sensed the effects of the meal had improved his odds, he broached the reason for their meeting. "So, tell me about FOAM."

Aubrey seemed reluctant to break back to business. She set down her fork and chewed a moment, getting back into character. "Well, we're California-based, as I'm sure you are aware. Hollywood, to be exact."

Kent did not stifle his smirk adequately.

"Hollywood is the center for a lot of progressive thinking."

"More like the center for a lot of high-profile people with too much money."

"If that's what you want to believe, I'm sure I won't be able to convince you otherwise."

"Sorry. I'm listening. Go ahead."

Aubrey started again. "FOAM is a group of individuals bound by the philosophy that, among other things, all animals are entitled to the same rights as feebleminded humans."

Kent marveled at how she could maintain such a self-assured air while making what he considered such an asinine statement. A voice inside Kent's head whispered, *Zealot, zealot, zealot.*

"We promote religious traditions of earlier times, the Earth Mother, the Matrix-Creatrix, Gaia, Pan, Diana. Man linked as an integral component to the rest of the animal kingdom."

Kent closed his eyes, pinching the bridge of his nose as if warding off a headache. "That's an easy position for the ultrawealthy of Hollywood to take. It is a very unsettling thought for any of us who understand and love animals. We get it that mankind needs their sacrifice for our food, clothing, and recreation."

"Like we really need to eat meat. And zoos? Horse racing? Dog racing? Rodeos? You could live without them. Easily."

Kent shook his head. "Not easily." He paused. "Then there is the matter of animals in research."

"Research can be done with computer models."

"That is simply not true. Control of diseases from smallpox to diphtheria and a hundred others occurred because of animal testing."

"They did not have computers back then."

Barry cleared his throat loudly, and simultaneously both adults remembered he was there.

"Sorry, Barry. We kind of got caught up. Didn't mean to leave you out." Kent searched for a neutral topic to include the boy. Finally he said, "I guess you get to travel a lot. That's got to be fun, right?"

"I've been on every continent except Antarctica."

"I bet not many kids in your school can say that."

"I'm homeschooled, which is probably the weirdest thing about me. At least most other kids think so. Except the ones who think being a vegan is more weird."

Kent gave his *no-big-deal* look. "Where's your house?"

"Anaheim. It's a great house. Big. Lots of rooms and a pool." The boy's expression became wistful. "Seems like we've been away for a long time."

"Judging from your shirt, you're into music, huh?"

"Yeah. I collect a lot of tapes, and I've been to more rock concerts than any kid I know."

"That's for sure," Aubrey said it with a smile.

"What about sports?"

"Basketball mostly."

"Lakers?"

"UCLA Bruins."

"Maybe someday they'll play Syracuse in the NCAA tournament."

"They your team?"

"Of course. Go Orange!"

Barry snickered. "I feel sorry for you. The Bruins are back. Syracuse is flat."

Kent's eyebrows squirmed into a wave of indignation. "No way!" He took a sip of his coffee, studied the boy. His thoughts drifted away from sports. "You like being a...what is it...vegan...vegetarian, or whatever?"

"It's okay. I've been one my whole life."

"Don't have much to compare to then, do you?"

Out of the corner of his eye, Kent saw Aubrey's posture become more rigid. The she-bear guarding her cub.

"Mom is one, so I became one. I never really felt like I missed anything, if that's what you mean." He remembered something and laughed. "Plus there was Mom's Otis story." He looked at Aubrey as if this was her cue. "Tell it, Mom."

Aubrey shook her head. "Not now, Barry."

"Come on, Mom."

She started to protest again and then sighed. "What the heck?"

Kent pushed back in his chair and crossed his arms, settling in for a story. The soft light and mismatched furnishings made her look more childlike than Barry.

"I guess I need to set the scene for you with a little background on my early home life. My parents were killed in a car accident when I was about the age Barry is now—somewhere out on those Iowa highways where everyone drives a hundred miles an hour. I have a mental image of them, but I'm not sure how much is true memory and how much is from pictures I've seen and stories I've heard. After that, I went to live with my father's brother's family outside of Des Moines."

She let out a little laugh that was an unsuccessful attempt to hide the emotions that went with the memories.

"I didn't fit in very well. They were rugged farmers, heavily into football and tractor pulls. I was from the city. Uncle Walt always believed my mother had taken advantage of my dad's post-Korea blues and led him down the primrose path." She made a gesture like Kent should understand. "She was an actress and a real knockout."

She paused a long moment. "I reminded Uncle Walt of my mother, and he was going to make sure I followed the straight and narrow."

Barry reached over and took a gentle hold of his mother's arm. "Mom, don't tell it so sad. That's not what I wanted. Tell it funny. You know, like you used to when I was little."

Aubrey rolled her eyes to the ceiling, and released a calming breath. She started again, only this time there was a much more musical tone to her voice, and Kent warmed to it.

"Anyway, in case you didn't already know, in Iowa, meat is a really big thing. Beef, poultry, you name it, but especially pork. My Uncle Walt mostly grew corn and soybeans, but for a cash crop he had a couple hundred hogs. And," she shook her head as if the thought of it amazed her even after all these years, "like all good Iowa kids, my two cousins, William and Oakley, and I belonged to 4-H and raised a pig each year to show. One year I made the mistake of naming mine. Otis. Things were never the same after that. It became a *Charlotte's Web* kind of relationship."

Aubrey glanced at Kent. "You know the old rule: Never name anything you intend to eat."

"Oh, boy," he said.

Aubrey nodded. "Otis did all right at the fair, but not good enough to get a stay of execution. So sure enough, when fall came around, and I was dreading it, I saw Uncle Walt and the boys setting up the meat hooks and the vat in the barn. I spent the whole rest of the afternoon with Otis. I didn't even come in for supper. My cousins couldn't believe it. Finally, Aunt Margaret came and got me at bedtime. But at first light I was right back out there. I know Aunt Margaret felt bad for me, but she and I both knew it would be hopeless to argue with Uncle Walt."

Aubrey sighed deeply and gestured with palms up. "That afternoon when I got home from school, I ran straight out to Otis's pen, and he and about ten of his pals were gone."

There was a grievous silence.

Finally Kent said, "That's a sad story."

"It is, except that's not the end. I think all kids go through that to some degree at some time. But what really locked me in as a vegan was the incessant teasing from my cousins. Every time we had pork, which was often, William and Oakley would start mock crying for

Otis or say something else to hurt my feelings. I wanted to just run away from the table, but Uncle Walt was a firm believer in thanking God for all the bounty he'd given us by not wasting any. I had to sit there until I ate every bit of food on my plate, including Otis. It was awful."

Aubrey mustered a laugh for Barry's sake.

"That's how I became a vegan. I've stayed one and promoted it ever since because, with time, I recognized there are a lot of more important reasons for not eating meat. Even more important than Otis."

Her tone had such finality to it that it effectively brought their meal to a close.

"And that's the Otis story," Barry said.

Kent guessed the boy had heard countless versions of the sordid tale since he was old enough to sit still. The pathos was gone now for him. It was just another funny family story. Kent signaled the waiter for their check.

"Let's go ride around some more. See the sights of Jefferson."

Aubrey seemed relieved at the suggestion.

CHAPTER 8

LUCINDA QUIVERED WITH EXCITEMENT. SHE
pressed her nose on the window of the truck as she watched Kent,
Aubrey, and Barry approaching across the Wheat Sepal's parking lot.

"Barry, let that ol' fleabag out, will you? See if she'll eat this."
Kent held out the carton of tabbouleh that had been next to his plate
during lunch.

He could not remember the last time he had dined with a
woman and child. It reminded him of the old days with Mary and
Emily. It was a good feeling.

Barry flashed his mother a hopeful look. "Can I?"

Aubrey nodded half-heartedly.

Barry grabbed the container. "Will she eat it right out of
the box?"

"Take her over in the grass," Kent said. "Lucy, go with Barry."

Aubrey and Kent leaned against the truck watching boy and
dog. Barry held the carton over his head, laughing and fending off
Lucinda as he walked.

"Don't put your hands near her food while she's eating.
Sometimes they'll bite," Aubrey said. Then she caught herself. "Sorry,
I get wrapped up in this parenting thing."

Kent smiled, eyes still on the pair. "He could put his head down
on the plate. She wouldn't bite."

Lucinda sniffed the gooey wheat purée Barry set before her,
raised her head, and cast a bewildered look at Kent.

"Sorry, girl, that's all I have. It's good for you."

As if to demonstrate her loyalty, the big dog dove into her meal.

"She prefers hamburgers."

Aubrey released the musical laugh again.

"How'd you get involved in this FOAM thing anyway?"

"One thing led to another, I guess. A few years after the Otis affair, I left Iowa for Chicago. Became a model, if you can believe that."

Kent could. Easily.

"Then I decided to do the Hollywood thing—you know, become an actress. I never really made it in showbiz, but I met a lot of interesting people. Influential people. Eventually, I married one of them. It didn't work out, but that's how Barry came into the picture. For a few years I drifted. Professionally that is. And personally, I guess, too. I was searching for where I fit in. About that time, the animal rights movement began picking up steam. The rest is history."

"You're not married now?"

"No. It's me and Barry." She stared, soft focused, out at the boy. "I don't know what I'd do without him."

"Yeah. He seems like a nice kid."

She looked square into Kent's eyes the way she had at their first meeting, but this time he noticed a gentleness, a melancholy warmth, that wasn't there before.

"How about you? Any family?"

Talking about himself usually made Kent uncomfortable, but somehow he felt different with Aubrey. Opening up to her wasn't too bad, like there was a chance she would get it and figure out what he was really like, and maybe even understand why he held his beliefs about animals. "I've got a daughter, Emily. She's nine. She lives with her mother. I wasn't too successful with the marriage game either."

"Too committed to your work?"

"I hate to admit being so stupid, but that's it. I dug my own grave."

"You miss her a lot?"

"Terribly. In that regard, Lucinda doesn't cut it."

"You're pretty good with self-analysis. You should come to California, the land of shrinks and therapy groups—touchy-feely heaven."

"Makes my blood run cold just thinking about it." He was relieved when Lucinda finished her health food and came bounding over. "Load in, girl. We're headed back."

Kent took a different route home. He guided the car slowly along a narrow ribbon of macadam that snaked its way through hills and valleys. They passed several dairy farms, and Kent pointed out a herd of cows loafing on a green knoll shaded by a fence line of old maples.

"You realize that if you eliminate farming, you can forget having the ready supply of milk, ice cream, cheese, and the rest of the dairy products Americans have learned to expect. Same for meat."

"There are alternatives."

"Yeah, right."

"You tell me how you love and respect animals, and then in the next breath you tell me you condone their abuse."

"I don't condone animal abuse! But I don't criminalize all animal use. And, by the way, FOAM resorts to some pretty criminal activities too!" He really didn't know how that statement had worked its way into his consciousness and out of his mouth. But it was too late to retract it.

"What?" Aubrey said, obviously caught off guard.

"You know what I mean! Your group doesn't mind crossing the legal line once in a while."

"I don't know what you're talking about."

"I'm simply saying that FOAM breaks the law to accomplish its goals."

"That's not true! We work within the law. Always."

"Always?"

"Yes. Always!"

Kent brought the truck to an abrupt stop along a wide stretch of shoulder. With both hands still on the wheel, he turned to look directly at FOAM's leader.

"I suppose you know nothing about an anonymous note my receptionist received."

"I don't know about any note. And we certainly didn't send one."

"Yesterday?"

"Not yesterday. Not ever!"

"Well, Sally, my receptionist, got a note telling her to quit working for me. It also implied my clinic might get torched. You don't know about that?"

"That did not come from FOAM, I can assure you. Hate mail and threats of violence are not our style. If that was the way FOAM worked, I'd be outta there."

Aubrey's simple disclaimer deflated him.

"We've got the police working on it," he said with more confidence than he really felt. "They'll find out who sent it."

"I hope they do!" She glanced back at Barry to see that he was paying attention. "FOAM always works within the law."

Kent steered back onto the road. Frustration lapsed into a silent stalemate for several miles.

Finally, Kent said, "I just thought of a place I should take you. You ought to see Jefferson's new animal shelter. It's state of the art."

"State of the art animal shelter. Kind of an oxymoron, wouldn't you say? Like Copithorn's animal-care supervising veterinarian." Except this time there was no hostility.

"You never let up, do you? You want to see the pound or not?"

"Sure. I'm up for a shock."

Aubrey wasn't sure if she was delighted or galled that the Dewitt County animal shelter was not shocking. In fact, it was hospital clean and well lighted and ventilated. She guessed four hundred animals held, hopefully temporary, residence in its three wings—about half cats, half dogs. There were a few grumps, but mostly smiling pet faces. Amazingly, she didn't hear a single cough!

They proceeded along a row of pens, each housing a small pack of motley dogs that piled forward in a jiggling mass of excitement to greet Barry. Kent expected the usual *I want one*, but the boy seemed content to squat near the cages and speak soft words of encouragement to hopeful eyes, while soft pink tongues moistened his fingers through the wire.

At the far end there was a couple with two young children engrossed in a family debate over which pup to adopt. And closer by, a slender black man was scooping small dogs into a large crate he had apparently brought with him. Kent watched him grab several. He worked rapidly, seemingly paying no attention to the characteristics of any of his adoptees.

"Where'd a rural county come up with the money for a facility like this?" Aubrey asked. Her question broke Kent's attention from the curious way the man was collecting dogs.

"Good luck, mostly. The state wanted to put a highway through where our old one was. Our lawyers got us top dollar out of that, and then we got a couple of matching contributions from local philanthropists. And we had a few fund drives."

"This place is really nice."

"We work hard to keep it that way."

"You must have a big crematorium."

"No, damn it! I mean adoptions. Give us some credit, will you!"

"I will when I figure you deserve it."

Kent shook his head in an *I-can't-win* gesture. Then he noticed a woman hosing a dog pen ahead of them. As they approached, he said, "Connie Hirt, meet Aubrey Fairbanks. Connie is the shelter director."

The middle-aged woman wiped her hand on her sweatshirt and extended it. "With FOAM, right? I've heard a lot about you."

Aubrey shook her hand. "I imagine. And not much good either."

"Actually, not so bad. Depends how you look at it. We are animal lovers too. We just differ with you guys on how and how much. You know what I mean?"

"Sort of," Aubrey said.

Connie drew her forearm across her brow, buckled her knees in exaggerated weariness, and looked at Kent. "Business is booming lately."

"That's good, I'd say."

"I can't remember ever placing pups and cats so fast."

"Don't knock it."

"Oh, I'm not."

The shelter director paused and toyed with the nozzle of her hose, appearing to consider whether or not to mention something else. Finally she said, "It's just a little strange. Like that guy over there." They turned to where the man had been snatching up pups, but he was gone. "He must have just left. Did you happen to notice he took several dogs and one cat?"

"Yeah. I was watching him. He took quite a few."

"There's been a few of those." Connie shrugged her shoulders. "I mean, usually we get the family with young kids making a big thing out of deciding on their next pet. Takes a couple of visits sometimes. You know what I mean? But lately we've had a run of guys by themselves. They stop in, pick out a bunch of pups and cats in five or ten minutes, and leave."

"Did you ask any of them what they were doing with all these new pets?"

"Not really. They say something vague like they're getting hunting dogs or barn cats.

"You know who that guy was?"

"Nope. Don't recognize most of them."

For a moment, Kent searched for a logical explanation but could find none. "Like you say, it's odd." Then he remembered something else. "By the way, I promised Maureen Philips that I'd alert you that her dog, Bear, is missing."

"She already called." Connie pointed with a thumb over her shoulder. "I put her name with Bear's description on the bulletin board. That's another thing. Come look at this."

Connie led Aubrey, Kent, and Barry back into the entry foyer. She waved at a corkboard wall, every inch cluttered with multicolored posters, handwritten notes, and three-by-five cards pleading for the return of lost animals. "I never saw so many missing pets!"

"Strange. Sally mentioned the same thing about the lost and found board at our clinic."

"Dognappers," Barry said. There was youthful intrigue in his voice.

Connie gave a short laugh. "In Jefferson?"

Kent felt Aubrey's eyes burning him.

CHAPTER 9

AFTER THE ANIMAL SHELTER TOUR, KENT dropped Aubrey and Barry back at the Red Horse and moved Lucinda to the front seat. He drove back toward his clinic thinking about all the questions Sally would have. She'd want every detail. Was Aubrey Fairbanks a bitch one-on-one too? Did he find out about the anonymous letter? Did he convince Ms. Fairbanks that people owning animals is okay? Some of the questions would be easy. Some would be impossible.

It had been an interesting afternoon to say the least. He doubted he'd made any real change in Aubrey's attitude. But the big thing was, he genuinely liked her, to his amazement. She was a complex woman with a simple clarity of purpose. The combination intrigued him. And he honestly believed she liked him. He had felt it when her eyes softened and had heard it in her laugh. He wanted to see her again.

He liked Barry too. He was a typical adolescent pushing his way out from under his mother's wing. Just a boy—Kent smiled to himself as the image of Barry and Lucinda in the backseat returned. Aubrey genuinely loved the kid, no doubt about that. Unfortunately, she bound him with her dogma and overprotectiveness. Allergies, schmallergies—it was as obvious as the nose on his face, the boy needed a friend. A dog! That's what Aaron Whitmore would have said. Yep. He could hear Aaron saying it, *Get the boy a dog. That's what he needs.* Aaron's solution to any problem was to connect with nature. Why hadn't it worked up at Cuyler Lake?

As he pondered that, an uncontrollable impulse rose from the corner of his heart where he had stowed his mourning for Aaron. He slammed on the brakes and cranked the steering wheel, causing the truck to spin into a jostling, creaking 180. He took off toward Aaron's cabin like a fox being chased by a pack of hounds.

Lucinda whined nervously.

The driveway to Aaron's cabin was a narrow ribbon formed by two parallel tire tracks and a center mound that grabbed the undercarriage of any vehicle that traveled it too quickly. Kent scraped bottom a time or two before pulling to a stop in the dooryard under a massive white oak, from which many a deer had hung.

Kent surveyed the sparse plot of grass surrounding the cabin. Aubrey was right—it did need mowing, but still, he resented her saying so. He felt protective of the old building. Aaron had built it himself and boasted proudly that it was a real log cabin, not some prefab job ordered off a lot and assembled in a week. He had cut the logs, oiled them, seasoned them, and built every stick of it himself. He and Claire had lived in it for thirty years. It was Aaron's cabin.

Kent stepped onto the covered porch that spanned the entire front. There was a pair of high-back wicker rockers, forest green, placed so that Aaron and Claire could watch the bird feeders that hung a few feet out in the yard. A hand-hewn table between them held a pair of berry-picking baskets and several Hubbard squash. Birds chirped nearby, wondering why the feeders were empty.

Kent reached up to a log ledge above a pair of snowshoes that hung on the cabin's face. He ran his fingers along it until he found a key. He inserted it into the lock and pushed his way into the cabin.

Immediately his nostrils filled with the familiar, sweet fragrance of pine logs, wood ashes, and gun oil. The layout was simple, to the right, a large kitchen, to the left, a living area complete with a woodstove on a stone hearth. Kent couldn't remember ever seeing it without a fire this time of year. There was a bedroom and bathroom in the rear and an open loft over them. Though the furnishings were rustic, the cabin was clean, and when Aaron was there, always warm and inviting, a place Kent loved to visit.

He glanced at the twelve-point buck mounted by the hearth. Aaron's pride and joy. He scanned shelves laden with books of woods lore and a rack of polished hunting rifles, and he smiled at the sight of Aaron's old AM tube radio. The place was a study in Adirondack decor except for a shiny new IBM Selectric on Aaron's oak desk. Kent stepped to it and searched the otherwise barren desktop. Nothing. He pulled open the top drawer and jumped back with a start.

"Jesus!"

The image of his mother smiled back at him.

Guardedly, he lifted the frameless picture into better light and examined it. It was June Stephenson Mays, all right. He guessed she was in her midthirties and casting a warm glow at the camera from her seat on a porch swing. The edges were worn as if the photo had been held many times in caring hands. In the lower right, in his mother's looping cursive, he read: *To Aaron, the man I came to know too late. Love always, June.*

For the first time Kent ever, a feeling of betrayal toward Aaron welled up inside him. How could he have missed a relationship between his mother and his mentor? He studied the picture once more, then carefully placed his mother back as Aaron had left her. He racked his brain for a better explanation. None came. As he thought about it, he pawed through the rest of the desk.

In one drawer, under a sheaf of typing paper, he pulled out a clean, new manila folder, opened it, and again was shocked. His half brother's cold eyes stared at him. This time the picture was small, fuzzy yellow with age, and framed in print. It was a newspaper article from a decade ago. Bold type above Maylon Mays's mug shot read: JEFFERSON MAN SENTENCED FOR ANIMAL WELFARE VIOLATIONS.

He shuffled through several more articles in the folder. "What the heck?" he said into the empty cabin. "What was Aaron up to?"

● ● ●

Aubrey Fairbanks sat alone in a corner booth of the Red Horse Inn's taproom. She contemplated the gilded letters on the mirror behind the bar, THE GROGGERY. Soft light, deep mahogany, and old brass made it dark and cozy. She leaned back against the wall and looked down at her legs sprawled full length on the bench. Still nice and firm, no cellulite. She rocked toward the black-glass tabletop and stared at her reflection—just a little too full for the camera. She'd have to watch that.

She lifted her empty glass, rattling its sludge of fruit and ice at the barmaid.

Without coming from behind the bar, a tiny, sienna-skinned woman with Indian cheekbones made a questioning expression and mouthed, "A*nother?*"

Aubrey nodded. She poked through the fruit at the bottom of her glass with a long fingernail and then slurped a soggy cherry into her mouth. She'd have to be careful of these. Nowhere did it say vegans couldn't have a drink, but at the same time, nowhere did it say old-fashioneds, fruit muddled, wouldn't make vegans as fat as anyone else.

She was glad Barry had gotten caught up in his movie upstairs. It was nice to be alone for a while. She was torn in too many directions these days—a single parent, demands of work, living out of hotels. And Barry's schooling. She hadn't realized the magnitude of the task when she had opted for homeschooling. *Home*schooling? That was a laugh. *Hotel* schooling would be more accurate.

She did a slow take of the room. Empty. Almost. Still early. There was a collegiate-looking couple quietly nursing beers in a corner. The only other patron was a man at the bar, his back toward Aubrey. Stringy brown hair squeezed from under his baseball cap and draped onto meaty shoulders. He was big but slouchy. Dark tanned arms and neck would place him more in a country music-blasting roadhouse than in the understated ambiance of the Groggery. He engaged in heated conversation with the barmaid each time she passed near him. She looked around nervously when the man's gravelly whispers became too loud. Both conversed angrily, with much gesturing and disgruntled expressions.

Aubrey was halfway through her drink when she leaned her head back against the wall and closed her eyes, languishing in rare solitude.

It was an abrasive, throat-clearing grunt close by that aroused her from dreamy tranquility. She snapped open her eyes to focus on the stranger from the bar looming over her, leering at her legs. Reflexively, she recoiled them under the table.

"How long have you been there?"

"Just long enough for a look."

His eyes were embedded in dark sockets above a matted beard. He emitted a musty odor, like a kennel suffering an outbreak of distemper.

"I was wondering if I could talk to you a minute." His lips twitched in and out of a wry smile.

"I'm really not looking for company."

"This is business."

"Business? What kind?"

"It'll only take a minute. Can I sit down?"

"Give me a little more information."

"It's about Copithorn. I can help you with your problem there."

"I don't have a problem. Copithorn has a problem."

"Whatever. You want to see them stop hurting animals, don't you?"

"Keep talking."

"Can I sit down?"

Aubrey reluctantly signaled him into the seat across from her. "Yes, I'd like to see Copithorn quit experimenting with animals."

"Well, wouldn't it look bad if they found somebody's pet dog in there?"

"Who are *they*?"

"The police. And what if Copithorn had a fire?"

Aubrey leaned away from the man's foul breath. "If I get your drift, you're suggesting something way too extreme for our organization."

"I'm not asking you to do nothing. I'm just asking if it would look bad."

"Forget it. We'd be the number-one suspects."

"Me and a few friends have a personal reason to see Copithorn take some heat." He shook his head in disgust. "And it ain't because they hurt poor little animals."

He said it in a way that made Aubrey think he would probably enjoy seeing animals suffer. It angered her, and the idea of this boor tying FOAM to some personal vendetta angered her more.

"Listen. I don't know what you're talking about, and I don't want to know. If you've got a problem with Copithorn, you deal with it. Leave me, and FOAM, out of it."

The barmaid appeared next to the table and pointed at the man. "Is he bothering you, miss?"

"Never mind, Tammy," the man said before Aubrey could reply. "I'm outta here. We're done talking."

The little woman watched him move slowly out the door. Then she turned to Aubrey with an embarrassed look. "I'm sorry, ma'am. He don't mean nothin'. He's just drunk. I'd ignore him if I were you."

Aubrey's eyes shifted from the stranger to the barmaid and back. She said nothing but sensed the last thing she should do was ignore him.

CHAPTER 10

KENT SAT AT HIS DESK, HUMMING "STARS AND Stripes Forever" as he rifled through a pile of window envelopes. His back was to Sally, who was addressing postcard reminders to owners whose pets were due for vaccinations.

"The bills never stop," he said almost cheerfully.

"Amazing, isn't it?"

"Seems to me that we haven't been busy enough to run up these kinds of bills."

"It has been sort of slow lately. Want me to take my car out and hit a few dogs and cats? You know, stir up a little business?"

"If you do, you've got to be accurate." Kent kept the black joke going. "You can't kill them. No money in that."

"What you want, then, is just a real expensive fractured leg?"

"Now you've got it. One for the morning, one for the afternoon for a week or two. That ought to get our cash flow where we want it."

Their sarcasm was interrupted by the telephone. Sally answered it. As Kent half listened, he turned to Lucinda. "Don't worry, girl. We're not really going to hit-and-run any of your buddies."

From her rug, Lucinda rolled her brown eyes but did not dignify his remark with a tail wag.

"It's Merrill." Sally stretched the phone cord so Kent could take it.

"Morning, boss."

"You sound cheerful," Merrill said. "Must be you haven't heard what happened last night."

"All is well as far as I know."

"Copithorn burned last night."

"What?" Kent said into the phone loud enough to make Sally turn.

"Not the whole place. They had a big fire in the research wing. Destroyed it. Firemen are still at the scene, but it's gone."

Kent stared at Sally, phone to his ear. He slipped his palm over the mouthpiece. "There was a fire at Copithorn last night."

"You're kidding!"

He repeated what little Merrill had just told him. Then he said into the receiver, "Where are you now?"

"At the station. But I'm headed back over there to meet the arson boys. I thought I'd pick you up on the way."

"You figure it's arson?" He knew the answer before he asked.

"Does a bear shit in the woods? That's why I need to talk to you."

"FOAM is on the list of suspects. Right?"

"Wrong. FOAM *is* the list of suspects. I need to know about your meeting with their gang leader…whatever her name is."

"Aubrey Fairbanks. I was going to call you to tell you I didn't think Aubrey…er, Ms. Fairbanks was likely to overstep the law." He hesitated. "Guess I was wrong."

"Very. She's overstepped the law, all right."

"How much damage is there?"

"Lots of cooked puppies and bunnies mostly."

"Jesus."

"A million and a half will probably build the place back."

"I can't believe they would do that. Did I ever buy into her line of bull. Yeah, Merrill, stop by and pick me up. I'll be ready."

How gullible can a person be? He had believed her! Or maybe he'd simply wanted to believe her.

● ● ●

Kent scowled through the window of Merrill's cruiser, oblivious to the background chatter of the police radio. Village scenery was an irrelevant blur as it passed. All he could think about was how he'd been duped.

Merrill didn't help. "So you figure you misjudged her, huh?"

Kent kept his eyes aimed out the window. "I admit I am the ultimate sucker. She told me, 'Violence is not FOAM's style. We work within the law.'" His voice was dripping with sarcasm. "What a crock. She's just as evil as the rest."

"You should have known, brother. That's why you're not a cop, I guess. You're not cynical enough. You've got to remember, they're guilty until proved innocent."

"I'm learning."

"Yeah. Well, don't take it too hard. We'll get to the bottom of this mess. You could say, we'll ferret out the perpetrator."

Merrill's weak pun caused Kent to shift his gaze toward his brother. He countered the chief's simpering grin with a look of disgust.

"Sorry," Merrill said. "Anyway, tell me about your meeting with Ms. Fairbanks."

Kent thought momentarily. He could feel his anger tainting the image of Aubrey and her FOAM cohorts. "They believe all animals should be wild, no domestication of any type. And they are against any use of animals by man."

"Any at all?"

"Any. They have a lot of quasiscientific jargon to support their position. And they expound alternatives to animal use. Most of it wouldn't work."

"But they think it will."

"Right. They play heavily on human emotion. You know, tug at a person's heartstrings. 'How would you like to be in the poor little bunny's place?' kind of thing. Make every issue a matter of rescuing the helpless, suffering animal. Then, to top it off, they throw in religion as a wildcard that gives them an unfair advantage."

"Religion?"

"Yeah. They flaunt religion as their reason for action. Except, instead of the usual, 'God is on our side,' they say the opposite. 'There is no God. We are not made in his image. We have no immortal soul. We are just animals in the big picture of nature—creatures of the Earth Mother, like all the rest."

"Sounds like a neo-pagan cult to me."

Kent's eyebrows V'd into a questioning look. "Neo-pagan cult?"

Merrill smiled slyly. "Pretty astute, huh?"

"From you? Yeah. Where'd you get it?"

"Actually, I'm reading a book about the rise of Nazism. It calls Nazis neo-pagans. They believe the same crap— man is just an animal, no different from a rat or a cockroach."

"That's about what it boils down to, now that you mention it."

Merrill wheeled the police car through the gate at Copithorn. Last week's picketers were now replaced by a police guard. An officer waved them through.

Ahead, Kent could see a thin gray plume of smoke floating skyward out of a charred window frame. All else was strangely still. Scorched cages and furnishings extracted from the building sat among hoses crisscrossing through puddles in the parking lot next to the burned-out building. Firefighters stood in small groups talking or were quietly stowing their gear.

Merrill rolled down his window as a firefighter with a chief's insignia on his helmet slogged over. The acrid odor of burning chemicals and electrical fire rolled into the car. Lucinda, in the backseat, sneezed hard.

"Hi, Tod. Looks like you guys are winding down."

"We are. Not too much more we can do." Tod thumbed toward two men in trench coats conversing beyond the firefighters. "The investigators take over from here."

"Any ideas?"

"It'll be arson for sure, if that's what you mean. The fire originated in at least two, possibly three, spots."

Neither brother showed surprise.

"You figure it was the animal rights people?"

Merrill kept his tone neutral. "Time will tell. Can we look around?"

"It's okay with me if you go in, Merrill, but I'm not sure I can let you in, Kent. Official personnel only. You know what I mean?"

"I'm Copithorn's animal-care supervisor. There're animals in there. Right?"

"Lots. But I don't think you can help them."

"I'll take a look anyway. I need to make a report."

The explanation was enough to satisfy Tod. He waved them through.

"You're getting pretty assertive in your old age," Merrill said as they walked toward the rubble. "It's about time. I like seeing the old Kent."

"Yeah? I hadn't noticed."

Ahead, Kent saw Stef Copithorn. She picked up their approach.

Her hands were locked on the lapels of an ultra-suede overcoat, pulling it around her like a kid hiding in bed. Red circles glowed under each eye. "Morning, gentlemen," she said.

"Hi, Stef. I'm sorry about all this," Kent said. It sounded hollow. "You okay?"

"As good as I can be under the circumstances."

"Right. Do you need anything?"

"Yeah." She gave a short sad laugh. "A research wing."

"Whole thing gone?"

"I'd say ninety-five percent, after a quick look-through."

Kent used his toe to nudge a blackened stainless steel water bowl that lay on the macadam. "This never should have happened."

"It's not your fault, Kent."

"I talked to her. Yesterday. To Aubrey Fairbanks, that is. They're a bunch of selfish, vicious thugs. I didn't know it then, but I do now. We'll get them."

Stef did not seem so confident. She stared blankly into the smoldering remains of her research building and said nothing.

Kent drifted away as an insurance adjuster approached Stef and introduced himself.

"Let's have a look inside," he said when he caught up to his brother.

They entered through a steel fire door warped by the heat. A lone fireman remained inside watching for flare-ups. He looked at their footwear.

"In those street shoes, you better stay away from the back corner. Still pretty hot back there. The rest should be all right."

They stepped carefully through sodden black ash and heat-mangled debris. The flat black that coated the walls seemed to swallow the beam from Merrill's flashlight.

Kent tried to remember the layout from their tour a few days ago. "This must have been a rabbit ward. Right?"

"I think so." Merrill forced open a cage door. Its hinges were twisted out of alignment by the heat. He studied a bundle of singed fur huddled against the back. "Yeah. This is a rabbit all right."

Kent stepped over and confirmed it. He shuddered at the thought of the creature's last moments of life. "Talk about cruelty to animals. What do they think *this* is?"

"Hey. They probably figure it's the cost of making a statement. Sacrifice a few for the good of the many."

They pushed through the burned-out rooms one after another. Like most veterinarians, Kent had a strong stomach for gore, but he felt it rolled as they entered the dog ward they had toured with

Stef. Each cage held a canine victim frozen in a hideous contortion. Some had died with paws outstretched through the bars, some had attempted to burrow into corners, all whose expressions were discernible had died in terror.

He noticed a canine body lying on its side across a lab counter. It must have been there during the fire, he thought. Hair on its side was almost completely burned away, and charred flesh and skin was exposed. It seemed smaller than the others.

"What time do they figure the fire started?" he asked.

"Haven't pinned it down yet. Sometime after midnight they think."

"That's odd."

"How so?"

"There's a body here on the counter. Why was it left out? It must have been dead before the fire. Right? Or it wouldn't be there."

"Maybe for an autopsy in the morning."

"Maybe. But I imagine they'd have left it in some sort of cooler. At least it would be in a plastic bag." Kent gently elevated the tiny creature by the tip of a rigored toe. "I don't see the remains of any plastic underneath."

"Got me."

Kent let it go. "Who knows? Let's get out of here."

The air outside smelled like springtime on a trout stream in contrast to the burned-out lab filled with soot. Kent scuffed the ash off his shoes in a patch of grass. "Now what?"

"We begin our investigation. Of course."

"Meaning what?"

"Meaning"—Merrill gave his brother a direct look—"don't expect an answer overnight. You let me do my job. We've got a systematic approach to this sort of thing."

"Think you can nail the bastards?"

"Probably. We usually do." Merrill climbed into his cruiser. "You want me to drop you back at your clinic?"

"Yes. I need to get cleaned up before I head over to the Red Horse."

"What you got going there?"

"I'm going to pay another visit to Ms. Fairbanks."

Merrill groaned. "Don't do anything to compromise our investigation. You got it?"

"Got it."

"And if you get any info that may be important, I'm the first to know. Got it?"

"Drive."

CHAPTER 11

KENT AND AUBREY FAIRBANKS FACED OFF FROM their positions in heavy leather chairs in the Red Horse's lobby.

"You certainly reeled me in. I actually thought you were sincere. Maybe misguided, but at least honest. 'We would never send an anonymous threat letter.' Right. You convinced me that you weren't some lunatic—you were honorable. Then you go and pull this crap."

"As I told you before, I know nothing about the letter to Sally. And we don't start fires. I assure you, the Freedom of Animals Movement was not involved in either."

"You must realize you're the gold-plated suspect here."

Aubrey leaned forward and gestured with both palms up. "Of course. Which is one reason why we would not do it."

"Except zealots crave publicity. You run around the countryside like mad dogs, rabid with your cause."

"We work *within the law*!"

"Uh-huh." Kent stared at one of Jefferson's ancestors on the wall.

"Look at our record. Civil disobedience, yes, but no violence. No felonies. And certainly no crimes against animals."

"You've got that right—this was definitely a crime against animals. You should have seen all those burned-up dogs and rabbits and mice and ferrets. It would make you vomit. They died the worst death anybody could imagine."

Kent watched as the horrific picture contorted Aubrey's face. She sank back into her chair. It was the first time he'd seen her defeated, the first time he'd uttered words that stabbed into the essence of all she believed. Instantly he felt ashamed. "I had no right to say that to you."

For a long moment, she let her eyes fix on the ceiling. Finally, she shifted them down to look at him squarely. "I'm going to tell you the only thing I know that may have a bearing on the case. Last night, I was having a drink in the bar right here in this hotel. A guy comes up and starts talking about wanting to help FOAM stop Copithorn."

Kent was cautious. "How?"

"He mentioned a fire. He didn't say so, but he was definitely implying that he, or they—he spoke of his friends—could cause a fire there."

"Why'd he want to help?"

"He didn't say. He just said he and his friends had a grudge or something. He said it wasn't because Copithorn hurt animals. Then he said, 'Wouldn't it look bad for Copithorn if the cops found *pets* being used for research there?'"

"He said he had a grudge?"

"Yes. I told him I wasn't interested and ended the conversation without giving him a chance to explain any more. The guy looked like trouble from word one."

"Did you get his name?"

"No."

Kent looked a little skeptical. "Describe him."

"Midthirties. Big. Overweight. Dirty. Brown hair onto his shoulders. A beard. He was pretty drunk. That may be why he seemed so mean."

Instantly, a mug shot of the man fitting Aubrey's description flashed into Kent's head. "Figures he'd be drunk. Was he with anyone else?"

"No, I don't think so. But he sat at the bar for a long time, and he seemed to know the barmaid. Actually, she came over and apologized for his intrusion afterward."

"A little woman with dark features?"

"Looked like an Indian. You know them?"

"That's Tammy Mays. And the guy had to be Maylon, her husband."

"Poor girl."

"May-May is his nickname. He's one of our local ne'er-do-wells. Tammy is always bailing him out of trouble. Tell me again what he said about finding pets at Copithorn."

"Only that he figured it would look bad for them."

"And he never said why he wanted to help FOAM?"

"Right."

Again Kent stared at Jefferson's ancestors…who stared back but offered no help.

"Pets at Copithorn," he said. "Pets at Copithorn." He drummed the arm of his chair with his fingertips. Then turned and looked at Aubrey—through her. "Pets at Copithorn," he said for the third time, this time loudly.

"What?"

"I might be able to substantiate your story." He stood up. "I've got to go."

"Why?"

"They'll start the cleanup as soon as the investigators are done. Then it'll be too late."

"Too late for what?"

Kent spoke over his shoulder as he strode toward the door. "I'll tell you later. I'm headed back over to the fire."

● ● ●

As he sped toward Copithorn, Kent bounced his theory off Lucinda. "It makes sense." Lucy half stood on the seat, bracing in the turns like a sailor on rough seas, and glanced nervously at Kent, then the road, then back at Kent. "Aubrey's story would explain what Merrill and I saw this morning. It's definitely a long shot, but something about that woman makes me want to believe her. Weird. Isn't it?" He reached over and stroked the red hound. "You listening?

His track record was pretty bad when it came to reading women. What the hell made him think he knew what was going on inside her head?

The truck's engine groaned as it climbed the east hill out of Jefferson on Route 20, accelerator to the floor. Aubrey had described May-May and Tammy Mays accurately. It would be pretty unlikely she'd connect them just by chance. That fit. And May-May certainly was the type to cause trouble. Lord knew Kent's whole family could attest to that.

A picture of Copithorn's burned-out research wing flashed back to Kent. If the inspectors were done before he arrived, he'd lose his chance.

"Can you believe this is happening, Lucinda? This was going to be a nothing job."

Lucinda studied him with her wet brown eyes and listened. "You were supposed to keep reminding me never to get mixed up with another woman."

He pulled through Copithorn's main gate just as two official-looking vehicles with insurance company logos pulled out. He skidded to a stop as close to the rubble as he could park and jumped from the truck while it was still rocking. On the sidewalk, several fire inspectors argued about wiring. He was glad to see Merrill had come back too.

The police chief backed out of a heated conversation with another man in uniform when he saw his brother.

"What's up?"

"I need to check something out. Can I go back in there?"

Merrill shrugged. "It was okay before, ought to be okay now."

"It will only take a minute. I won't disturb anything."

"No matter, the big cheeses are done anyway. What you looking for?"

"I'm not sure." Kent stepped into the blackness of the research wing and then turned back to the chief. "Can I use your flashlight?"

Merrill pulled the long black light from his uniform belt and handed it to him.

Kent wove his way along the same path they had taken earlier, Merrill at his heels. A feeling that he was regaining control of his life overcame him as he stabbed the beam at the darkness. If he could just be right about this, he'd be over the hump. Then he was at the dog ward, and to his relief, the tiny canine body that they had noticed earlier was still lying on the countertop. Kent drew close, holding his light within inches of it.

Now he could see it. Now it seemed obvious. He let himself breathe again.

Merrill recognized his brother's agitation. "What? What's so different now?"

"Nothing's different. I just see what I didn't see before." He pointed toward the body. "Look. It's not a beagle. It's too small, and its conformation is all wrong. Too fine boned. Remember, Stef said they only use beagles at Copithorn." He gently grasped the rigored foot for the second time that day and carefully rolled over the burned animal.

"Okay. I get that," Merrell said.

"The fur underneath didn't get burned."

"So what?"

"It's *white*! That's what." With two fingers, he teased up a lock of the dog's coat. "This hair is close to six inches long. Way too long for a beagle."

Kent shifted his light to the dog's neck and found the remains of a delicate rhinestone collar. He held it in the beam so Merrill could see it. "Wouldn't expect to find one of these on a research dog, would you?"

89

The yellowing light reflected off a nickel-size, silver name tag. Kent cleaned it with his thumb and bent close to read it. "Son of a bitch. I knew it!"

"What?"

Kent read the inscription. BEAR. I BELONG TO MAUREEN PHILIPS, JEFFERSON, NY. 555–6741."

As Merrill grasped the significance of Kent's find, confusion exploded into anger. "How did you know about this?"

Kent continued to examine the little dog.

"Goddamnit, Kent. Did Fairbanks tip you off?"

"Actually she denied knowledge of any of this."

"Bullshit."

"I'm telling you, she denied the whole thing."

"And I suppose you believe her?"

"Yes. And this proves she's telling the truth." He pointed at Bear's remains.

"Jesus Christ. What does she have to do, bring you along while she sabotages the place?"

Kent studied the tiny canine cadaver, giving his brother a moment to calm himself.

"The very fact that we found Mrs. Philips's dog here substantiates Aubrey's story."

"And what's that, may I ask?"

Kent recapped Aubrey's encounter with May-May at the Groggery. When he was finished, Merrill recapped the recap.

"Let me get this straight. Ms. Fairbanks told you this guy, who sounds a whole hell of a lot like May-May, came up to her out of the blue and offered to burn down Copithorn for her? Just like that?"

"More or less."

"And he said something about letting the cops find some pets?"

"Yes."

"That he had some grudge against Copithorn?"

"Maybe."

"I gotta tell you, it sounds like a crock to me. Even May-May, our long-lost, pain in the ass brother isn't that dumb. And why, if I may ask, didn't she mention any of this to me when we questioned her?"

"I don't know. Maybe she doesn't trust cops. Maybe she hadn't connected the two yet."

"Or, more likely, she hadn't thought up the crazy story yet."

"How would you explain a Maltese, recently reported missing, turning up dead on a countertop in a research center?"

"I wouldn't try yet. And I sure as hell wouldn't buy the only cock-and-bull explanation we have so far. Think about it from May-May's angle, your half brother in the same town you live is a cop. Would you pull shit like this?" He let that sink in a minute then turned and headed from the rubble. "Let's get out of here."

"I'd like to have Bear autopsied at the vet college in Ithaca. Will you authorize it?"

"Be my guest."

Kent secured two plastic trash bags and a supply of ice from the company cafeteria and a few minutes later had Bear double bagged on ice, ready for transport.

"Have one of your men take this to the vet school right now," he said, handing the slick black bundle to his brother. "I'll call down there with the medical history and alert them your guy is bringing it in. Don't tell him what's in the bag. Don't let anyone else in on it."

"Got it," Merrill said. "And where are you going?"

"To ask some more questions."

"Remember what we agreed. Don't get in the way. And report in!"

"I agreed to that?" Kent said, and headed toward the atrium at a brisk walk.

● ● ●

Out of the corner of the same window in Stef Copithorn's office where the two of them had reminisced about the old airport, Kent could see the burned-out windows of the research wing. He told Stef about his discovery and waited for her reponse.

"I don't know why Maureen Philips's dog was in my building. Don't get any ideas, either. Copithorn Research does not use dognapped pets for our projects. Never have, never will. Period." Her face was haggard, and Kent sensed her determination was waning. "This whole thing is going to cost the company millions. It had to be FOAM." Her tone fell to brokenhearted. "I always played by the rules. I'm not insensitive to animals. Why are they doing this to me?"

"Could someone get in? Breach security?"

"Probably. We've got a security system, but it's not Fort Knox."

"No reports of anything suspicious last night?"

"No."

"But someone could have gotten a small dog in without being detected."

"Sure. There are ways. Anyone who generally knew our operation. Probably not a guy off the street, but maybe a delivery man…or a disgruntled employee."

"You have many of those?"

"Which? Deliveries? Tons. Every day. Disgruntled employees? A few, I suppose. Like any business."

"Could someone from a different division, say shipping or accounting maybe, get into R&D?"

"All employees have free run of the place when they have their ID badges on."

"The fire investigators been in to see you yet?"

"Briefly. I'm sure they will be back. I guess officially it's not arson until they get some test results."

"Don't worry, it will be."

"Great." Stef's flat tone betrayed her frustration. She stepped to the window and pressed her forehead to the glass. "I don't need this, Kent."

"Keep it together. You're tough. You're the one who built this place, remember? We'll get this straightened out."

Stef nodded, ran her dark nails along her temples. "I guess I just wait. What else? Right?"

"You run your business. Stay busy. As for me? I have a couple more stops to make. Keep in touch."

As Kent pulled onto the highway, he noticed a beat-up pickup parked off the road in front of Copithorn. He would not have given it a second thought had he not seen the lone driver quickly drop something from his eyes. It looked like a pair of binoculars. He squinted at the truck as he passed, but glare on the glass obscured his view. What little he could see of the man's features triggered a vague sort of recognition.

"Who would be watching Copithorn?" he asked Lucinda as he searched mental files for the face. "Where have I seen that guy before?" The memory came running back like a hunting dog whistled in. "That was the guy who was getting all the dogs at the animal shelter the day Aubrey and I were there!"

He pulled to the right edge of the road, only half looked over his left shoulder, and wheeled the truck into a tire-screeching U-turn.

"Lucinda," he said, "it's time to find out more about that guy."

Lucinda perked up in her seat. But when they approached Copithorn's front gate, the pickup was gone.

CHAPTER 12

KENT KNEW WHERE TO FIND TAMMY MAYS midafternoon on a weekday. She'd be waiting tables at the Jefferson Diner for a few more hours.

There were no cars there when Kent pulled up. When he entered, the diner was as empty as its parking lot. Quiet before the onslaught of supper customers. He saw Tammy sitting on a stool with her back to the counter, pivoting absentmindedly back and forth and drawing deeply on a cigarette. He thought he caught a flicker of alarm cross her face as he approached.

"Hi, Tammy. You look like you've had a long day."

She dragged again on the cigarette. "And I'm only at the halfway point."

"Tending bar at the Red Horse tonight then?"

The petite waitress extended a darn good-looking leg and stared at it. "I hope these old dogs can hold out."

The slit in Tammy's otherwise plain waitress uniform revealed the lower third of her thigh. It was, no doubt, an alteration she had made to increase tips.

"You have a minute to talk to me?"

She stubbed out the cigarette and exhaled a breath of smoke toward the ceiling. "Sure, Kent," she said with no enthusiasm. "What can I do for you?"

"Actually, it has to do with something that happened over at the Red Horse the other night."

"Yeah? What?"

"You run into that animal rights activist woman who's been around lately?"

"I've seen her a time or two. It would be hard not to. She's staying at the inn."

"Did you happen to talk to her in the bar?"

Tammy pulled a pack of cigarettes from her pocket, tapped one out, and slowly lit up again. "She was there. Southern Comfort old-fashioneds."

"What?"

"That's what she was drinking. Southern Comfort old-fashioneds, fruit muddled. A bunch of them."

"Was she drunk?"

Tammy shrugged. "What's drunk?"

"Was she by herself?"

"I didn't pay much attention."

"Tammy, come on. A pretty stranger like that with a big-city rep wanders into little ol' Jefferson, and you don't pay attention? You remembered what she was drinking."

Tammy shrugged again, said nothing.

"Was it busy?"

"No."

"You remember what you want to remember."

"What's your point?"

"Was your husband there?"

Tammy's expression grew dark. "May-May? Son of a bitch. He stopped by to say hello." She took a long drag.

"What's he up to lately?"

"Same old big-talking, little-doing May-May."

"Was he drunk?"

"I couldn't tell you. He's been drinking so long I don't know when he's drunk and when he's sober. He was the same as usual, if that's what you want to know."

"Did he talk to Ms. Fairbanks?"

"I don't remember."

"They didn't argue or anything?"

"Not that I recall."

Kent had another thought. "You see May-May cutting letters out of any magazines lately?"

The strange question stopped Tammy for a second. "He's outgrown that stage. He's more into Matchbox cars and BB guns now."

Kent didn't laugh. "Then you don't know anything about him pasting together an anonymous threat letter?"

She held the cigarette up, studying the thread of smoke that curled from it. "To who?"

"Never mind. If you don't know about it, it doesn't matter."

"I don't know a thing," Tammy said, as if her thoughts had drifted to another place.

"Where was May-May last night?"

Tammy narrowed her eyes. "Jesus, Kent. I thought you were a vet, not a cop. You trying to be like Merrill or something?"

"Not a chance."

"Well, go ask May-May yourself if you want to know where he was. He's your brother."

"Half brother."

"Okay, half brother."

"Ms. Fairbanks told me a guy whose description fits May-May talked to her at the Groggery."

"I don't doubt it. May-May hits on every lone skirt he sees. Except I think even he'd know she is out of his league."

"She says he propositioned her."

Tammy's snicker registered a mixture of jealously and disgust.

"Not the way you're thinking. He offered to help her sabotage Copithorn."

"Meaning what?"

"Sounded like he had some kind of a grudge. You know anything about that?"

"Nope. You know, Kent? It kind of surprises me that a guy who's always been one of us, loyal to the town and all, would take up with someone like her. An outsider, I mean, and working against what you do, for Pete's sake. You a vet, and her against people having animals."

"I'm not *taking up* with anybody. I'm just trying to figure out who's responsible for all those dead animals at Copithorn. That's my job."

A wry smile tipped Tammy's mouth. "Doesn't have anything to do with you being divorced—and lonely—for a long time, and now suddenly you're the middleman between two hot single women?"

"When'd you get your psychology degree?"

"Night school. Behind a bar."

When Kent was back in his truck, he said to Lucinda, "So Tammy isn't talking—if she knows anything, that is. No use me even thinking of talking to May-May. He's been in enough scrapes with the law to know to keep his mouth shut. Why would he do it, though? May-May is no animal rights activist, that's for sure, and he wouldn't do it unless there was something in it for him." Kent grabbed his dog's soft dewlap and massaged it gently in his fingers. "Lots of questions. Huh, girl?"

Lucinda gave his hand a reassuring nuzzle.

He drove away, wondering if he really did feel some subconscious pleasure in being the middleman between Stef and Aubrey.

Lucinda eased her head down into his lap, thumped her tail once, and was instantly asleep.

● ● ●

Sally's usual verve was returning. Finally. She had plodded around the clinic in a deep funk ever since receiving the anonymous letter. But today, she stood at her usual place against the wall of the operating room reading aloud from the newspaper as Kent worked to remove a grotesque cancer from along the shoulder blades of an ancient boxer.

An informed source said that the remains of a locally owned dog were found in the debris. Though badly burned, the pet was identified as a Maltese named Bear, belonging to Maureen Philips of Jefferson. Ms. Philips said Bear had been missing for several days.

Except for an occasional disapproving cluck of his tongue, Kent listened in silence as Sally read the reporter's account of Copithorn's fire. She folded the paper in half and continued:

Does this mean there is truth to the rumors that Copithorn uses pets for experiments? Does the company support dognapping? When Philips was asked what recourse she would take, she stated only that she was too distraught by the loss of her beloved pet to consider any action at this time.

Kent rested the heels of his glove-clad hands on the draped patient and stared at Sally.

"What?" she said.

"There has to be some kind of an informer. Where would that reporter have gotten his information? The only ones who knew about Bear were Stef, Merrill, and me. I talked to Aubrey Fairbanks right after the fire, but I didn't mention the pet connection. The police officer who transported Bear to the diagnostic lab didn't even know what was in the bag. Stef promised me she wouldn't tell a soul, and I believe her. I was thinking, *Why did Merrill tell the reporters about it?* It just struck me. He didn't. He wouldn't. Somebody else did."

Sally slowly lowered the paper. "You mean this is true? The article is correct? I thought you were going to say the whole thing was made up. Why didn't you tell me about Bear?"

"Merrill and I agreed not to tell anyone at all. And look what happened. Somehow the press got hold of it. So who would tell them?"

"I wouldn't even guess."

Kent made small circles in the air with his scalpel, like a teacher coaxing an answer out of a reluctant pupil.

"The person who put the dog there in the first place, of course."

"Someone *planted* Bear at Copithorn?"

"That's what I'm beginning to think."

"Why?"

"They—he, she, whoever—*wanted* him to be discovered." Kent spoke confidently now, as if saying it made it true.

"Why?"

"To discredit Copithorn."

"Someone set up Stef?"

"It looks like it. That's why they left Bear in such an obvious spot. I couldn't figure that out. In a lab situation, to leave a specimen out on a counter overnight? No plastic bag, no refrigeration? It didn't fit. And, that's why he had a name tag on his collar. I ask you, if you stole a dog, would you leave the rightful owner's ID on it?"

"Only if I wanted his identity discovered," Sally said, as she began to catch on.

"Exactly! Whoever is trying to embarrass Copithorn would *want* Bear's identity discovered. And when they thought it hadn't worked, that no one had noticed there was a pet inside, they called the newspaper themselves to get things rolling."

"Wow. So who is 'they'?"

"Good question." Kent went back to his surgery as he pondered the possibilities.

A few minutes later, he was finished and drying his hands. "Could be FOAM if Aubrey is lying, or it could be May-May if she's telling the truth."

"Which would mean, from what you've already told me, that Tammy is lying," Sally said.

"Right."

Before Sally could continue she was distracted by the sound of someone opening the front door. She peered around and saw Merrill slowly, cautiously creeping into the clinic, as if avoiding some imaginary pathogen.

"Well, look who's here. A rare visitor indeed." She made no attempt to hide her sarcasm.

"Hello, Sally," Merrill said.

"Watch out for the dog piles," she said and laughed as Merrill went up on his tiptoes.

Tentatively, he proceeded into where Kent was operating.

"Hey. You can't go in there. You're not sterile. Then again, maybe you are."

"Hi, Merrill. Nice of you to stop by." Kent's tone communicated his boredom with their cat-dog act. He noticed the newspaper under his brother's arm. "I bet I know why you're here."

"I bet you do." Merrill extended the paper toward Kent while keeping a close eye on the boxer whose incision loomed before him. "I thought we had an agreement."

"What was that?"

"That you'd keep me informed."

"I agreed to that?"

"Yes you did. And so what's this?" Merrill tapped the paper.

"That's what I'd like to know."

"Meaning what?"

"I did not say one word to anyone."

"Then who did?"

"Not you?"

"Of course not me," Merrill said. "I wouldn't give a reporter the time of day."

"Must be some *informed source.*"

"And who might that be?"

Kent shrugged but didn't answer.

Merrill twisted around in place, eyes searching. "Where's your phone?"

Sally pointed toward her desk then helped Kent finish the boxer and return him to his kennel.

A few minutes later, Merrill slammed the receiver down. He radiated a policeman's contempt for reporters.

"He wouldn't tell me anything. Confidentiality bullshit, you know. But he hemmed and hawed enough that I'm sure he didn't verify his source. He just went with it. He wanted the scoop. So we're back to square one."

"Not really. We can at least figure Bear was a plant."

"Did I miss something? A plant? As in framing somebody, not a green growing thing, I assume."

"Yeah. Sally and I figured it out. Bear wasn't on the lab counter because Copithorn had dognapped him. That's just what they wanted us to believe."

Merrill was lost, and it made him uncomfortable.

"Who's *they*?" he asked.

"*They* is whomever it is that wants to embarrass Copithorn by making it appear the company snatches dogs off the street for research. They planted Bear. That's why they left him where he would be found. But when there was no report of a pet found in the fire, they figured we missed the setup. So they tipped off the newspaper to be sure the word got out."

101

Merrill returned the confused look of a youngster watching magic tricks.

"I'd say Copithorn Research is off the hook as far as dognapping is concerned," Kent said.

Merrill stuck both thumbs into his thick leather uniform belt and stared through his brother. "It works. I guess. Now what we need to do is figure out who *they* is."

"And why they planted Bear," Kent added as he scrubbed blood off a hemostat. "If it turns out to be FOAM, the obvious explanation is to discredit Copithorn and prove to the world that they were right, cosmetic companies use pets for research. However, if it is someone other than FOAM, what motive would they have?"

Merrill was suffering from information overload. "I thought you were going to let me in on anything you found."

"I would have. Eventually. The question is, did FOAM do it, or is Aubrey telling the truth and someone else did it?"

"Yeah, well I have my bias on that one," Merrill said.

Sally waggled a finger at Merrill. "Cops are not supposed to be biased."

"Cops are human."

"Some more than others."

"I'm going to call the diagnostic lab to get the postmortem results on Bear." Kent looked from Merrill to Sally. In a parental tone he said, "Do I need to stick you two in separate cages while I'm in the next room?"

"We'll be all right. Make your call," Sally assured him.

A few minutes later Kent reentered the room where Sally and Merrill maintained an uneasy truce. "Head trauma. Blunt object to the frontal bones." He tapped the center of his forehead theatrically. "They guess something like a ball-peen hammer."

"Right between the eyes," Merrill said, impressed by the thought.

Sally shuddered. "Gruesome."

"For sure," Kent said. "And, since we know they're not doing any head trauma studies at Copithorn, we can be pretty sure someone killed Bear and put him there to be found."

Sally shook her head in disbelief. "That person is sick."

"Doesn't it strike you as unlikely that animal rights people would use such a disgusting method?" Kent asked.

Merrill held two palms up. "So that leaves us with the mystery person Fairbanks told you about. The one who's probably our dear old brother, Maylon Mays."

"Half brother."

Merrill headed for the door. "I think I'll pay him a visit. Middle of the day…good chance I'll catch him at home."

"The hard part will be waking him up."

"Right. You got a cattle prod around this place?"

After Merrill left, Kent and Sally worked their way through a session of appointments. Kent treated ear infections, skin problems, and a lame German shepherd that he was pretty sure he'd be seeing again when the owners worked through their denial of a torn knee ligament. The hit of the day was a litter of four teacup Chihuahuas getting their first vaccinations. Sally could hold all four in one hand. Only difference was today Kent did not spend as much time as usual chatting about grandchildren, Florida trips, and the client's own health issues.

At one point, when there was a break in the action, she glanced over at a large wall calendar. "Today's your mom's birthday. Did you remember?"

"Of course," Kent lied. A spasm of guilt rose from his stomach and settled around his heart.

Sally sounded worried. "Did you get her something?"

"Some perfume," he lied again.

"Good for you. Don't forget a card. That's the most important part."

"I've got it covered."

Before Sally could say more, the front door opened, and a tall, stick-thin African American man who was not scheduled for an appointment stepped in.

"You got any penicillin I can buy?" he inquired as if he was apologizing for the intrusion. His voice was soft and very deep.

Sally studied the visitor from his engineer's-capped head to his worn Big-K sneakers. There was not an ounce of fat on him. He had a ragged gray scar running along the hairline at his right temple, a poorly healed wound from long ago. His prominent Adam's apple quivered nervously in his throat. It rose and fell like a barometer of his mood.

He seemed so harmless that Sally couldn't help but smile. "You must be new around here. I know all of our clients."

"I moved here from the other side of Syracuse. Took a farm job. My name is Bo Davis."

Sally tried not to stare. There were very few African Americans in Jefferson.

She extended her hand. "Pleased to meet you, Bo. I'm Sally. What was it you wanted?"

Bo's big hand engulfed Sally's in a gentle greeting. "Penicillin. One bottle will do. And a couple of syringes. And I'd like some suturing thread."

"Suturing thread?"

"Yeah. What vets use to sew up cuts."

"What are you, some kind of do-it-yourselfer?"

He laughed. "Not really. I'm taking my dogs bear hunting in Canada. Sometimes they get hurt, and there's no vet anywhere close."

"Yeah. That could be a problem. We have penicillin and suture material. I'll get you some."

As she stepped toward the medicine closet, the front door opened again. The person who filled it this time made Sally forget Bo Davis entirely. Her surprise was a hundredfold greater than when Merrill had lowered himself to his surprise visit earlier.

"G-good af-afternoon, Ms. Copithorn," she stammered.

The charismatic exec's face drew into a soft scowl. "Come on, Sally. It's Stef. Remember? I went to school with you and your sister."

"Right. Sorry. You surprised me." Sally shuffled the clutter on her desk into some semblance of order as she spoke.

Stef accepted the apology with a smile. "Is Kent in?"

"I'll get him." Shock prevented Sally from saying more.

Kent nearly knocked Sally down trying to smooth his crumpled smock while rounding the corner from the exam room. In his eagerness to welcome Stef, he never even noticed Bo Davis, who shrank behind a dog food display almost out of sight.

"They've taken Armani," Stef said. Her voice was matter-of-fact, but there was an undertone of alarm.

Kent gave her a confused look. "Armani?"

"My cat, Giorgio Armani."

"I didn't even know you had a cat."

"He's always been healthy and never leaves my house, so I never brought him to see you. He's a Himalayan. Mostly white with orange tips on his ears and feet."

"A flame point. Who took him?"

Stef shook her head. She spoke with deep motherly concern. "I don't know. More harassment from FOAM, I guess. Mostly he stays inside, but every morning I let him out on the patio for a few minutes on a cord. Today when I went to bring him in, the cord was cut right near the snap, and Armani was gone."

"You didn't see or hear anything?"

"Nothing." Stef dug through her purse, found a tissue, and dabbed her eyes. "He's a friendly cat. He'd go with a stranger without a fight. He loves everyone."

"And you're sure the cord was cut? It didn't just break?"

She balled the tissue, replaced it in her purse, and took a deep breath. "Cut clean. I checked it carefully."

"What type of collar did he have on? Any tags?"

"A red leather harness, no tags. If I find the person who took him, I'll press every charge in the book."

"Yeah, well, let's get him back first. Did you call the shelter, or dog warden, or Merrill?"

"Not yet." Stef's expression became quizzical. "You can't call the police for a missing cat. Can you?"

"You can call. I'm not sure how much good it'd do."

Bo Davis, who had been listening quietly, seemed distracted and oddly disappointed when Sally handed him the medicine and suture material. Slowly, he withdrew his wallet, took out some cash, and paid. Moving like someone returning to an assembly line after a cigarette break, he departed, keeping his back to Kent and Stef.

Sally turned back to her boss and Copithorn's CEO. "Maybe it is time to get the police involved, Kent," she said. "This isn't an ordinary missing pet. It could be tied in with the fire and whole FOAM thing."

Stef clicked her tongue. "*Could* be? It's *got* to be!"

"Besides," Sally said, "this brings us back to all the missing pets we've noticed around Jefferson lately. What's going on with that? The police might be able to help."

Kent pulled the stethoscope from around his neck and placed it on its designated wall hook. "Merrill did say he wanted to know if we came up with anything. I'll give him a call. Sally, you contact the shelter and post a notice on our board too. We'll see if we can make something happen."

After his last appointment, Kent sat at his desk pondering the significance of Armani's disappearance. A hazy picture of the thin, dark stranger lingering in the waiting room crept into his mind.

"Sally, weren't you waiting on someone while I was talking to Stef?"

Sally was making entries into the daily ledger, she did not look up. "Yep. Never saw him before. Said his name was Bo something."

"What did he want?"

"Just some medicine."

Kent let the image of the man roll in his head until finally it focused. The connection jolted him. "Are you kidding me?"

"What's the matter?"

"I think that was the guy who was getting pups at the dog shelter and spying at Copithorn!"

"Spying at Copithorn?"

"Yes. I saw someone, and I'd swear that was the guy, studying the Copithorn fire scene the morning after the fire. He took off before I could talk to him."

Sally turned him a helpless look. "He paid cash too. There's no receipt to trace."

"That makes three times I've seen that guy slinking around, and we still don't know who he is."

CHAPTER 13

THE SHOUTING MATCH WAS ALREADY IN PROG-
ress when Kent entered the diner. Owner-manager Eugene was leaning on his elbows, face to face with a youngster across the counter.
They snapped insults back and forth at the urging of several patrons
who obviously considered it wonderfully entertaining. The boy who
had gotten the proprietor's hackles up was Barry Fairbanks.

"Have you ever seen the Chicago stockyards?"

"No-o-o-o!" Eugene said.

"Well, I have. Cows crammed in pens so tight they can't move.
No food. No water. They get stuck with electric shockers by big goril-
las like you who think it's funny to see one get trampled when it
falls down."

"Listen, kid. All I know is meat tastes good, and it's good
for you."

"Right. Tell that to the parents of the kids in Oregon who died
of *E. coli* after they ate at some fast-food dump a couple of years ago."

The veins surfaced on Eugene's forehead like snakes. "That was
an exception."

"Exception. Bad meat kills hundreds of Americans every year
and puts thousands in the hospital."

When Kent eased up behind Barry and put a hand on his
shoulder, the boy whirled, fists up and balled.

"How about joining me over at a table?"

Barry relaxed when he recognized Kent. "Hi. I didn't see you come in. Sure, Dr. Stephenson, I'd like that." He nodded toward his adversary. "Beats talking to this knothead."

The remark brought a round of laughter.

"Knothead, is it?" Eugene said and reached to grab Barry, but the boy was too quick and sidled out of reach without much effort.

Kent held up his hand. "I can handle him, Eugene." He turned Barry away from the counter. "You aren't going to win any popularity contests around here if you keep up like that."

"Like I care."

Kent guided Barry to one side of a booth. "Where's your mom?"

"She's gone for a couple of days."

"Gone?"

"Yeah. She's holding a rally at some rodeo in San Diego."

"Rodeo?" It took Kent a second to catch on. "Right. FOAM doesn't go for them either, huh?"

"Grown-ups whose mental development arrested at the cowboy stage. Snapping calves' necks with a rope fascinates them."

"Uh-huh." Kent picked a plastic menu from behind a bowl of sugar packets. "You staying by yourself at the hotel?"

"Yeah." Barry flashed a defiant look. "But before you flip out, I've got the number of the hotel she's staying at. She left me enough money and a pile of homework to do. I've done it lots of times. I'm fine."

"I wasn't worried in the least."

"I get good grades, you know. I still have to take tests even if I don't go to regular school."

"Anyone can tell you're a smart kid, Barry."

"Homeschooling is harder than most people think."

"I don't doubt it for a minute. Did you eat yet or just get right into that pissing contest with Eugene?"

Barry cast a scowl toward the diner's owner, who happened to be looking their way. "No."

"Good. I'm buying." Kent replaced the menu and turned to the daily specials board.

It was then he noticed another boy sitting at the end of the counter, near the kitchen door, a half dozen stools from where Barry had confronted Eugene. He was hunched over a soda, sucking on a straw casually, and watching the waitresses. AC/DC T-shirt, baggy black jeans, chain looping from belt to wallet, and thick-heeled boots. Some of his hair was long, and in some places it was shaved to his scalp. His face boasted several piercings, his arms several tattoos.

"Nathan," Kent said loud enough for the boy to hear across the room.

Nathan turned and gave him a keen-eyed look. A smile tried to surface, but it would have been uncool.

Kent waved him over.

The boy slid off the stool, bent, grabbed a skateboard that had been braced on the foot ledge. He sauntered over, board in one hand, drink in the other. James Dean couldn't have done it better.

"Nathan, there's someone I'd like you to meet." Kent gestured toward his table companion. "This is Barry Fairbanks. Barry, Nathan Gaines."

Nathan inspected Barry openly. "I caught him in action with Eugene. The antimeat guy." There was approval in his voice.

Barry extended his hand. Nathan hesitated for an instant then took it. They shook firmly. Manly.

Kent slid further into the booth. "We're about to order. How about joining us?"

Nathan eased himself into the booth. He looked across at Barry again but didn't speak. Then he nodded up toward the counter and the manager. "You're right about one thing. Eugene is a knothead." The faintest of smiles flickered around his mouth, lit his eyes, and then disappeared.

"The world is full of them."

"You got that right."

Kent glanced toward Eugene. "I don't know. He's not so bad."

"He's a control-freak dork," Nathan said. "Pushes everybody around."

Kent knew Nathan was referring to Tammy Mays, his mother. He scanned the room and found her serving a table in the corner. Changed the subject.

"Barry's new in town. Thought maybe you might show him around. 'Hang out' is the term, right? Listen to some music. Maybe do some skateboarding."

Both boys looked at the veterinarian and then at each other. Rolled their eyes.

"You a skater?"

"I have a board." Barry noticed the scimitar on Nathan's wrist. "Awesome tattoo."

Nathan held it closer for him. "Check out the blood. I had the guy do it red to look real."

"My mom won't let me get one," Barry said, his words dripping with envy.

"My mom's pretty cool about it. My stepdad is the one who's the pain in the ass. Says it looks like I'm trying to be a tough guy."

Kent turned from the specials board. "Not much for a vegan up there, Barry."

"I'll just have a salad."

Kent gave Nathan a conspiratorial glance but directed a question to Barry. "Did you ever eat a hamburger?"

"No."

Kent took up his menu again and scanned it. "Doesn't mean much when someone argues against something he knows nothing about."

"Mom would cut my head off."

Kent contemplated for a few seconds more. "What the heck." He waved Tammy Mays over from behind the counter.

When she was close enough, she looked from her son to Barry to Kent. "You taking in all the strays now-a-days, Kent?"

"How about one of these cheeseburgers with everything for me and a plain hamburger for Lucinda. Barry here's trying to decide if he wants to take the plunge. Nathan, you order what you want. I'm buying."

"Oh. The rich uncle," Tammy said with mock surprise.

Nathan ordered a burger and fries.

Tammy tapped a pencil on her pad. When Barry took too long, she made an executive decision. "For you, son, our deluxe double burger is on the house."

"There you go. Opportunity knocks," Kent said.

Nathan's shoulders rose and fell in a chuckle that made no sound.

Barry didn't move.

"Go ahead and get it for him, Tammy. If he doesn't eat it, Lucinda will."

Minutes later, Tammy returned with their orders. She placed a massive burger in front of each of the boys. "And a plain one for our girl outside," she said handing a bag to Kent.

She pointed at Barry's deluxe burger and waited impatiently. "That baby's dripping with everything any kid ever wanted."

Barry stared nervously at his plate.

Tammy took advantage of the lull. "Kent," she said in a quiet voice, "I guess you've noticed all the pets missing around town lately."

Nathan flashed her a wary look.

Kent snapped his attention from Barry but moved carefully. "As a matter of fact, I have."

"Well, it would pay to follow up on it."

"Meaning what?"

Tension rose in Tammy's voice as Kent forced her to put it in words. She spit them in an angry whisper. "Meaning the only reason I'm telling you this is because I've known you all my life, and you've always been fair with me. I can trust you. I think. And I hate to see the animals suffer."

Nathan scowled at Tammy. "Ma. Give it a rest!"

"What animal suffering?" Barry asked.

"Never mind," she fired at both boys. "Kent, take a ride out to our place sometime. Be careful. And I didn't tell you a thing." She gave Nathan a defiant look, tore off a slip for their lunches. She slapped it on the table and headed back behind the counter.

"What was she talking about, Dr. Stephenson?" Barry asked.

"Forget her," Nathan said. "She's being a jerk today."

Kent stared thoughtfully in Tammy's direction. "I'm not sure, Barry. And would you do me a favor? Call me Kent or Doc, maybe, not Dr. Stephenson, please?"

"Sure, uh, Doc."

"And Nathan." His eyes still followed Tammy. "Whatever your mother is, a jerk isn't one of them."

Barry picked up the burger with both hands and took a bite. For a moment he chewed equivocally, then broke into a bulged-cheek smile.

"Pretty good, huh?"

"Great, actually."

Kent glanced at Nathan. "See, I told you."

Barry took several more mouthfuls without stopping to make conversation. Lucinda was not going to get that burger.

"Better than a spicy bean burger?"

"Much," Barry said, a little confused at the discovery.

Kent got another idea. If he'd had a handlebar mustache, he would have twirled it. "What are you doing tonight, Barry?"

"Nothing. Homework, probably, and some TV."

"Want to go coon hunting with me and Lucinda?"

Nathan buried his face in his hands and smothered a laugh. "Oh, man. No. Doc, you definitely have brass balls."

Barry froze, burger poised inches from his mouth "Hunting?"

"Raccoons."

It was as if Kent had invited him to Mars. "I've never been hunting."

"I figured as much. Want to try?" Kent motioned at the burger. "You never know what you'll like till you try it."

"Hunting. Raccoons," Barry said slowly. "I guess so."

"Nathan. How about you coming along too? If May-May will let you. I mean chores and all that stuff."

"He doesn't have any say in what I do."

"Okay. You want to come along?"

"Sure. I'm in."

"Good! I'll pick up the two of you around eight in front of the Red Horse. Wear good footgear. I'll have everything else."

After the boys left, Kent worked his way to the cash register. As the cashier dropped change into his hand, he made eye contact with Tammy across the room. Her expression reminded him of the frightened rabbits he and Merrill used to find in their box traps.

● ● ●

On his way to the nursing home, Kent stopped at the pharmacy and bought a card and a bottle of Chanel No. 5.

He pulled into the visitor's lot just as a group of nurses came out of the building. They were chatting merrily and sucking cigarettes the way miners suck air after being trapped for a week.

Their father had smoked. He had died of throat cancer when Merrill was seventeen and Kent was fourteen. Twenty-two years he ran the Jefferson Lumber Company. June handled the books and the two boys helped out after school and summers in the lumberyard. Good memories.

After he died, the memories got grim. June struggled to keep the family together and the business going. It was a losing battle. By the time she finally resigned herself to selling the lumber company, there was just enough equity to fund Merrill and Kent's college educations.

Eventually, June remarried. The lucky guy was Clifton Mays, a hill farmer from one town over who was more oxlike than anything in his barn. He managed to get one son out of her—Maylon, a.k.a. May-May.

Clifton complained bitterly about money wasted on college. Never considered that route for May-May. He did his best to drive a wedge between the three boys. And succeeded.

May-May hated both his half brothers, though he focused his animosity mostly on Kent. Kent was a veterinarian and May-May considered himself to be an animal expert.

After June went to the nursing home—expenses paid by Merrill and Kent—May-May took over his parents' farm. Clifton was last known to be living out his golden years in a trailer park in central Florida. No way would he remember his wife's birthday.

"Happy birthday, Mom!" Kent said as he entered her room.

She was in her wheelchair, ready to go to the dining room. The nurses had dressed her even nicer than usual. On her white blouse was an enormous pink corsage. It covered half her chest.

"Thanks, honey," June said, twisting her head to look up at him. "It's nice of you to remember. I heard you've been busy."

He adjusted the tiny plastic oxygen tube taped in place beneath her nose. "What have you heard?"

June's eyes twinkled with a mischievousness he loved to see.

"I read the paper, and I get visitors, you know." She caught her breath. "I heard about the Copithorn fire."

"You never miss a trick."

"You bet I don't." She glanced down, giving her condition an appraisal, and then released a laugh that sounded like a songbird. "It

115

just takes me a little longer now." She rested a minute. "You find out anything more about Aaron?"

Kent remembered the tattered picture of his mother in Aaron's desk and its amorous note. He considered asking her about it but decided not to do it on her birthday.

"Not yet. Merrill and I are working on it."

"There isn't a shred of truth in what they're saying." She reached for his hand and clinched. It felt like a chickadee gripping a perch. "I'm telling you, Aaron Whitmore did not kill himself!"

"I guess we're all surprised, Mom, but how else would you explain it?"

"Murder!"

"Murder? Why? Who would kill Aaron?"

"I don't know, but I do know he didn't shoot himself."

"Mom, it was Aaron's own gun on a lonesome lake where he used to like to fish. Maybe he just got tired of being alone."

"Don't tell me about being alone. I know all about it, and Aaron wasn't. He had friends. Lots of them. He was busy hunting and fishing and writing. Sure, Claire is gone, but he wasn't lonely."

"So why then? Who?"

"I said I don't know. That's up to you and Merrill to find out." Her eyes burned with conviction. "You've got to."

"Okay, Mom," he said, trying to sound confident. "We're looking into it." He touched her corsage lightly. "Let's not let it ruin your birthday."

"Hold on. I've got one more piece of business before I forget."

Kent shook his head. Chuckled. "What's that?"

"The Copithorn fire. And all that animal experimenting protest."

The humor went out of Kent's expression. "What about it?"

"I'm glad you're working with Merrill and Stef."

"The old crew. Like high school again."

"They need your help."

"Did Merrill say that?"

116

"Heavens no. He came by today." She raised her corsage lovingly, tried as best she could to catch its scent. "Brought me this. But you know he'd never ask for help. That's why I'm glad you're there for him."

"So that's how you know so much." Kent was relieved that his brother had remembered their mother's birthday.

"He only told me what he wanted me to hear." Her eyes squinted into slits. "He told me about how interested you seem to be in that Aubrey Fairbanks."

"Professionally."

"I hope more than just professionally! She's gorgeous. You deserve gorgeous."

"Mom, please."

"Nobody's trying to marry you off, Kent. We just want to see you enjoying life again."

"I live among a tribe of matchmakers."

June smiled broadly.

A nurse's aide entered and announced dinner. Kent wheeled his mother to the dining room while the aide walked beside her. June was given the place of honor in front, where all birthday celebrants were placed. Lights were dimmed, and everyone sang "Happy Birthday." A cake with candles was brought out. June seemed genuinely pleased to be remembered. She ate well. Kent picked at the tray of food they had brought for him.

He handed her his gift while they were finishing the cake and ice cream. "Happy birthday, Mom."

The next few minutes were occupied with opening first the card and then the perfume, which June raved about as if it was the first time she had ever received such a novel present. They chatted about family and friends, his daughter Emily's plans, how things were going at the home. Eventually the small talk waned. Thoughts of current events in Jefferson seeped back into their minds.

"Did Merrill mention anything about May-May?"

June's surprised expression was an answer. "Is that boy of mine in trouble again?"

Kent shrugged, angry with himself for ruining the moment. "We don't know just yet. But his name came up in the Copithorn investigation."

June struggled to straighten herself. "How?"

"Aubrey Fairbanks. The gorgeous one? Says he approached her before the fire and indicated he might be willing to help her burn the place."

"Then she admits to being part of it?"

"No. Actually she claims she told him to take a hike."

"Maybe I don't like her as much as I thought I did."

"She's still gorgeous."

"Beauty is only skin deep."

"Listen to you now."

June considered the news about May-May quietly. "I guess, as much as I hate to admit it, being his mother and all, I wouldn't put it past him." Her voice trailed off sadly.

"To make things worse, Tammy caught us at the diner and, without giving any details, said I should stop up at the farm. Apparently, May-May's got something going on up there."

"What?"

"I don't know. I haven't made it out there yet."

"I wish that boy could stay out of trouble. What did I do differently with him than with you and Merrill?"

Kent wanted to tell her it wasn't her. It was Clifton who messed up. Instead, he said, "It's nobody's fault, Mom."

"What do you think, Kent? Do you figure he did it?"

"I don't know. May-May's done a lot of dumb things in his life, but I can't imagine he'd burn Stef's business."

"By Jesus, I hope not. If he's not careful, he'll wind up in jail again."

"Except we're talking arson here. He'd go up a long time."

"Would it do any good for me to talk to him? I could call him up, tell him to stop by. He still listens to me, you know."

Kent knew better. May-May hadn't listened to his mother, or anyone else offering good advice, since third grade.

"No. Let's not show all our cards just yet. You know how he always says he's the first to get blamed whenever anything goes wrong. We won't give him a chance to start that. I'll stop out at the farm tomorrow and see where that leads us."

He helped the aides get June situated back in her room, and they visited a few more minutes. As he stood to go, June took his hand. Her eyes held the look of a mare afraid for her foal. "Kent, you be careful. May-May can be very dangerous if he's cornered. He's got his father's wickedness."

"I will, Mom." He kissed her cheek gently. "Happy birthday."

CHAPTER 14

KENT STOPPED HIS TRUCK IN THE GLOW OF A
streetlight a few paces from the Red Horse Inn. Barry pushed himself
up from the curb where he'd been sitting, trotted over, and climbed
in the passenger seat. Lucinda stuck her head over the seat and licked
his ear.

"Ready to add coon hunting to your library of life's experiences?" Kent asked.

"I think so."

"No sign of Nathan yet?"

"Nope."

"He should be here any minute."

They waited in silence for a while, Kent watching for Nathan,
Barry stroking Lucinda's muzzle.

Then Barry asked, "You're Nathan's uncle, right?"

"Yes. Well, maybe not officially. His stepfather is my half
brother, if you can follow that."

"Uh-huh."

"You met his mother—Tammy, the waitress? She had Nathan
when she was real young."

"At least he has a father."

"Where is yours?"

"Long gone."

"It's been tough for Nathan. He and May-May don't get along
very well."

"He seems pretty cool."

"As I said, Nathan's got his problems, but he's resourceful, and he's in there plugging away. The trouble is he's basically on his own."

"That doesn't sound so bad. His mom let him get a tattoo."

"Believe me, you would not want to trade places with Nathan."

They became silent again, both pondering that possibility. A candy-apple red 4x4 pickup came from behind, slowed, and then pulled to the curb just in front of them.

It was jacked up at least a foot higher than Kent's truck. Knobby tires bulged from the wheel wells. A whip antenna lilted from the momentum of the stop. Light from the streetlight played off its polished chrome and highlighted POWER WAGON in bold letters across the tailgate.

"Wow. Look at that truck!" Barry said, as the rumbling of its glass-pack mufflers ceased.

Dark tinted windows hid the driver, but Kent knew who it was. "Speak of the devil," he said, half under his breath.

Barry glanced over at him, then back at the truck. "Who's that?"

"May-May himself."

"Nathan's stepfather?"

"In the flesh."

The big truck's door opened. A heavyset man with long hair and beard, tired work clothes, and a sullen expression stepped down on wobbly legs. He gave Kent's truck a narrow-eyed once-over and then turned without acknowledging it. He wobbled around the front of his truck, balancing himself by running a hand along the hood. He negotiated the Red Horse Inn's seven stone steps unsteadily and disappeared inside.

"Must be Tammy's working at the Groggery tonight," Kent said.

"He looked pretty drunk."

Kent let the comment go.

They were staring at the truck's gleaming tailgate when a hand emerged. Like a small mammal emerging from its burrow, it poked out from under the black canvas tonneau cover, felt its way along the tailgate, and tripped the latch. The tailgate fell open. Nathan rolled out, eased the tailgate back up quietly, and stepped quickly to Kent's truck. Kent cranked the motor. "I told you he was resourceful!"

Barry held the seat forward as Nathan slipped in with Lucinda. "What were you doing in there?"

"Sorry I'm late. May-May messed me up. He decided to start his drinking at home tonight. He didn't leave the house when I figured he would."

"Why were you in the back of the truck?"

Nathan gave a sly look. "I sneak rides from May-May all the time. He still hasn't figured out that he is my main ride to town if Mom is working."

"Why don't you just ask him for a ride?"

"I'm grounded. At least, he says I am."

"Oh."

"Plus I don't want him to think I need him for anything."

"Well, anyway," Kent said as they headed for the forest, "you made it. And we're off to hunt some coons."

● ● ●

Kent eased his truck, pitching and rolling, along a single lane road through the darkness and dense hardwoods up in the state land. Both boys kept their eyes fixed on the tiny wedge of visibility created by the headlights. They stopped as the road dwindled to an overgrown logging trail. Lucinda, vibrating with excitement, nearly trampled Nathan.

Kent shut off the engine. Listened to the night sounds. Stared into the darkness. "Quiet, isn't it?"

He heard Barry swallow hard.

"How do you know where you're going? It's blacker than black out there."

"Don't worry. I've got lights. Here's how it works. Up ahead is—"

Barry cut him off. "Doc, this isn't a snipe hunt, is it?"

It took Kent a second to catch the boy's drift. His heart sank. He glanced back and saw a mix of surprise and sympathy on Nathan's face, too.

"No, Barry, it is not a snipe hunt." Then, as his eyes adjusted to the moonlight, he could see the fear in Barry's eyes.

"Jesus. We wouldn't do that to you!"

Barry didn't move.

Kent remembered the boy's remark at the Wheat Sepal on the day they met. *Other kids think I'm weird.* He suspected Barry had been the butt of many a cruel joke because of his mother's politics.

For a second, Kent thought he might have to call off the trip. Then he reached down and took a huge ring of keys from the ignition and handed them to Barry. "Don't lose these," he said. "You've got the keys to the truck, my clinic, my house, and a pile more. Nathan and I don't want to walk home."

Barry massaged the keys in his hand and mulled over Kent's gesture of good faith. Finally, he drew a deep breath and blew it out. He jammed the key ring into his jeans pocket. "I'm in."

Kent started again. "Now, as I was saying, ahead there's a section of hardwoods that goes up the hillside. On top is a cornfield. Most of it's been chopped for this year. Coming down from the left is a pretty good size stream. Perfect coon-hunting terrain. As soon as I open the door, Lucinda will be off like a shot. We'll get our gear and kinda follow along behind her. Ready?"

"Ready," Barry said with genuine enthusiasm.

Kent opened the door, and Lucinda hit the ground at a full run into the night.

Barry stared after her. "How the heck are we supposed to follow that?"

"Stand still and keep your ears open."

Kent opened the rear of his truck and pulled out three hard hats with lights attached. "Have a miner's hat," he said, handing one to each boy. "The battery pack goes on your belt."

From a worn leather gun case, he extracted a Remington .22 rifle with scope. Immediately, Barry's dubious expression returned.

Kent frowned at Nathan. Gestured toward Barry. "Looks to me like he's never been around a rifle, huh?"

"Nope," Barry said.

"Don't worry. They're safe enough if you obey the rules. I'll carry it tonight."

Kent held up one hand, signaling for quiet, then cupped his other hand around his ear. "Hear that?"

"I can hear Lucinda yipping, if that's what you mean," Barry said.

"That, my friend, is no yip," Kent said. "That is the trailing bark of a well-schooled coonhound. Music in the night woods."

"Sorry." Barry listened again. "Does sound kind of neat."

"That is the ultimate understatement."

"How far away is she?"

"I'd guess a quarter mile."

"She's on the trail of a raccoon?"

"Yep. Put it this way, if she's on a deer trail, I'll wring her neck."

Suddenly the tenor of Lucinda's voice changed from an even cadence of staccato barks to a series of long slow howls.

"She's got him." Kent said.

"How do you know?"

"Did you hear her voice change?"

"Yes."

"That's her treeing howl. Beautiful, isn't it?"

"I guess so," Barry said, beginning to like the game.

Kent charged off into the darkness. "Let's get moving."

Fifteen minutes later, huffing for breath, they found Lucinda braced against an ancient beech tree singing up into its branches.

"There's a coon up there?" Barry asked between breaths.

"You can bet on it." Kent handed him a square flashlight. "Here. See if you can spot him."

Barry clicked it on and squinted as the powerful beam exploded through the night. "Man, that's some light."

"Shine it up in the branches. Look for the reflection off a pair of eyes."

It took several minutes of systematic scanning limb by limb before Barry held the beam on two iridescent points glowing in a sea of blackness thirty feet above them.

"Told you so," Kent said. "Lucinda would never let me down. Keep your light right there, and I'll dispatch him."

"Dispatch him?"

Barry's inquiry was followed by a crisp snap, like a small fire-cracker, in the darkness beside him. He jumped.

"Yep. Right between the eyes," Kent said.

Branches rattled, and twigs fell from above into the leaves. There was a heavy thud. Lucinda pounced on the coon, but it did not move.

Barry and Nathan raced over to investigate. Nathan hefted the beast with one arm and turned it for Kent to see. "You got him!"

"We sure did," Kent said. "You guys, me, and Lucinda."

Barry watched eagerly as he learned the art of skinning an animal. Kent tucked the pelt into a plastic bag, washed his hands in the creek. He brushed off a seat on a convenient rock, broke out a bag of sandwiches. Passed it to the boys.

"I wish Aaron was here with us tonight," he said, hand-feeding tidbits to Lucinda. "He'd have been proud to see a couple of young guys like you in the woods."

"Wasn't that the guy they found dead the day we got into town?" Barry asked, chewing.

"Yes. He was a great man. A real good friend of mine."

Nathan's voice came out of the darkness. Deep, bitter. "He was an asshole."

Kent had never known a single kid, not one, who didn't like and respect Aaron Whitmore. "Why do you say that, Nathan?"

"He was a control freak. Just like Eugene."

"No."

"If you weren't moving like him, you were nobody."

"That's not true."

"He kicked me out of Scouts because I wouldn't wear one of his faggot uniforms."

"He was trying to make you into a team player. Follow a chain of command. It's a good lesson."

"He was a do-gooder old fart. It was about time somebody knocked him off."

Kent's voice became a low hiss. "What makes you think somebody knocked him off? The police said it a suicide."

Nathan said nothing, but the silence that hung in the air spoke volumes.

"You know something about Aaron's death, Nathan?"

More silence. Then weakly, "I don't know nothing."

"You'd tell me if you did though, right?" It was more of an order than a request.

Nathan flashed him a defiant look. "Now who's being a control freak? I told you, I don't know a damn thing about what went on at Cuyler Lake."

The three of them ate sandwiches in the dark, taking in the sounds of the brook and breeze. The smell of moldering leaves.

***

The next morning Barry raced around getting caught up on his studies and finishing laundry chores before his mother returned from the rodeo rally. The whole time he thought about the night before—Lucinda baying in the distance, the night woods, the kill. It had been a wonderful night. He rubbed his fingers over a stinging scratch on his cheek. A battle scar. The hours of that night had gone faster than any he had ever experienced. Wet feet in the creek. Firing a rifle for the first time. Elation tempered with pathos, as each raccoon fell. Running after the baying hound and laughing with Nathan at sad-faced Doc as they stumbled through the blackness and branches. It had been a night like no other. It was the first thing he mentioned to his mother when she walked in the door.

"You what?" She could not believe her ears.

"I went on a coon hunt with Dr. Stephenson and a kid named Nathan."

Aubrey dropped into a chair in slump-shouldered despair. "Barry, how could you?"

When he saw how his words stung her, he wished he had kept it a secret.

"Mom, it wasn't like that. It was exciting, not cruel. We spent most of the night in the woods, but it wasn't scary. It was awesome. We saw deer and owls, waded through streams in the dark, it was amazing!"

"Did you, ah…get…any raccoons?"

"Four."

"Did you actually…?" She searched for a euphemism.

"'Dispatch' is the word Doc uses. And yes, I did one. He taught me how to shoot a rifle."

"Oh, God!" Aubrey said, burying her face in her hands.

"Mom, that was the only part I didn't like. And Doc said that was okay because he didn't like that part either. But it was okay as long as you used what you dispatched."

She knew what she was about to hear and dreaded it. "The fur, right?"

"He taught me how to skin a raccoon."

Aubrey winced visibly and then shook her head wearily as Barry told the rest of his tale.

When he left, she flopped onto the bed, pulled a pillow over her head, and lay there, deflated, appalled at her son's enthusiasm, disheartened by the ease with which he had disregarded all that she had taught him. And furious at Kent.

After a long while she pushed the pillow aside. Between clenched teeth she said, "That man is going to answer to me for this!"

● ● ●

Kent sat across from Aubrey in the diner, where they had agreed to meet for lunch. She picked at a limp spinach salad. He had a BLT.

"So did you get the rodeo banned in Southern California?"

"Actually no, but we haven't given up on that yet either."

"I'm sure."

"The reason I asked you to meet me for lunch has nothing to do with the rodeo." Aubrey cut her eyes around the diner to be sure no one was within earshot. She leaned forward, elbows on the table, and struggled to keep her voice down. "It has to do with Barry, you son of a bitch."

"He's a great kid."

"He told me you took him raccoon hunting, for Chrissake. Now I'm asking you, wasn't there at least the slightest suspicion in your head that I might disapprove of that?"

Kent leaned back, putting space between himself and Aubrey's long fingernails, which dug at the tabletop like bear claws.

"Actually, I saw a bored young man and felt it was an opportunity to—"

"An opportunity to what? To undermine all the values that I have instilled in my son since birth? An opportunity to get at me through him? Or just a vindictive man's opportunity to screw up a nice kid?"

"None of those!"

"I gotta tell you, Kent. I am really pissed!"

"Give me a chance to explain."

"Explain? Bullshit!" She was shaking. Rage and frustration churned in her eyes. "And you know what really frosts my ass? He *liked* it! That little SOB son of mine liked hunting with you."

"Of course he did! I made sure he did. That's my point. The kid is at the age where his natural instinct to hunt is peaking. You're like some overprotective old she-bear. Cut your cub some slack."

"So what do you suggest? I just let him go against everything I believe in?"

Kent leaned toward her. His words were gentle but firm. "I suggest you go where your conscience leads you and give Barry a chance to go where his takes him. After all, if your way is as virtuous as you'd have us believe, Barry will come around to it on his own. He's a smart kid."

"Is that supposed to be a challenge?"

"I suppose it is. Of sorts."

"Why the hell does Barry like you, anyway? What does he see in you?"

Kent shrugged. "I think it's Lucinda he likes."

For a long moment she stared at him, through him, eyes probing, trying to figure out what made him tick.

Kent watched the rigidity gradually go out of her body. A faint sparkle flickered in her eyes.

"There's more to the pair of you than just Lucinda," she said.

Kent held that thought for an instant, celebrating the prospect that such a beautiful woman could be intrigued by him. He took the safe route. "While you're not screaming at me, can I change the subject for a minute?"

"If you are careful."

"Remember Tammy Mays, the waitress at the Groggery? She was there when the guy came to you about setting a fire at Copithorn?"

"Yes."

"She works here too. Days."

Aubrey glanced around the diner nervously.

"Don't worry, I haven't seen her today. Must not be her shift. Anyway, the first time I talked to her she denied everything."

"Why am I not surprised?"

"Wait a minute. Then yesterday, right here in this very booth, she admits to me that, in fact, it really was her husband, Maylon, who talked to you about pets and a fire at Copithorn."

"It's about time."

"Yeah, well. Then she goes on to hint that there may be something happening out at their place."

"Their place?"

"They have a small farm."

"What sort of *something*?"

"She wouldn't say."

"Why'd she have the change of heart?"

"All she said was she was letting me know because she doesn't like seeing animals suffer."

"What's that mean?" Aubrey weighed the information for a moment. "So what are you going to do?"

"I was going to call Merrill, but I changed my mind."

"Who's Merrill?"

"My brother, who incidentally, is Jefferson's police chief." Kent paused. "Remember? You met him the day of the Copithorn protest."

"That was your brother?" Aubrey's face broke into revelation. "I'll be damned. Your brother is the cop who tried to roust us when we were picketing?"

Kent nodded.

"That explains a whole lot of things. No wonder we can't make any headway in this town."

"It doesn't matter. I decided I'd check it out myself."

"What did you find?"

"Nothing yet. I haven't had time to get out there. But since you and I were going to meet today, I figured I'd see if you wanted to come along. After all, FOAM ought to be interested in who started the fire. Right?"

Aubrey's brow drew into a series of deep creases. "I'm supposed to go check out some woodchuck's dump up in the hills, on a tip from his wife, who lied once already, with a weird veterinarian who's trying to mess up my kid?"

"Well put."

The corners of her mouth drew back in confusion, deepening her dimples. "There's something about you that grows on a person. I haven't figured it out yet."

Kent fixed on her gray-blue eyes. "I'm telling you, I'm as loyal as an old hound dog if you give me a chance."

"I'm against pet ownership. Remember?"

"Are you coming, or not?"

"I've done a lot of dumb things in my life. Might as well add a trip into the boonies with you to the list."

CHAPTER 15

TEN MINUTES OUTSIDE OF JEFFERSON, KENT turned down an unmarked dirt road that crossed a muddy creek then twisted its way up a wooded slope. At the top of the hill, it broke out of the trees and ran alongside a series of semi-abandoned farm fields, mostly overgrown and crisscrossed by thick hedgerows.

Aubrey studied the terrain. "When you get here, you're at the end, huh?"

"You mean of the road?"

"Whatever."

"Not much going for it," Kent said, scanning the tired acreage. "Better for deer hunting than farming. Nice view of the valley, though. That's about it." He pointed off into the panorama beyond the windshield. "Looks down on the Indian reservation."

"I'm thinking that would appeal to May-May's type."

On their right, they passed the remains of a large vegetable garden. Decimated by frost, its withered spires of tall weeds rose above blackened tomato plants and beheaded cabbages. Beyond, a gaunt gray donkey searched already close-cropped grass along a circumference formed by his tether.

"Where are all the junk cars?"

Kent pointed left. "You can just catch the tops of them along the hedgerow over there."

"Whew. I was worried."

Aubrey's humor was lost on Kent. He was awash in memories. Bad ones. Of coming home from college to this dreary place. Of seeing his mother degraded by an overbearing husband. Of watching May-May stealing away what should have been the best years of her life with his incessant run-ins with the law.

They pulled to a stop in front of the farmhouse. It was almost as large as the swaybacked barn and sat among a bevy of canted outbuildings like a mother hen surrounded by her chicks. Years ago when Kent had spent time here, it needed painting. It looked like no one had bothered to take a brush to it since. Patches of bare wood were exposed where the chalky white paint had flaked away. Many of the clapboards were askew or missing. In the dooryard was the green skeleton of a John Deere 3020 tractor, its engine long ago eviscerated.

"Dammit," Kent said.

"What?"

"May-May's truck isn't here. I was hoping to talk to him."

"That might not be so bad. It'll give us a chance to look around."

"Remember," Kent reminded Aubrey of the story they'd concocted while driving. "If he is here, you figured out that he was the guy from the bar by asking around. You just wanted to ask him a few questions. I agreed to bring you out. Okay?"

"Right."

"Don't push him."

"Me? Push?"

"I'm not kidding." Kent knocked on the door several times then thumped it hard enough to rattle the loose panes of glass. No response.

"No one home."

"Good. Can you see anything inside?"

They both put their faces to the window and explored the expansive country kitchen. A mound of dirty dishes and old magazines covered a grimy metal table with a Formica top in the center of the room. More dishes rose out of the sink. Along the far wall was a gun rack bristling with weaponry of many lengths and calibers. Empty cereal boxes and papers littered the floor.

"Your average dump," Aubrey said.

"Nice gun collection."

"Ah, yes. I forgot who I was with."

"Silk purse from a sow's ear." Then, "Well, would you look at that?"

"What?"

"There's a pair of scissors and some tape on the table. And some of those magazines have been cut up. Looks like old May-May has been making anonymous threat letters."

He turned and looked at Aubrey just in time to see the blood drain from her face as she realized the level of danger had just increased. "We going inside?" she asked.

"No. Tammy said it had to do with animals. If there's anything to see, it'll be in the barn." Quietly, watching in all directions, he guided her around behind the house.

"What are all those hutches?" she asked, pointing to half a dozen tin-and-plywood boxes next to the barn.

Kent had already stopped. His eyes were also fixed on the cubicles. "Doghouses. For pit bulls." Under his breath, he said, "May-May, you damn fool. You can't be serious."

In response to strange voices, a dark-colored resident came slinking out of each domicile dragging a heavy chain. Lifeless canine eyes studied the intruders. None made a sound.

Aubrey took an involuntary step backward and then squatted for a better view. "Those dogs look awful. They don't even bark."

"Don't get them stirred up."

"They are so thin. God. They don't even move like dogs. They must be starved."

When Kent did not reply, she ripped her eyes from the dogs and turned to him. His attention had shifted to a wooden-spoke wheel fixed horizontally two feet off the ground by an axle that was anchored in a drum of cement. He gave the folk-art helicopter a push. It spun freely.

"I'll be a son of a bitch," he said. "After all these years. I can't believe he's at it again."

Aubrey rose from the ground. "At what?"

Kent tugged on a heavy rope that hung from a nearby tree limb. A gnarled piece of inner tube dangled from its end, waist high. "I'd never have thought it."

"You going to let me in on this?"

Kent strode away without answering.

"Where are you going?"

"I want to look inside the house."

She caught up with him as they stepped onto May-May's front porch for the second time.

"I thought you didn't want to go inside."

"I changed my mind." He tried the worn latch.

Kent raised a finger to his lips, signaling Aubrey to be quiet. But the door chattered loudly across warped floorboards when Kent pushed his way into the kitchen, louder than her voice. The air inside smelled faintly of wood smoke, but the quaint country fragrance was overpowered by a musty, unkempt smell.

"Get some of those magazine clippings," he said, pointing to the heaped table. "We'll look for a match with Sally's note."

While Aubrey worked at the table, Kent rummaged through a wicker basket of bills and miscellaneous mail. Most of the bills carried past-due messages.

He was studying the names of the addressees when he heard a sound. A distant cow bellow? From the way Aubrey looked at him, she heard it too.

Then it came again. From inside the house. A moan? It was coming through a closed door off the kitchen.

Aubrey was closer. She reached to open the door. Kent lunged to stop her, but his foot caught in the tangle of debris on May-May's floor, and he fell forward. His shoulder crashed against the door, throwing it open. He ended up sprawled inside the room from which the sound emerged.

On all fours, he scanned the room and saw nothing threatening. He looked up at Aubrey. She was braced in the doorway staring at a sagging brass bed along one wall. There was a horrified look on her face.

Kent shifted his eyes to the bed, but from his low vantage point he could see only the ratty gray pinstriping and ticking of a worn mattress. There was no sheet or blanket.

The moan came again.

He wished he'd brought his .38. He raised his head high enough to see the surface of the bed and instantly recognized the cause of Aubrey's horror. There was no need for a gun. Huddled on the bed like an abandoned kitten was Tammy Mays. She was shivering violently. Eyes wide, revealing the whites. She moaned again.

Kent crawled to her. She lurched back when he touched her arm. Gently, Kent pushed back a lock of hair pasted with sweat to the tiny woman's forehead. "Jesus, Tammy. What happened?" he asked in the tone he had perfected for soothing distraught animals.

Tammy maintained her mix of terror and disorientation.

There was a purple bruise covering her left cheek. Her lips were cracked and swollen, coated with dried blood. Her cotton dress was torn loose at the shoulder, exposing her left breast. A grotesque red welt spread from near her nipple to her ribs and armpit.

Aubrey slowly sat on the edge of the bed. The level of fear in Tammy's eyes rose. Aubrey eased the torn dress back up over Tammy's chest and gently straightened the skirt that had ridden up to the top of the battered woman's thighs. There were more bruises on her legs. The gesture seemed to calm her. She took a faltering breath and exhaled through chattering teeth.

"What happened, Tammy?" Aubrey said.

Still she did not answer.

Kent stood, stepped toward the door to the kitchen. "I'm going to call an ambulance. She's in shock."

Tammy reached out for him with both hands. "No, Kent. No doctors. No police."

"You're hurt. You need a doctor."

She drew a second breath. Deeper. Winced as it caught on her ribs. Exhaled slowly. "Just get me a glass of water."

Kent hesitated, questioning the wisdom, then honored her request. When he returned, he handed Aubrey a threadbare washcloth and gestured for her to wipe Tammy's face with it.

He handed Tammy the glass of water, which she downed completely without looking up. It revived her. Grunting, she pushed herself into a sitting position as Aubrey fluffed a flimsy pillow behind her.

Kent asked the obvious. "This is May-May's doing, isn't it?"

Tammy's cracked lips curled into a painful smile. "You think I fell in the bathtub?"

Kent didn't laugh. "Why? What the hell is going on?"

"He's big, I'm little. What more can I say?"

"A lot more!"

Tammy adjusted the cold compress Aubrey had put on her forehead. "Take it easy, Kent. You're making my head hurt more than it already does."

"Okay." He backed off. "But I want some straight answers."

Tammy flashed him a look that signaled she had been bullied all she was going to be bullied. "Hey, brother, or brother-in-law, whatever. Any information I give you is because I want you to have it. Got that?"

"We can't help you unless we know what's happening."

She looked back and forth between her nurses, registering uncertainty. "I doubt you can help me anyway."

Kent pointed out the window where he could just make out the pit bull hutches through the smeared glass. "You must have figured

I could do *something*, or you wouldn't have told me to come up here in the first place."

"What do you think is going on? You're the amateur detective."

"I don't *think*, I *know*. I was just out by the barn. May-May's got dogs. He's got a cat mill greased and ready. Hell, there is fresh spit on the jaw rope. The dumb son of a bitch is going to find himself in the hoosegow again if he's not careful. Before it was a misdemeanor—now it's a felony. And this would be his second fall."

Tammy patted her lips with a fingertip and then puckered them, testing the discomfort level. "Don't think I haven't tried to tell him that. But he hears what he wants."

"Why? Fifteen years ago, that was good ol' boy stuff. Find a dog, rough him up a little to make him mean, put a few bucks on him, and get drunk watching him get chewed up on a Saturday night. I can't imagine anyone doing dogfights anymore. People don't put up with that stuff. Makes them sick. Makes *me* sick."

"It's different this time, Kent!" Tammy leaned toward him, winced, and eased back.

"What's different?" Aubrey asked, lost at the edge of their conversation. She was amazed that the two of them seemed to know what the other meant.

"I'll tell you about it later, when we're out of here," Kent said.

Aubrey gave him a cool look but sat back to listen.

"It's not just an evening's sport like it used to be," Tammy said. "Now it's big money. Serious money."

Kent shook his head. "You know? That makes it worse. It was a revolting pastime even when it was a so-called sport. At least someone got some sadistic pleasure out of it. But for plain old money? To let dogs do that to one another? That's about as low as you can get."

"We're not talking 'plain old money,' Kent. This is big! Real big."

"Yeah, right. How big?"

"Across the United States, Canada, and Mexico. There's a good chance the Mafia is in on it. Lots of white-collar types."

"Sounds like May-May's giving you a crock of shit."

"This is no shit," Tammy said. Her voice took on a pleading quality. "The whole reason I told you what was going on is because he's in over his head. Believe me. If he gets himself killed, that's his own damn bad luck and his own business. But he's dragging me down too."

"You're a part of this?"

Tammy spread her arms wide, displaying her battered body. "Does it look like I'm part of it?" She accepted Kent's apologetic look. "The whole idea of it makes me want to puke. He's spending every cent of his money, and mine, on dogs. Buying training stuff or gambling on them. Shit, we've never been very solid, but now we're about to lose the farm. He's peddling marijuana he grew out back just to make ends meet, and I think he's doing a little street work for some penny-ass dealer friends of his. I've just had it. I want the hell away from it all. And I don't give a shit if he does get pissed off."

"Why don't you take it to the police?"

Tammy spread her arms again. "I just *mentioned* the police, that's all, just mentioned them, and look at me. I'm telling you, Kent, he's crazed. May-May was always a little quick to fly off the handle, but never like this. He beat the hell out of me." She carefully eased the front of her dress open enough to peek at her bruised bosom.

Tammy's confirmation that May-May had done this to her made Kent want to tear into town, find him, and clench both fists around his half brother's throat. He'd watch May-May's eyes bulge as he strangled the life out of him. He'd watch spit dribble down the bastard's beard and listen to the gurgle of his swollen tongue stifling his last scream.

Tammy broke the thought. "Besides, Merrill isn't going to do a damn thing but laugh at some screwy story about big-time gamblers and dogfighting coming to Jefferson. Especially from a two-bit squaw like me."

"What do you mean 'coming to Jefferson'?"

Tammy looked at Aubrey and waved weakly toward the kitchen. "My cigarettes are on the counter. How about you grab me one?"

As Aubrey left, Tammy said to Kent in a voice just loud enough for Aubrey to hear, "I always wanted to be waited on. Never figured it would be by a hotsy-totsy Hollywood actress." She coughed when she laughed.

Kent was relieved that Aubrey showed no response.

Aubrey returned, tapping out a smoke. Her eyes cut to Kent as she dutifully held a match.

Tammy filled her lungs, rocked her head back, and let the smoke emerge from her open mouth at its own pace as she figured how to tell the whole story.

"All right. Here's how it goes. A couple of years ago, May-May and a few of his pals went big-game hunting down in Texas. What do they have down there—wild boars? Something like that. Naturally, the hunt was a bust because they spent most of the time passed-out drunk. But somehow they stumbled onto a dogfight. Well, May-May is sometimes a big talker, if you haven't noticed, and he starts shooting his mouth off about how he used to fight dogs up in New York and got busted for it. Paints this picture of himself as a big-time hoodlum." Tammy interrupted herself to take another drag on her cigarette.

"So anyway, he ends up buying a couple of pit bulls from these guys, and presto, he's back in business. Only this time it's strictly for money, and he's got his connection to the big league."

"He's been building up a pack of dogs ever since," Kent said.

"He's buying and selling all over the country."

"Who's he work with around here?"

"No partners. Just got one guy helps him out. A real dumb black guy named Bo something. Yeah. May-May's playing it real cool." She struck imaginary quotation marks in the air. "If you'd wandered down into the woods you'd have seen his whole setup. He's got a couple of kennels' worth of bitches and pups. Let's see, he's got a treadmill and several crates of little dogs and cats he picked up from who knows where for training."

"That explains all the missing pets."

"Yep. I'm sure he's going through a lot of them. He's even got a practice pit."

Tammy pointed at an empty tuna can on the windowsill. Aubrey handed it to her. She tapped off her ash. "He's heavily into getting ready for this big fight they've got planned."

"When is it supposed to happen?"

"No one knows exactly. Not yet anyway. That's the way they work it. Sometime in the next few weeks though."

"Right here in Jefferson?"

She took one last pull on her cigarette, so deep it made tiny popping sounds, and then butted it in the tuna can.

"That's what May-May says. My big-mouth diplomat husband managed to convince the hotshots that they ought to hold their national championship in the east so they can promote their sport here." Her voice hissed with contempt. "This area could use more dogfighters, you know."

"Like hell."

"These guys are really serious, Kent. It's no joke." Tammy paused, debating whether to put all her cards on the table. Finally, almost inaudibly, she said, "That's why they burned up Copithorn."

Aubrey, who had stayed at the periphery, snapped to attention.

"What?" she and Kent said in unison.

Tammy leaned back nervously. "That's why they torched the cosmetics factory and left the little white dog in there so the police would find it."

"Why?" Kent could not believe he was actually hearing what he had desperately wanted to hear. He gave Aubrey a look of relief. "It wasn't FOAM that started the fire."

Aubrey's expression said, *Of course not.*

"For a distraction. Call it a smokescreen," Tammy said with a dismal chuckle and pointed at Aubrey. "They had the good luck of having these idiotic animal rights Californians stumble into town."

"I don't get it," Kent said.

"I guess May-May and his buddies got wind that some other humane group is snooping around about dogfighting, so May-May decided to give them something else to think about."

Kent held up his hand. "What did you just say?"

"I'm telling you, and I could get killed for this." She spoke slowly, exaggerating her enunciation of each word. "May-May and company started the fire at Copithorn to get these other guys going after FOAM and away from the dogfighters."

"There is *someone else* investigating dogfights around here?"

"Yep."

He massaged his brow, letting this new information sink in. "We've got *two* animal rights groups hanging around town?"

"That's what I said," Tammy said. "I can't remember the name of it, but May-May had a magazine they put out. That's what caught my eye in the first place. He was actually reading something besides *Penthouse*. When I asked him about it, he said he wanted to know his enemy." She laughed. "A regular General Patton, wouldn't you say?"

Kent and Aubrey didn't laugh.

"Pretty ballsy move for old May-May. I'd be proud of him if it weren't for the fact that he's into killing animals."

"He's going to get himself killed."

Tammy shook another cigarette out of the pack Aubrey had left on the bed. Lit it. "Well, the ball's in your court now." She turned to the wall and closed her eyes. Smoked in silence.

"I'd feel better if you'd let us drive you to see a doctor," Kent said.

Tammy did not respond. Aubrey said, "I can help you find a safe place to stay."

Tammy still didn't answer.

Kent nodded toward the door, and they slipped quietly back to his truck. On the road he asked, "Am I supposed to feel like crap because of what May-May's doing with the dogs and how he hurt Tammy, or am I supposed to feel good because we've got a witness who can testify that FOAM didn't start the Copithorn fire?"

Aubrey shrugged. "I'm going for the 'feel good' option myself."

CHAPTER 16

MERRILL PIVOTED IN HIS GRAY STEEL DESK chair…slowly, back and forth, like an oscillating fan, but he sure as hell wasn't blowing a cool breeze. The tiny office was stifling. He touched an electronic box and ordered the duty officer, Janet, to hold his calls.

"Okay, Kent. We're all here, as you asked. It's your show. Take it away."

Kent looked left and right at Aubrey and Stef and then back to Merrill. Both women were glistening. Merrill seemed oblivious to the dead air. "I figured I'd have to talk to all three of you about this, so I might as well do it at one time. Then maybe we can formulate a plan."

"A plan for what?" Merrill asked.

Kent held his course. "You questioned May-May about the fire, didn't you, Chief?"

"For what it was worth, yes."

"Where?"

Merrill pointed. "I was in this seat. He was about where Stef is."

"You didn't go out to his farm?"

"No."

"You should have. He's got a bunch of pit bulls and fighting equipment out there."

Merrill's eyes narrowed. "What were you doing at May-May's farm?"

144

"Snooping around. Tammy tipped me that he was up to something. So I…" he glanced at Aubrey again, "*we* went to see what we could find out."

"You two went out to May-May's farm together. Alone. Sweet Jesus!"

"I already told you on the phone, *I* was out there. That's where we found Tammy—all beat up. She told us all about a big fight coming to Jefferson. She called it the national championship. And this time May-May's not in it just for a little something to do. He's got himself mixed up with some real high rollers. They want to promote dogfighting in the east."

Merrill's face twisted into a look of disbelief. "Come on, Kent. Is this Maylon Mays, a.k.a. May-May, ne'er-do-well of Jefferson, we're talking about here? May-May who got busted years back for the same game? He couldn't pull it off back then, even small time. No way could he do what you are saying. Think about it."

"He's doing it, all right," Kent said. "Tammy had too many details. He's got some big money backers and he's doing it."

"Details like what?"

"Like he burned Copithorn."

Stef spun her head from a resting stare to fix on Kent. "May-May started the fire?"

"And they planted Bear, Maureen Philips's dog, inside to discredit Copithorn."

"Why?"

"To get attention away from themselves. Apparently, there is some *other* humane group on their tail."

"Did Tammy say anything about other missing pets? Besides Bear Philips, I mean?" Stef's voice held the terror of a mother asking about a missing child. "Anything about Armani?"

"Nothing specifically," Kent answered as gently as possible. He knew he had to tell her. She would settle for nothing but the truth. "A dognapping ring usually accompanies dogfighters because they use dogs—and cats—for training."

"I don't get it. For training?"

Kent turned to Aubrey. "Remember that spoke-wheel thing that looked like a modern-art helicopter behind May-May's? That's a—"

"Cat mill," Merrill said. "He's got a cat mill?"

"Yes. Along with a lot of other training stuff."

Merrill shook his head and said, "So Armani is probably—"

Kent sucked in a loud breath and glared at his brother, interrupting Merrill's comment.

Stef clenched the arms of her chair so hard her nails made a blackboard noise. "What the hell are you guys talking about? A cat mill? What's that got to do with Armani?"

Kent gave Merrill a you-jerk look.

"The chief is going off half-cocked, as usual. We don't know what happened to Armani yet. He's just speculating because a cat mill is a machine used to exercise fighting dogs. It's like a horizontal wheel with spokes about five feet long and maybe this high off the ground." Kent gestured to just below desktop height. "What they do is leash a fighting dog at the end of one spoke and then dangle a cat just out of reach on the spoke in front of him. A pit bull will run himself in circles for hours trying to get that cat."

"What happens to the cat?"

Kent swallowed hard. "In the end, they give the cat to the dog as a reward. But we don't know that happened to Armani."

"Oh, Armani," Stef whispered.

Aubrey reached over and took her hand.

Kent caught Aubrey's eye. "FOAM ever go after dogfighters before?"

"I thought that stuff died out years ago."

"Well, if you want a cause—a *real* anticruelty cause—forget what you're doing now and go after the dog men."

" I can't believe that stuff still goes on," Aubrey said, amazed at her own ignorance.

"They've gone underground. And with good reason. It's a sickening sport. What these crazies do is take perfectly normal Staffordshire terriers and train them to be maniacal killing machines."

"Using things like the cat mill," Stef said.

"Right. But that's not the half of it. Tell them, Merrill."

The chief squirmed again as visions of the hideous sport came to mind. "It all starts as pups," he said. "They look for what they call gameyness. Really what it means is aggressiveness. Then they encourage it and develop it. They teach the pups to attack and fight by killing rabbits, then kittens, and then small dogs...and so on. What's the word for it, Kent?"

"Blooded."

"That's it. *Blooded.* By the time the dogs are two years old, their natural gameyness has become a drive to wage war even in the face of annihilation."

"These people should be castrated," Stef said.

Aubrey nodded. "That's one thing we agree on."

Merrill stood and slowly crossed his office to a water cooler. He poured himself a cup and returned to his seat without offering any to the others. "The trainer leads a dog up to twenty miles a day with his arm out the window of a pickup truck, the poor animal trotting alongside on a leash."

Stef's neck drew down into her shoulders as a chill of revulsion skittered up her spine. "You're kidding! Twenty miles? A day?"

"Yep. And then these guys will make their dogs hang by their teeth from a piece of hose or inner tube to build up their jaws."

"That was the rope with the inner tube attached we saw at May-May's," Aubrey said.

"Uh-huh."

"God. The whole thing makes me nauseated."

"All right. Let's go on to the next thing. What are we going to do about it?" Kent knew Merrill would respond first.

"You know, folks, what I said originally still holds true," Merrill said. "Sure, this whole thing sounds mysterious, diabolical, exciting, what-have-you, but in the end it's probably just hearsay bullshit. Just May-May—and Tammy—blowing smoke. Personally, I find the odds of this really happening to be one in a million. Think about what we're saying here. A scofflaw from the hills out by the reservation puts together a clandestine national championship criminal activity? And then he torches a major business as part of his plan? I mean, it all sounds intriguing, I'll admit, but when you boil it all down, it's pretty far-fetched. Wouldn't you say?"

"You didn't hear Tammy tell it. You'd believe it," Kent said.

Merrill crumpled his paper cup. Tossed it under his desk, presumably into a wastebasket. "Probably should forget it, but probably shouldn't, either. I'll tell you what I'll do. You three give me a day or two. I'll find Tammy and get what I can out of her. Then I'll tell you what way we ought to go with this. That make sense to you?"

"See if you can find out anything about Armani too, please, Merrill," Stef said.

"Agreed."

Kent walked a few strides behind Stef and Aubrey as they left the station. He studied the two women. He couldn't hear what they were saying, but for the first time, their body language was that of friends, comrades. Tammy was right, he did like being the middle-man between these two beautiful women.

He and Aubrey stood together, watching Stef drive away.

"Stef asked if you and I would have dinner with her tonight," Aubrey said, keeping her eyes on Stef's taillights.

"You and me? As if she considers us a couple? Where?"

"At her place. I don't know about the couple part." Aubrey wove her arm into the crook of his elbow and walked close. "She said I can bring Barry, but you can't bring Lucinda."

"Isn't that kind of discriminatory? I'll have to find Lucinda a sitter."

"I think I'll find something for Barry to do too. He's bored with adult dinners."

"Hey. Let's be practical here. How about we let the two of them entertain each other?

"You'll have to give her a bath."

He held the truck door for her. "A bath! She doesn't need a bath."

Aubrey turned a sappy, coy look on him, fluttering her lashes.

He let out a sigh of defeat. "If you insist," he said, and headed his truck back to the hotel.

Kent walked Aubrey into the Red Horse lobby just as Barry and Nathan crossed the room dribbling skateboards with one foot. They ignored the desk clerk's severe look. "Hi, Mom. Hi, Dr. Stephens… er, Doc," Barry said. "Nathan's going to show me some new moves in the parking lot. Recess. You know?"

Aubrey hooked his arm, brought him to a stop. "You get your schoolwork done?"

"Most of it," Barry said, flipping the board up with his toe, catching it clean. "Nathan, this is my mom."

Aubrey let her son go, extended her hand to Nathan. "So you're the other coon hunter."

"Yes, ma'am." Nathan smiled wider than Kent had ever seen.

Barry waved over his shoulder as they pushed through the lobby door.

"Your mom is pretty," Kent heard Nathan say as the door closed behind them. Then Barry opened it again. "Nice to see you two together. I thought you might have had a wicked fight." He disappeared, smiling.

"Great kid," Kent said. "But that's all I'll say for fear of getting your hackles up again. I enjoyed your company this afternoon."

Aubrey led him toward the stairs to her room. "Don't leave so quickly," she said. Her eyes met his. "You already have my hackles up again."

Her room had vintage furnishings that he did not even notice. Slowly, purposefully, she triple-locked the door. She moved to the window and drew the blind without taking her eyes off him. His heart began sending pulses to his brain like waves crashing on a beach. He rubbed his fingers against his palms, feeling the moisture. It had been so long. She was such a beautiful creature.

Aubrey stepped to him and brought her arms around his neck, pulling him toward her, covering his mouth with her lips. She writhed her breasts across his chest in a slow sway. She nudged him toward the bed. Slowly, she teased her sweater over her head and shook black curls onto her shoulders. Then she pressed her weight against him and they melted onto the bed.

Years of self-denial gave way as Kent made love to this woman who moved like a doe in a misty morning meadow. When they were finished, he sank back into the covers, only to have his desire restored as she rolled against him stroking and nudging. After a second time, they lay together awestruck by the power of passion to transcend their differences.

They stayed there on their sides, facing each other. Casting blurry gazes into each other's eyes. They did not talk for a long time.

Finally, Kent said, "What kind of a chance is there for two people as different as we are?"

"I was asking myself the same question."

"What did you decide?"

"I didn't. Except that I'm willing to give it a try. All the old clichés come to mind— opposites attract, one day at a time, all that stuff." Then a smile flickered across her face. "Besides, I'm from California, remember? Anything goes."

Kent was silent for several very long seconds. When he finally spoke, his tone was deep and somber. "Well, I'm from upstate New York, where we are not so flippant." He took a lock of her hair and brought it to his nose, inhaled her scent, and watched her brow furrow with uncertainty. He held the moment. Finally, he said, "I'll have to consult with Lucinda on this."

Aubrey warbled a laugh that was music.

Eventually they became quiet again as thoughts of the day's adventure returned.

Aubrey pulled herself up, fluffed a pillow against the headboard, and leaned back, tucking the sheet into her armpits.

"Kent?"

"What?"

"How do you know so much about this May-May guy?"

"What do you mean?"

"Right off the bat you knew he was the one who approached me at the Groggery just by my description. Then you knew where to find him. You know his wife, Tammy, and what her work schedule is." She ticked off each clue with her fingers. "At first I wrote it off as the small-town, everybody-knows-everything-about-everybody lifestyle, but then you knew too much about May-May's farm, like where the junk cars were, and you walked around the place like you'd been there a dozen times before. You didn't act like someone sneaking around on someone else's private property. Then Tammy called you 'brother-in-law.' What's that all about?"

Kent lay there without moving, deciding whether to level with her. Why not? They were a team now. Relationships were built on honesty. Besides, it was the truth. She'd find out sooner or later anyway. And aside from it being a family embarrassment, there was no reason not to tell her.

He sat up next to her and took her hand. "He's my half brother."

151

"What?"

"He's my half brother. My mother is his mother."

Aubrey leaned away from him to better study his face. "Why didn't you tell me before?"

He shrugged. "May-May's farm is my stepfather and my mother's old place. I lived there on and off during the summers while I was in college."

"Jesus. First you just happen to mention the village police chief is your brother. Now you tell me the village crook is your brother too."

"You asked."

"Well then, let me ask again. Do you have any other brothers? Politicians? Priests? Pro athletes? Anything like that?"

Kent huffed a laugh through his nose. "No."

"How about any sisters?"

"No sisters."

"You're sure now?"

"Yes."

"Okay. That's settled."

After a brief pause, Kent made a dubious expression. He held up one finger as if suddenly remembering something. "I have this uncle…"

"Go jump!" She pushed him off the bed.

CHAPTER 17

MAY-MAY SAT IN THE FIRST ROW OF MAKESHIFT bleachers in a barn on a remote farm somewhere in Texas. He turned to the burly clod wearing tattered Carhartt coveralls and a three-day beard who was sitting next to him. "What you got for time, Leon?"

The man kept a blurry-eyed watch on two warrior dogs locked in combat fifteen feet away. "They've been at it almost half an hour so far." He leaned toward May-May, grinned. His teeth matched his Carhartts. His breath was sour with whiskey and tobacco. "That red's got your dog pretty good, ain't he?"

May-May squinted through the smoky darkness and into the pit in front of him. "Like hell. You just keep watchin'!" he said with more confidence than he felt. "That leg hold don't mean nothin' to Little Jake. He's got three others, and besides, that dog'll tire. He can't breathe good the way Jake's got hold of his belly."

The grating crack of enamel daggers crushing a leg bone spread a knowing smile across Leon's face and taxed May-May's bravado.

A soft whine bubbled through blood and slobber around Little Jake's clenched teeth, but he held on. Gamely he tossed his head back and forth on neck muscles quivering with fatigue, trying to widen the rent in the red dog's belly, trying to spill his adversary's guts for the honor of his master.

"Won't take long now," Leon said. "Broken leg's too much pain." He sucked hard, retrieving a dribble of tobacco goo that had escaped his lips. "Makes 'em go shocky real quick. I've seen it before."

May-May's vantage point was from behind his corner of the pit. The dogs were up against its plywood wall. He could not see them well, but he did not need to. He could tell by the crowd's reaction that things were not going well for Little Jake. He chugged the rest of his beer, crushed the can angrily, and tossed it with the half-dozen others between his feet.

"I'm doubling bets on my Jake!" he shouted up to the crowd, as if such a brash show of confidence would inspire his dog.

A short, barrel-chested man rose from his position at a long ringside table. Beads of sweat glistened along his receding hairline. He wore an expensive gray wool suit, but that was his only resemblance to a gentleman. His dark eyes were fired with bulliness.

"That's against the rules, May-May! You know it. Betting's closed."

"Tell him, Mr. Ross," someone goaded from the crowd, but Lester Ross eased back into his seat without another word.

May-May waved him off as if he didn't care. But he did care and did not make his offer again. He sat brooding, raking soiled fingernails back and forth in his beard.

His boldness drew several laughs and sarcastic remarks from the raucous crowd. They'd been around long enough to know the end was in sight for this match.

Another ten minutes of ominously silent combat continued in the cold dimness of the Texas barn before Little Jake, exhausted and in shock, released his hold on the red dog. He let his head drop to the sodden rug.

The red dog's handler shouted, "That's it! That was a turn, ref. Come on!"

Obligingly, the referee yelled for both handlers to corner their dogs and rammed his parting stick between them. "Get 'em back, boys. Get 'em back. Three minutes. Then we'll see if the brindle can scratch."

May-May watched in silence as Bo grabbed Little Jake by his scruff and slid him to his corner across the pit's rug floor, which was coated with blood, saliva, and urine. Both of Jake's front legs were useless, hanging limp and twisted. The dog lay shaking and gasping, as much from fear of humiliation as from pain or fatigue. He had disappointed his master. Bo worked feverishly trying to revive the vanquished pit bull, wiping him with cool water and Listerine.

"Time's up!" the referee said. "Face your dogs, men." He dragged the side of his boot along a strip of duct tape that transected the ring. "Here's the scratch line. See it? Billy, you hold your red back. Bo, your dog's gotta cross this here line since he's the one that turned," the referee explained, as if there was a soul in the crowd who did not already understand what it meant to scratch. "If he don't, he's out."

Bo pivoted his dog toward the red one, but the fiery aggressiveness in Little Jake's eye was gone. In its place was a disoriented glaze. Bo straddled him, both hands on his scruff and rousted him. "Come on, Little Jake, he ain't got you yet. Git out there. You can take him." He shook him hard.

"Let him go!" the ref said.

Bo gave Jake a hard shake and almost shoved him to the line, but there was no need for anyone to call foul. Without taking another step, Jake dropped his hind legs to a crouch, turned his gashed and swollen face to Bo, and ignored his opponent's frantic attempts to attack.

The ref declared the red pit bull the winner. The crowd roared. No one heard Bo Davis whisper, "I'm so sorry, Little Jake."

May-May stood, pointed at Little Jake, and addressed the crowd. "That there brindle pit's for sale. He's still a champion even if he did lose tonight. Make me an offer. I don't want his sorry ass around my place no more. Anything reasonable I'll take."

No one spoke.

"Bo, take what's left of him out to the truck. You hear me?"

Bo obeyed, too disheartened to argue. May-May yanked his worn wallet from his pocket by its chain and began divvying up to the players he owed. "The bastard let me down," he said to no one in particular. No one seemed to care.

He waded through the unruly crowd, tripping on empty beer cans and ignoring facetious remarks from other pit-fighting aficionados. He breathed a deep breath of the moist night air as he approached his truck and recognized Bo's silhouette in the moonlight. His skinny corner man was hunched over the tailgate. When May-May got close enough to look in the bed, he could see Bo was washing wounds on Little Jake's semiconscious body.

"What you doin'?" May-May asked.

Bo quickly wiped away the tears that had rolled down his cheeks and continued to work a damp cloth gently over Little Jake. "Just cleaning him up."

"No need to."

"Why not?"

"Cause if no one wants to buy him, you're gonna shoot him. That's why."

"Ah, May-May, ain't no need to do that."

May-May swung his heavy forearm at Bo, backhanding him and sending him reeling away from Little Jake. "I told you I won't have no losin' dogs around! It looks bad. People'll think we breed dogs that can't fight."

"But like you said, he's still a champ. Even after tonight."

"Only now he's a loser, too," May-May said without the least compassion for the dog that had given him his heart and soul. "That's why ain't no one from in there comin' out here to buy 'im.".

"Well, then, maybe I'd buy him," Bo said.

"The hell you will!" May-May gave the ground a scuffing kick, sending leaves and pebbles flying at his helper. "You live in the trailer up behind my place, which means he'd still be in my sight. You ain't bringing him there, and that's that." The more he thought about it, the more angry he became. "Hell with it. Take the worthless piece of shit out in them woods right now and plug him. And don't bring him back. Got it?"

Without waiting for an answer, May-May stepped around the truck into the darkness, turned his back to Bo, and began working down his zipper.

"Come on, May-May. He's a gamey dog. I can bring him back for you."

"I don't want him! Shoot him, dammit!" May-May said over his shoulder as he urinated on the truck's tire.

Bo swallowed his frustration and resigned himself to the task. He slid his lank arms under the dog and lifted him against his chest. Little Jake offered no resistance. His front legs swung like grotesque pendulums as he was carried into the woods.

May-May turned, legs bowed, pulling up his zipper. "And bring me back his collar!" He straightened, collected himself, and then noticed the outline of a man approaching in the dark.

"Tough luck in there tonight," came Lester Ross's voice.

"Yeah. Shouldn't have happened, Mr. Ross," May-May said, feeling the front of his jeans to be sure all was secure.

"Sorry I had to bring you back into line about the betting on your dog. Nothing personal, you know. But rules are rules."

May-May wiped his hand on his shirt and shook the one Lester Ross extended. "I can take it," he said with forced levity.

"I'm sure you can. You didn't get where you are being somebody's patsy."

May-May squared his shoulders in response to the flattery. Lester's tone became businesslike. "I was hoping you'd have a little better showing tonight. Would have gone a long way to build interest in the national championship. Everything we do from here on out is aimed at building the nationals. You realize that, don't you?"

"We'll do better from here on out, Mr. Ross. You can bet on that."

"The very fact that we're holding the tournament in your area puts you in the hot seat."

"I know that too." May-May was glad there was darkness to conceal his nervousness.

"There's a lot at stake here. A huge amount." Lester's voice dropped. He spoke as if he were revealing something very confidential to May-May. "I think I mentioned to you at the last fight that I have a business associate in Boston who is very interested in what we're doing. *Very* interested."

May-May nodded his head rapidly, eager to be included in the dealings of such powerful men. "Yep, you did."

"I was on the phone with him just today. He indicated that if the national championship goes well—you know, lots of people, lots of action, lots of money—he'd probably jump in with some major backing." Ross paused to let May-May grasp the idea. "If that happens, I promise you, the sport of pit fighting will explode in this country. And"—he punched May-May lightly in the shoulder—"you and I are in on the ground floor."

May-May swallowed hard and reminded himself he was a high roller too. "Don't worry. It'll go off without a hitch."

"I'm counting on you. A lot of people are counting on you. I'll be in touch." Lester walked back into the darkness.

● ● ●

On the long drive back to New York, May-May said to Bo, "I can see I'm gonna have to be keepin' an eye on you with the training. You didn't come close to gettin' them dogs fit enough." He pounded the steering wheel with a fist. "How do you expect Lester Ross to figure we are worth our salt if we don't do no better than what we did?"

"Mr. Ross knows we have good dogs," Bo said.

"No he don't! And even if he did, how is he supposed to convince all them big guys that we deserve the national championship?"

"I dunno."

"Well, you best be thinking about it, 'cause it's coming if I have anything to say about it." He remembered what Lester had said. His voice took on a dreamy tone. "The future of dogfighting in the whole US of A rests on the next national championship. Either it stays small-time, or the hotshots get in and get serious, and dogfightin' hits the big time. We're gonna be a part of it."

Bo stroked a hand through his hair. "Man. Can we handle all that?"

"You better believe it! And we stand to be in on the ground floor, Lester says. We're the guys'll make the biggest amount of money."

CHAPTER 18

MAY-MAY WATCHED JERRY, THE GRAY-HAIRED barkeeper, paint endless swirls on the bar's surface with a sour rag. He listened to backwoods patrons honk out gravelly, coughing laughs at dirty jokes and tell lies about ignorant bosses and would-be sexual conquests.

Years ago, Kolbie's Tavern had been a respectable outback watering hole. Fishermen in summer, hunters in the fall, loggers and snowmobilers in winter. Nowadays, it was an embarrassment to the countryside. Way out in the middle of nowhere, it was surrounded by miles of woods, lakes, swamps, and abandoned farms. That was the only thing unique about the place. It was also the reason it appealed to May-May and his dog men.

He rotated on his bar stool, rose unsteadily to his feet, and wobbled to a pool table with a gouge in its felt. He fished his jacket out of the many piled on the table. It reeked of smoke and stale beer.

"Come on, Bo," he said. "We're outta here."

Jerry stopped polishing long enough to give the pair his usual advice. "You boys go straight home, now. You hear me?"

"Like hell," May-May said. "Nothing much to go home to. Not tonight. I think I'm going to pay a visit to a long-legged friend of mine. See if she likes my work."

The old bartender shook his head. "That sounds like trouble to me. You be careful."

May-May drove his pickup well under the speed limit, both hands gripping the wheel. Occasionally he closed one eye to consolidate both road lines into one. He hated the way cops hung out near the bars late at night, always trying to ambush him. Always looking for a chickenshit DWI bust.

Bo braced gnarled hands on his knees that almost bumped the dashboard. "Who's your 'long-legged friend,' May-May?" he asked as oncoming headlights showed his nervous grin.

"Miss Fairbanks," May-May said, pride of ownership in his voice.

Bo's grin dissolved into a frown. "The lady that's after Copithorn?"

"The one and only."

"I doubt you'll get to first base with her."

May-May swung a beefy arm and caught Bo in the shoulder, tearing the thin man's gaze from the road. "You might be surprised. I'm gonna ask her what she thinks of our little bonfire over there. That ought to get me on the inside track."

Bo's Adam's apple rose then fluttered back down. "You get anything off her, it'll be a miracle."

"You watch and see." May-May turned his pickup truck in behind the Red Horse Inn. "I hope she's in her room," he said and pulled into a shadowed corner, hidden by a mounded green dumpster.

"Why you parking way back here?"

May-May let out an exasperated huff. "I can't just waltz in the front door this time of night, stupid. I'd get recognized."

"So how you gettin' in?"

May-May leaned close to the steering wheel, cast his eyes upward at the inn, and pointed to a second-story window. "Tammy said Miss Fairbanks is in 206. That window is 206. It pays to have a wife who works in the building you want to sneak into." He let out a wet laugh.

Bo's Adam's apple rose higher and settled back with more vibration this time. "You're sneaking in the window?"

"Yes, sirree. Won't hurt to scare her a little. May be kind of a turn-on for her. At least she'll get an idea who she's dealing with."

"Good Lord." The hired man pulled his tattered cap down over his eyes. "I'll be here when you get back." His tone made it clear he held no hope of a successful outcome to his boss's plan.

May-May scaled an ancient fire escape and crept across a small roof. He eased his way to the window of room 206 and peered through the glass. Nothing but blackness. She must be sleeping. His eyes widened at the titillating thought. He forced his fingers under the sash, slid the window up gently, and listened. Not a sound.

He pivoted, stepped one leg and then the other over the sill, and then ducked his head into the darkened room. He listened again, letting his eyes adjust. Suddenly, like a demon condensing out of nothingness, Lucinda's face appeared in front of his so close he could feel her breath. She snarled a primordial warning to get out. May-May was instantly sober as a preacher. He stared point blank into Lucinda's eyes. They gathered light and reflected hatred. He could count her teeth, glistening with saliva against curled lips. Instinctively, he screamed, but all that came out was a croaking gurgle. He turned to avoid a full-face bite and scrambled back toward the roof.

A thousand volts of pain roared up his leg, tripped along his spine, and crashed into his brain as Lucinda secured a crushing grip on his calf. He reeled and twisted to get away, but her jaws held and tore into his skin. He pulled himself through the window, dragging Lucinda with his leg, and yelled to Bo. He clawed his way onto the roof, kicking her face with his free leg.

There was a shout from inside. "Lucinda, let him go!" And suddenly his leg was free. Recoiling away on the pitched roof, he lost his balance, rolled down the slope, and fell to the ground a story below.

"Bo!" May-May forced the words out of his breathless chest. "Get the truck over here."

He heard the pickup's engine roar to life and tires squeal as he staggered to his feet. Bo pulled alongside, and May-May rolled himself into the bed. With the last of his strength, he signaled Bo to keep going.

Secure in the darkness of the cab as the truck sped away from Jefferson, Bo's face broke into a broad smile. He thumped the steering wheel with his palm. *Yes, sirree! Sometimes things go right, after all.*

●　●　●

Kent slumped, submerged among a litter of pillows on Stef's massive velvet couch. Her whole house was oversized. A Realtor would describe it as a sprawling contemporary, ceilings vaulted, lots of glass, angles oblique. Kent called it modern.

Dinner was fabulous. Stef prepared it herself, and even though it was vegan, it was as satisfying as any Kent had ever eaten. He turned his Amaretto slowly, studying the way it gathered the orange light flickering from the fireplace. Aubrey was curled at the other end of the couch, letting her thoughts drift with the soft chords of the Moody Blues. Her legs were drawn up so that the hem of her silver silk dress was at midthigh. Absentmindedly, she ran her nails lightly along her calf in long sensuous strokes. The cut of her dress was perfectly low across her chest, and she had accented it with a maroon-and-green paisley scarf. She was stunning. Kent felt a warm glow that was more than the liquor. He wanted that scarf—he wanted her!

He had not had a chance to follow up with Aubrey about their earlier encounter in her room. That had made him uneasy until, during dinner, he felt her tiny shoeless foot under the table. It stroked gently against his calf. The gesture was so sensual and so perfectly timed to his mood that it aroused him instantly. Without breaking conversation, Aubrey flashed him a demure glance laced with womanly humor.

"I think it was pure genius to let Lucinda babysit Barry," Kent said. He knew Aubrey would take the bait.

"Wait just a second, sir. My kid needs no babysitter, and I resent your implication that your dog could exercise better judgment than my son."

"Hey. I'm into animal rights. I see no reason my dog should not have a position of authority."

"Oh, boy. Here we go," Stef said and settled back to enjoy the banter.

"Lucinda didn't look too authoritative when you were sneaking her up the back stairs into our hotel room. She looked pretty timid."

"She was just out of her element. That's all."

"I hope she doesn't try to make Barry's room into her element."

"I can see Lucinda now," Kent said, "strewn across Barry's bed, shedding gobs of hair onto his pillow, fleas leaping in all directions."

"God, why would anyone want a dog even if it wasn't morally wrong?"

"You just don't see what Barry and I see in her."

"I guess not."

Stef was stretched on a thick throw rug in front of the fire. "Quiet times like this are when I miss Armani the most. He used to sit and listen to my problems. Never said a thing, just listened. God, I miss him. To think what could be happening to him." She looked as though she would cry.

Aubrey rose, crossed to Stef, and wrapped her arms around her. The two women rocked long and slowly in a ritual of grief and consolation. Kent watched misty beads of sweat form on Aubrey's back. Heat from the fire gave her skin a salmon shine.

He wanted to throw open the french doors behind him, let cool air rush in from the patio, but somehow he was paralyzed, immobilized with desire for Aubrey. The telephone's abrasive ring startled him back to reality. He glanced at his watch, it was nearly three in the morning.

"Who would be calling now?"

The women untangled, and Stef begrudgingly pushed herself to her feet.

"Heaven knows." She resigned herself to the intrusions all business owners endure. "I'll take it in the bedroom."

A few moments later she returned. There was an incredulous look on her face. "That was Barry."

Aubrey stiffened.

"He's fine," Stef said.

"What happened?"

"You are not going to believe this, but apparently, someone tried to break into your hotel room."

Instantly Aubrey was on her feet. "You're sure he's okay?"

"Absolutely. He sounded a whole lot less upset than I would be." She looked at Kent. "Barry said Lucinda chased the burglar away."

"Is he still on the phone?" asked Aubrey. "I want to speak to him."

"I told him he should talk to you, but he said he didn't need to and that he wanted to get back to Lucinda. You know"—Stef sounded mystified—"he sounded more thrilled than frightened."

"The dog is amazing," Kent said. "You told him we'd be right there, I hope?"

"Yes. He's to keep the doors locked and keep Lucinda beside him till he hears his mother's voice at the door."

Aubrey was already at the foyer collecting her coat and purse. "Thanks for a wonderful evening, Stef," she said. "I really mean it too."

Stef held the door for the pair. "I'll call you for a full report tomorrow."

Barry bubbled with excitement as he told Aubrey and Kent the story.

"Man, you should have seen it! I was sound asleep and all of a sudden I feel Lucinda shoot off the bed like she was after a raccoon and head into your room, Mom." Barry bounced one palm off the other in a gesture of something launching. "Then there's all this growling and yelling. I get in there, and Lucinda's got this guy's leg. She's trying to pull it in, the guy is trying to pull it out. And she's crunching him—hard." He grimaced and squeezed both hands into tight fists. "I didn't know what to do, so I yelled at her to stop. Boy, I wish I hadn't. I think she'd have chewed it clean off." He gave Lucinda an admiring pat on the head. The big hound nudged up against him. "Anyway. She let him go, and he disappeared. I think he actually fell off the roof." The boy laughed. "That crook had a bad night."

"Can you describe him?" Kent asked.

"Only that he was big. It was too dark."

"You didn't see any strange people or cars around this evening, did you?"

"No."

They questioned Barry for a few minutes before deciding that he had no information to give. They settled the boy into bed, and Lucinda jumped in beside him. Aubrey didn't protest.

"Got anything to drink up here?" Kent asked as he took a chair in Aubrey's adjoining room.

"Just some bourbon. Want one with water?"

"That'll do."

Aubrey poured from a bottle on the bureau, added water from the bathroom sink. She handed him a hotel tumbler two fingers full and collapsed onto the bed. "Ice is down the hall."

"This will be fine." He sipped in silence.

Aubrey lay on her back, eyes shut. Her taut facial muscles told Kent she was not asleep.

"Would it be too much to hope," she asked, "that a man breaking into my room is just coincidental bad luck, or would you guess it's somehow tied into everything else that's going on?"

"Knowing what we do? It would only be a guess. I'd say the thing to do is tell Merrill about it in the morning and see what he comes up with. I'm just thankful that Lucinda was here."

"Me too."

"Fleas and all?"

Aubrey rose onto her elbows. Her eyes showed a mother's gratitude for her child's safety. "She's earned her welcome anytime, fleas and all. I hate to think what could have happened."

"Well, don't, because nothing did. They're both in there safe and sound asleep."

Aubrey stroked the bedspread. "It's almost time to get up. You could rest here for a while. It would make me feel better." She caught his dubious look. "Just sleep."

Kent was too tired to debate the wisdom of accepting her offer. He stretched out next to her and slept as if in a coma.

* * *

By rushing through treatments and appointments, Kent made it to the police station by late morning. He sat in Merrill's office, wondering why'd he bothered to tell the chief about last night's break-in. Merrill signed a fistful of papers an officer brought to him, answered several phone calls, and fielded a half-dozen questions posed by heads poked through his office door, all while rebuffing Kent's speculation.

"Come on, Kent. These things go on all the time. Rich-looking tourists and businesspeople are sitting ducks."

"We're talking Jefferson here, Merrill, not New York or Chicago."

"It happens here too."

"But it's quite a coincidence, wouldn't you say?"

Merrill made a gesture of helplessness. "Not really. Aubrey Fairbanks is probably the most high-profile person in town. A single woman. She'd be a prime target."

Kent pushed the form he had completed across the desk back at his brother. "That's all I can do? Just fill out a report?"

Merrill slid it back. "Ms. Fairbanks has to sign it."

"Jesus, Merrill."

"I'll tell you what." Merrill reached for the telephone while he spoke. "Normally a written report would be the end of a deal like this. We'd just keep our eyes and ears open and look for stolen property, which there apparently was none in this case, to turn up. That's all our manpower and budget will allow."

"The ol' budget line again."

"Let me finish. I'm going to call the hotel. If the maid hasn't been through the room yet, for my brother and the new love of his life, I'll get a couple of guys from the state police lab to take a look. Lift some fingerprints maybe. Fair enough?"

Kent grimaced at the wall clock as Merrill dialed. Eleven o'clock. Why hadn't he thought to call off the maid?

He thumped the chair arm with the heel of his hand while his brother asked a few questions to someone at the Red Horse Inn and then politely apologized for the interruption and hung up. "It seems we're out of luck. Not only did the maid do her thing, but also as we speak, the hotel maintenance man is smearing his prints all over the window as he repairs the faulty latch. Hey, we tried."

Merrill hesitated, studied his brother's angry face. "I'll tell you something. Maybe it'll give you a lift. I'm planning to stop out and see Tammy today. Don't tell her that, if you run into her. She might take off. If I can, I'll see what May-May has to say."

"Well, that's something. See if you can get an idea where he was last night."

"Will do."

● ● ●

Kent was just finishing one of his pat lectures to a college-age woman on the importance of heartworm prevention and cuddling the puff-ball chow pup it was intended for when Sally informed him that his brother was on the telephone. He handed the proud owner her new buddy and took the phone with much greater haste than usual for Merrill's calls.

"I thought you might like to know how things went this afternoon," Merrill said. "At least you'd want to hear about it firsthand instead of in the paper tomorrow morning."

"Yeah, so what's up? You made it to the farm, I take it."

Merrill continued in his melodramatic drawl. "Oh, I made it all right. Just not on my terms."

"Meaning what?"

"Meaning an hour after I talked to you, we got a call about a farm accident, and do you know where it was?"

"Can we skip the guessing game, Merrill?"

"At Maylon's place. A fatality."

An invisible hand grabbed a fistful of Kent's intestine. "You're kidding me."

"As I live and breathe."

"Who got killed?"

"Tammy."

"Jesus Christ," Kent said, and it came out like a prayer. "What happened?"

"The way it appears, she got off a tractor to untangle some fence wire that was caught underneath, and it rolled over her. Crushed her head."

The grotesque image of Tammy dead under a tractor made Kent more angry than sick. "Where the hell was May-May?"

"In the house. And get this, he's laid up in bed with a bad back. Says he fell off a roof."

"No kidding." Kent's words dripped sarcasm.

"Funny thing was, he had one leg elevated with pillows and packed in ice. I could tell it hurt like hell when he moved it."

"I'll bet. Dog bites do hurt like hell. I wonder what roof he fell off."

"He didn't say."

"It seems to me that a farm accident would be a good way to disguise a murder."

"Like a blunt object to the head then plant the body under a tractor wheel? I thought of that."

"Yeah. And we know from Copithorn that May-May's pretty good at blunt objects to the head and planting bodies. At least dog bodies."

There was momentary silence from Merrill's end. "Killing a dog is a whole lot different than killing a person. Anyway, I tactfully told the investigators to be thorough. We'll have to see what they come up with."

"You have a chance to ask him where he was at the time of the Copithorn fire and the break-in to Aubrey's room?"

"As a matter of fact, yes. Surprise, surprise, he had an alibi for both. Gave me half a dozen names I could use to confirm them. And another thing, you told me about a cat mill and some other dogfighting stuff near the house. Remember?"

"Yeah."

"None there now. Not a trace."

"Goddamn outlaw."

Their conversation lapsed into details of the accident and how the people of Jefferson would react. It ended with their usual agreement to keep each other informed.

After he hung up with his brother, Kent busied himself around his clinic, but his thoughts were on Tammy Mays. She had been right on target when she accused him of liking his role as middleman between two important women. She said this time the dogfighting was different, that it was big, really big. Was she right about that too? Was it big enough to get her killed?

And what about May-May? Merrill said the cat mill and all his other dogfight trappings had disappeared. Was May-May starting to realize he was in over his head?

He pondered that possibility. Not likely.

CHAPTER 19

LESTER ROSS REACHED OVER TO THE COFFEE table and pulled a fat torpedo from a mahogany humidor. He slipped off the ring and squinted at the tiny print. Monte Cristo Number Two. He snipped it, then moistened it by running half of it in his mouth. He padded in sock feet to the front windows of his condo as he fired it with a gold lighter.

He stared out the expanse of glass that captured midtown Austin, a breathtaking inner-city stretch of the Colorado River with its stylized wharves, docks, and high-rises. He loved the city, its grinding noise, frantic pace, even the proximity to crime. It fueled his nervous, hyperactive temperament.

He had tried rural life, had actually been born into it, and he'd hated everything about it. Of course, the big difference between then and now was that now he was rich. Back then he was just the oddball son of Milton Ross, soybean and cotton farmer of Dawson Grove, Arkansas, in Chicot County—a stone's throw from the Louisiana border, a light-year from anything cosmopolitan.

As a boy, Lester was antsy, highly motivated, strangely fixed on his future. He was aloof and pretty much disliked by the rest of Dawson Grove's citizenry. He made no bones about it— he was going to make something of himself. That attitude just did not set well around Chicot County, where any attempt at self-improvement was considered uppity.

Computers came on the scene when Lester was fifteen. He became a charter member of the Dawson Grove High Computer Club. Unlike most of his benighted peers, Lester realized early that computers were the way of the future. He welcomed them with open arms, submerged himself in their technology, and mastered each new byte of information.

By the time he graduated, he and his computer had increased his father's profits in beans and cotton by 35 percent, a fact that pleased his father immensely and turned Lester from family embarrassment to family wunderkind.

Lester went on to Texas A&M, where he majored in computer science. Seven years after graduation, he sold his computer software company to Agri-Tech in Lincoln, Nebraska, for fourteen million dollars.

Lester loved city life, especially Texas city life. In Austin, rich businessmen were expected to wear cowboy boots, drink heavily, laugh too loud, and generally behave as if they were on a cattle drive. He liked to say, "I was always a Texan, it just took me a while to get here."

He drew deeply on his cigar and released a dense cloud of smoke. Shit. Why were these big-money types always so nervous? You'd think he was asking the guy to invest his last dime.

The thought of spending half a day in an airplane headed to Boston depressed him. But he had no choice. He had spoken with Dietrich Manning the previous night, and the conversation left no doubt that Manning was nowhere near convinced that pit fighting was a good investment.

Their ducks were in a row. He knew it, but he had to convince Manning of it. He'd talked to Maylon Mays and, surprisingly, the dumb woodchuck was doing okay. Preparations for the national dogfighting championship were proceeding on schedule—a fall date would be announced soon—in Jefferson, New York.

Lester smiled slyly. Stumbling on Mays at a dogfight a couple of years ago had been extraordinary good luck. Mays was just the pawn he needed to get a foothold in the east. And, with that foothold, he could get Dietrich Manning's backing. Then pit fighting was on the way up.

Yep, he had to go to Boston.

● ● ●

Lester's stomach was making wet, boiling noises in protest of airplane cuisine when the Boeing 737 touched down at Logan Airport. He chewed a few Tums while he climbed the Jetway into the terminal and picked up his rental, a Pontiac Bonneville. By four o'clock, he was easing along Route 129 between Swampscott and Marblehead past one majestic oceanfront estate after another, looking for 2746. His gut had settled into an uncomfortable bloat by the time he saw the gray stone entryway and wrought-iron gate that Manning had given as a landmark. He turned in, announced his name to the uniformed gateman, and proceeded along a quarter-mile drive through expansive lawn, ancient trees, and elegant plantings. It ended in a circle that passed throughout the porte cochere of Manning's gothic mansion. Lester took one look at it, steeped in history and aristocracy, and instantly hated it. His country-boy insecurities came crashing back, sending more waves along his bowels. He cursed himself for not finding a restroom before he arrived.

The door opened as he reached for the brass knocker that was shaped like a coiled snake. A maid, who actually looked sexy attired in a simple black uniform, white apron, and cap, escorted him beneath a massive crystal chandelier to a cherry-paneled library. He waited alone, glancing at old volumes on the shelves and snooping around for a bathroom. No success. He worked his feet into the nap of the oriental rugs, ran his fingers over the contours of a carved desk.

He had just made it around the room when the door through which he had entered eased open. A thin-faced man in his sixties with a pointy nose and beady eyes crept in like a ferret on the hunt. He wore a burgundy smoking jacket. His white hair was oiled back smooth. He flashed Lester a brief, twitchy smile.

"Good afternoon, Lester." The ferret scanned the room and then added in a whisper, "It's nice to see you. You didn't bring any dogs along for demonstration purposes, did you?" He let out a chattering laugh that made the dog man's skin crawl.

Lester shook the cold paw that was offered and thanked God he lived in Texas.

"Hello, Dietrich. Everything pretty good with you these days?"

Dietrich Manning formed his lips into a tight pout and shrugged. "They could be better." He picked a cut-glass decanter off a side table and held it up for Lester to see. "Brandy?"

"Sure, why not?" He would have preferred bourbon.

Manning poured two glasses and moved to one of two upholstered wing chairs in front of a fireplace stacked with white birch logs ready to be touched off. He waved Lester to the other one.

"It's a tough market out there," he said.

Lester nodded but did not know exactly what Manning meant.

"Gambling, drugs, girls..." Manning said. "It used to be easy pickings. But no more. Atlantic City and the Indians have taken the juice out of East Coast casino gambling. The market is tough now." He glanced at Lester for agreement.

Lester nodded again and sipped his brandy. *Come on, Manning, get to the point.* The brandy started his bowels roiling again.

"There's a lot of reasons, I guess. Hell, the government's on the verge of legalizing drugs. More competition—everyone's into drugs—blacks, Hispanics, even the cops. No code of ethics anymore." Manning stared into the brandy sadly. "And the girls. How do you deal in prostitution when the whole country's attitude is 'just give it away' anyway? No moral values anymore."

Lester gave a polite laugh at Manning's non sequitur. He wasn't sure if his host was joking.

"Then there's our damn legal system. Pick any level you want. Local? State? Federal? They've given law enforcement more latitude than ever before. I'd like to know where the hell the ACLU is these days. And the penalties are a hell of a lot stiffer than they used to be. You simply can't afford to get caught."

"Yeah, well crime ain't what it used to be, I guess," Lester confirmed, for lack of anything else to say.

Manning gave his guest an offended look. "I'm not joking."

"Sorry, Dietrich. I knew you weren't." Manning was so damn difficult to read.

"As a matter of fact, Lester, when you boil it all down, that's why you're here, isn't it?"

Lester gave an unsure nod.

"This dogfighting venture you've proposed. That's to fill the void created by those things I've just mentioned. Right? It's going to be a gigantic new market for us. Right? Isn't that what you said?"

At last, Lester was on firm footing. He forgot his intestinal urgings. "Yes, of course it is, Dietrich. That's exactly what it will be." He moved into his salesman mode. "Dogfighting is a perfect spin-off of casino gambling because of the types of people it attracts. There is a giant inner-city market potential because urbanites love exciting, rough-and-tumble sorts of gambling. Dogfighting makes football and boxing seem like competition solitaire. The cities have always been the bread-and-butter areas for gambling."

"But can people really get behind dogfighting?" Manning asked with the cold concern of an investment strategist. "I mean, get hooked, really enthusiastic about it?"

"It's gambling, isn't it?"

"Yes"—Manning cast a dubious look—"but dogs?"

"Hey. They race dogs, don't they? And horses?"

"True, but there's a tradition there. Convince me that the general public will root for some dog they know nothing about. We're not talking Lassie or Rin Tin Tin here."

Manning's denigration of his favorite sport stung Lester, but he wasn't about to let it show. He threw the last of his brandy to the back of his throat, held it there letting the liquor's acid burn before swallowing. Slowly, he placed his glass on the table. "They root for the blacks, don't they?"

The strange question caught Manning off guard. His ferret nose wrinkled. "I don't follow you."

"College and pro basketball—huge betting sports, right?"

Manning nodded. "Yes."

"That's the whites, your clientele, the general public betting on a bunch of mostly black guys. Everybody has their favorite team. They root for them like their lives depend on it." Lester stared directly at Manning with eyes that demanded an honest answer, "But do they *like* them? As people, I mean. Hell, no! They are just dumb, overpaid blacks who can be trained and enjoyed and then forgotten as soon as they're too banged up to put on a show anymore."

"I see your point. There's as much public sentiment for dogs as there is for blacks."

"In a nutshell, yes."

"Sounds pretty crude, but it's probably true."

"Damn right it's true!"

Lester became more animated as he pitched Manning for what seemed like the hundredth time. He rose from his chair, crossed the library, and poured himself another brandy without interrupting his speech.

"But," he turned to Manning and held up a finger for emphasis, "and this is the unique part, dogfighting also attracts a whole new segment of the population."

"Rural people," Manning said. The ferret was in a trance, mesmerized by Lester's enthusiasm for this land of milk and honey.

"Right! The fighting pit appeals to ranchers, and loggers, and migrant workers, and wildcatting cowboys because they are tough, independent types that relate to the never-say-die dogs that fight to the death."

Manning started to comment, but Lester stopped him with an outstretched palm. "Plus, pit bulls attract the white supremacists, paramilitary types. Skinheads, I guess you call them. It draws them out from under their rocks."

Manning cringed. Lester moved on rapidly.

"Now, let's face it, Dietrich, we could all do without the skinheads. They're pure scum. Let's call a spade a spade." He flashed a sly smile. "But they've got money, lots of it. And your guys might even be able to use dogfighting to make some inroads with them. Kind of a bargaining chip when you're battling over drug turf. I know the skinheads are a constant burr under your saddle that way."

Lester could tell by the look on Manning's face that he had him. So he stopped. A good salesman knew to quit once he made the sale.

Manning nibbled a fingernail. "This is an intriguing new concept. As you say, it has potential to capture a fantastic new market for gambling."

"Absolutely."

"I know that the machinery is already in place in Mexico on a large scale, and in Canada to a lesser degree. It makes sense that it should all come together in the United States."

"Unite the hemisphere, so to speak."

"Yes."

"Then, maybe the world!"

Manning's eyes glazed over. "I should live so long."

For a moment both men relished the thought in silence. Then Manning began in a reserved, businesslike tone, "All right, Lester. I'm ready to give it a try."

"Excellent."

"The way we'll play it is that my fellow investors and I will be watching the big fight. The national championship you call it? If it comes off well, if we feel it shows all the potential you say it does, we'll get in. We'll set up something with you so you'll have all the capital you need and access to our network. Fair enough?"

"Fair enough."

The ferret escorted Lester to his car, and their meeting was over less than an hour after it had begun.

As Lester drove to a hotel in Boston, his mood swung between elation and brooding depression. He had revived Dietrich Manning's interest, virtually locked in his support. That was reason to celebrate. But now he'd have to be extra sure everything went well at the national championship. More than ever, everything rested on that one meet.

He cursed under his breath, rubbed his paunch. He really didn't want to, but he'd have to make a side trip to Jefferson, New York. Tomorrow, before heading back to Austin. Right now, the very first thing he had to do was find a restroom.

CHAPTER 20

MAY-MAY MARCHED IN FRONT OF A ROW OF homemade cages along one wall of his crumbling barn. Like a military commander, he inspected his crop of warriors. Bo Davis followed meekly at his heels and bit his lip when his boss reached into a wire pen and hoisted a pup out by its scruff. May-May eyed the tiny creature with cold detachment—the materials of war. The potbellied mass of wrinkled fur pawed the air for a foothold, but true to terrier nature, accepted the pain in silence.

"See this pup? He's what we've been breeding for," Commander May-May said proudly. "Pups like this will get us some respect from folks like Lester Ross." The pup grunted loudly when May-May dropped it back onto the cage's wire-mesh floor. "That is if you can train a few of them decent. Jesus H. Christ, I sure as hell couldn't bear another showing like we made at the preliminaries down in Texas."

"I don't know," Bo said. "We looked pretty good in all the weight classes except Little Jake's."

"And that's bullshit. If you don't win the heavyweight division, no one wants to talk to you." May-May slammed the cage shut. "I told you that before. It's like boxing. Can anybody tell you who the welterweight champion of the world is? Hell, no. All anyone cares about is heavyweight. It's the exact same thing for fighting dogs. You can make a little money betting on lightweights, but if you want to get a reputation as a good pup breeding operation, you got to win with the big dogs."

"But we're still in it. We made the cut."

"Damn lucky for us. It sure wasn't your great training that got us there. Damn dogs weren't fit. No endurance."

"I just do what you say."

May-May dug into the breast pocket of his flannel shirt, pulled out a hand-rolled cigarette, and lit it. He took a long draw and studied the smoke curling from the tiny white finger as he held a maximum dose in his lungs.

"Well, we're going to be doing things different now. I'm taking a more active role, as they say." He smirked at his own wittiness. "I gotta keep a better eye on what you're doing."

"Whatever you say, boss."

"Damn right. And by the time we get a call about setting a date for the nationals, we'll have the most fit dogs those western boys ever seen."

He drew another breath of marijuana. Bo watched with apprehension as May-May's confidence mushroomed into swaggering braggadocio.

May-May took one last toke and twisted the butt into the ground with his boot. "Come on, Bo. We've got a lot of work to do and not much time to do it."

He led his assistant into a musty cinderblock offshoot of the main barn. A dented water heater and rust-streaked stainless steel tank were the only remnants of what once was a milk house. Empty dog-food bags were strewn about. Assorted containers of vitamins and supplements boasting outrageous claims and crusted mixing utensils revealed that the room's current use was as a kitchen for the dogs.

"I been too lax with you, Bo. I want to go over just what you been doing with my dogs. And I'd guess right here's a good place to start."

Bo stood in bovine silence.

"Well?" May-May said.

"Well, what?"

"Tell me about what you been feeding, for starters."

Bo stroked his chin thoughtfully, straining his brain for something that would satisfy his boss. Nothing came to mind, so he admitted the truth. "I been feeding regular old dog food, just like you told me."

"No extra vitamins and stuff thrown in for extra energy?"

"No. I quit them after you said they was too expensive."

May-May ignored the insinuation. "Pups getting the same?"

"Pups get puppy food. I get two or three bags of the biggest size they have at the feed mill each time I'm in town."

May-May gave his simple helper an exasperated look. "Now, you see? Right off, there's a problem. You ain't feeding our dogs to *win*. In Texas, some guys were telling me about what they feed. Supposed to be a secret formula, but they got bragging so much they let it out. They say it's specially made up for fighting dogs. Mostly it's raw meat, but there's a lot of vitamins and minerals mixed in for extra energy."

May-May let that information sink in before continuing. "And how often you feeding the dogs we're getting ready to fight?"

"Morning and night. Just like the rest." Bo's expression showed he fully expected to be corrected, and he was right.

"That ain't no good!" May-May said. "Out in Texas they told me dogs get more nutrition from what they eat if you only feed 'em once every two days."

"Two days!" Bo said in disbelief. "That's a long time to go without eating. You sure you got that right?"

"I got it right, and you do it. Hear me?" May-May jammed a thick finger into Bo's flat chest. "You got some gall claiming to know more than them guys who've been fighting champion dogs for years and years. You got to stop being so soft, Bo. You can't expect to have tough dogs if you ain't tough yourself and tough on the dogs. From now on, dogs in the keep get the new special feed mix. I got the recipe back at the house. And they get it every two days. Period."

"You're the boss."

"Right, I am," May-May said. "Now, what about training? Tell me what you been doing to get our dogs fit."

"What you told me to do. I ain't changed a thing."

"Tell me anyway. So I'm sure we're right."

"Okay." Bo took a deep breath, exhaled frustration. "Every day, each dog gets a couple hours on the cat mill. Sometimes a little more or less depending on how tired they get."

"You give 'em the cat at the end. Right?"

"Yes. Just like you said."

"Okay, good. But I want to change it to every two days now. They get the cat mill on the days they don't get the special food."

"What difference does that make?"

May-May gloated at his own cleverness. "Because they'll be hungrier. They'll enjoy eating the cat even more."

Bo accepted the grisly reasoning. "Now, you want any exercise on the days they don't get the cat mill?"

"Yeah. Road work. Work up to twenty miles at a trot behind your truck."

"No problem. I can handle that," Bo said as the prospect of a sit-down job while the dogs did all the work appealed to him.

"Okay then, go to it." May-May swung his arm in a large arc, indicating that he intended to watch his kennel man in action.

For the next hour, he observed carefully as Bo proceeded with daily chores at his lethargic pace. Young pups were fed dry commercial food as before. Then Bo threw several kittens into each pen containing several older pups. May-May watched with satisfaction as the hungry pack swarmed onto the prey and ripped the hissing kittens apart.

"They're getting blooded good now," May-May said with a smile. "No stalling when the kitten goes in. They're right on it."

Bo said nothing, just rubbed his hands on his thighs, venting nervous energy.

They moved into the largest room in the barn, a storage area capable of holding at least three tractors with implements. Now, instead of farm machinery, it housed the mature fighting dogs in a bank of kennels along a back wall and a cat mill in the center.

May-May surveyed the room. "Pain in the ass bringing all this stuff inside, but we couldn't risk it outside anymore. Not with all the police sniffing around."

"It's your own goddamn fault," Bo said.

May-May wheeled to face him. "The hell it is!"

"Well it is." Bo held his position. "You didn't have to kill Tammy. She wasn't gonna tell nobody nothin'. And if you hadn't, we wouldn't have all these cops around."

May-May pushed his face so close to Bo's that his beard brushed the front of his lean hireling's work vest. "That's bullshit, and you know it. She already talked. She talked to the good doctor. I got wind of it, and I asked her. She tried to, but she couldn't lie to me." May-May shook with rage, spitting the words at Bo. "She admitted to it finally. She said I wasted all our money on dogs and gambling. Hell. Told Kent because he was a person who likes animals. She didn't mean to get those FOAM people or the cops in it. Bullshit."

"I think she was telling you the truth." Bo tried to sound confident. "She really didn't mean to stir up no trouble."

"Well, what the hell did she figure would happen?"

"I don't know. Tammy is—was—a nice person. She didn't like what we are doing. Me and you both know that. She probably just figured Dr. Stephenson would be someone she could talk to about it."

"You listen to me real good, Bo. Nobody. Not Tammy, not my brothers, not you. Nobody is gonna mess up my shot at making it big with these dogs. You understand me? 'Cause if you don't, you might get clubbed in the head and found under a tractor wheel too."

"I'm not saying nothin' to nobody."

May-May took a calming breath and stepped back. "That's good. Because if I go up the river for fighting dogs, you'll go with me. Neither of us wants that. Right?"

"No way."

"So let's get back to it. Show me what you're doing with the dogs in the keep."

The sound of a car crunching gravel up the driveway interrupted their conversation.

"Who the hell?" May-May said as he headed toward the door to check it out. He watched a Lincoln Town Car pull up to the house. A solitary passenger disembarked and May-May's face spread into an astonished grin. "I'll be damned. It's Lester Ross himself."

He hurried to greet him. "Lester. Why didn't you say you was comin'?"

Lester was still in somewhat of a pout about having to detour to Jefferson. "I didn't know I was coming till this morning."

"Well, welcome to Jefferson, New York, home of this year's national dogfightin' championships." May-May beamed.

Lester smiled weakly. "As you can guess, that's why I'm here."

"I figured." May-May scanned Lester up and down, noting his tailored suit and cordovan boots. "You ain't exactly dressed for it, but do you want a tour of our operation?"

Lester sighed and then shrugged. "Why not?" He could tell May-May was dying to show him.

"Step right this way," May-May said proudly. Then as an afterthought he asked, "You want a beer or something to eat?"

"Think I'll pass. I had some on the plane." Lester glanced at his watch. "And I'm booked back to Austin in three hours, so I don't have a lot of time."

May-May looked disappointed. "Too bad. Well, let's make the best of it. In this barn are our dogs in the keep."

Lester followed May-May back into the soft light of the old barn. Bo, hearing them enter, uncurled himself from the cage he was leaning into.

"Bo, come over here," May-May said. "You remember Lester Ross, don't you?" He explained to Lester, "Bo here's my hired man. He works our corner too."

Bo's eyes narrowed, his lips drew back in a flat grin. He gently stroked the scar on his right temple. The other two men did not catch the rancor in his soft bass voice. "Oh, I remember Mr. Ross, all right."

Lester swelled at the black man's servile address. "How you know me, son?"

Bo seemed flustered for a moment but then caught himself. "From the fight we went to in Texas."

"Oh, right. You handled that Little Jake dog, didn't you?"

"Yes, sir, I did."

Lester looked back and forth from May-May to Bo. "Not to be too critical," he said with a concerned tone, "but I hope you boys can put on a better showing at the nationals."

"We qualified, didn't we?" Bo reminded their guest with more bite in his voice than necessary.

"Shut up, Bo. You keep your place here with Mr. Ross and let me do the talking."

Bo slipped into his Jim Crow mode, but his gaze was like one of the pit bulls, fixed on Lester Ross.

"As a matter of fact, Lester, I was just going over our training technique with Bo. How about a little demonstration?" Without waiting for an answer, he signaled to Bo. "Get Scorpion."

Bo stepped to a cage and pulled out a mature black male whose wide head was accentuated by powerful biting muscles that bunched like fists in each jowl. His protruding lower jaw displayed a row of pearl-white teeth and gave him an air of stubbornness. His vacant eyes seemed to have come to terms with life's struggle.

"I guess Scorpion here will be Little Jake's replacement. He's the best we got. I always said he could outfight Little Jake anyway."

May-May eyed the dog. "He better have more grit than Little Jake ever did. Else we might as well put a bullet in his head right now. Save us a lot of trouble."

Lester nodded.

"No. We don't need to do that," Bo said. "This boy will fight. You can believe that."

"What's he weigh now?"

"I'm not sure. Haven't had him on the scale for a week or two."

"Take him over, let's see."

The gladiator dog seemed not to care or even notice as Bo dragged him across the floor, lifted him by his harness, and suspended him by a hook that dangled from the scale. All three men watched as the needle on the rusty dial rotated three quarters around, vibrated, then stopped.

May-May spit between his boots. "The son of a bitch is up to fifty-eight pounds! I entered him at fifty. Somehow, between now and fight time, he's got to shake eight pounds."

"We can do that. No problem." Bo grunted reassurance as he lifted Scorpion down.

"Don't you take no chances. You work his ass off," May-May said, watching Lester's reaction out of the corner of his eye.

"He'll show you a workout," Bo said. He dragged him toward the cat mill.

He snapped Scorpion's harness to the end of a spoke, left the room momentarily, and returned stroking an orange tabby cat.

The scent of a cat locked the attention of every fighting dog in the place. Automatically, their ears flattened against their heads. All eyes fixed on the animal they had been programmed to kill.

Scorpion became a raving demon intent on destroying the bundle of orange fur. Bo secured a leather thong around its tiny chest and dangled the feline from a spoke in front of Scorpion. It swung inches out of his reach as he lunged against his harness.

"Let 'em go," May-May said.

Bo released the wheel, and Scorpion charged into an endless race around a tiny track to catch his wild-eyed, hissing prey.

Soon, saliva dropped from the dog's gaping mouth. He huffed grunts of exertion as all four legs strained to close the last few inches between jaws and cat flesh.

May-May and Lester looked on with satisfaction as the dog played the absurd game of chase.

"Man," Bo said. "Scorpion is definitely heavy metal, ain't he? When he gets excited…"

May-May swelled with pride. "Looks like a real fightin' dog. Give him an hour and then let him eat that damn cat."

Lester's spirits buoyed as he watched.

May-May led the way over to the jaw rope that now hung by a large wooden pulley from a barn beam instead of the tree limb. The shredded piece of inner tube, sticky white with dried saliva, still dangled at the end.

"How they doing with the rope?" Lester asked.

"Some take to it better than others," said Bo.

May-May cringed. "But they all get to where they can hang a long while. Right?"

"Most do."

Lester glanced nervously at May-May. "Most?"

"Yeah," Bo said. "Most of them, if I get them really worked up, they'll hang for half an hour or so. Once in a while you hit a stubborn one who thinks he's had enough after five or ten minutes."

Lester swatted the rope, sending it into an aerial snake dance. "Well, Bo, you can't have that and expect to have winners too."

"Bring out one of those stubborn ones and put him on," May-May said, anxious to put Lester at ease.

Bo fetched a dog they'd bought in Virginia. "Judas, here, he's a good example. Likes the cat mill, hates the jaw rope."

"Set him to work on it," May-May said as he loosened the end attached to a wall cleat and played out slack through a ceiling pulley.

Bo stuffed the inner tube into a five-gallon plastic pail full of chicken entrails and clotted blood and withdrew it dripping. Then, holding the rope near the bottom, he began flogging Judas about the head with the blood-sodden remnant of inner tube.

Lester stepped back to protect his suit.

For the first few blows, the animal cringed. After that he held his ground until, angrily, he grabbed Bo's whip in a vicious bite.

"There we go," Bo said, jerking the rope to test the dog's grip.

They shouted encouragement as May-May hoisted the future gladiator so that his hind toes just brushed the floor.

Judas writhed like a hooked fish lifted from the water. His neck muscles flexed hard left then right, trying to tear enamel knives through chicken-blooded rubber.

"Now we're getting somewhere," Lester said. "He's got to be able to hold there at least half an hour."

Bo pushed his cap back, rubbed his scalp, and swallowed hard. "I don't know he'll go that long."

"It's up to you to see that he does."

"How am I supposed to make him hold on, Mr. Ross?"

May-May crouched to within inches of the dangling dog. "Egg him on. Encourage him. Keep him fired up."

All three men bombarded Judas with every order of verbal abuse and encouragement for close to half an hour, but in spite of it, they could see his resolve slacking, his grip slipping.

"Goddamn it. He's quitting!" Lester said.

May-May loaded his cheek with a wad of scrap tobacco. Said nothing.

Judas dropped to the floor.

"Looks like egging him on ain't working," Bo said.

May-May spit brown goo onto the floor.

"I'll show you how to fix that little problem," Lester said. He turned to Bo. "Get me a piece of roofing tin. And do you have an electric fencer around here?"

"Yes, sir."

"Get them both then."

A few minutes later, Bo returned with the sheet metal and fencer. He noticed May-May had retrieved a length of wire.

"What you gonna do with all this stuff?"

Lester hastily attached one end of the wire to the fencer and the other to the sheet metal. "You watch and learn, Mr. Bo-Bo," he said. "Plug this in." He handed Bo the cord from the fencer as he slid the sheet metal beneath the jaw rope. May-May and Bo suddenly realized what their instructor had in mind.

Lester cranked the amperage selector to maximum. "We'll either toughen him up or kill him. Get him back up on the rope."

Reluctantly, Bo repeated the start-up procedure, and within minutes Judas was once again suspended. Except this time the electrified sheet metal roofing lay three inches beneath his hind feet.

Lester switched on the fencer. "Son of a bitch comes down on that, and he gets juiced up one leg, across his balls, and down the other."

"Ouch." May-May moaned and laughed at once. "That'd sure as hell make me hold on."

Within a short time, the already tired dog began to slacken his grip, until finally his toes brushed the deck. There was a short snap, like the sound of a matchstick breaking, and the air took on the smell of burned hair. Judas yipped through clenched teeth and tucked his feet up. But his jaws could not maintain their purchase. He touched the metal again, screeched loudly, and pulled up again.

May-May smiled approvingly. "See, Bo? You gotta be tough if you want your dogs to be tough."

"Yeah. Well, he can't hold on forever. Then what?"

Lester stared at the terrified dog with the emptiness of one who had not an ounce of compassion for any living thing. "You let him land good and firm on all four feet so he gets an idea of what happens if he don't hold on. Then you throw him in his cage to think on it."

At that moment, Judas's tired jaws gave way, and he crashed onto the sheet metal. The electricity rattled up nerves overriding any voluntary impulses. His muscles froze in a high-voltage tetany.

"Jesus, May-May, he can't move." Bo said.

Lester watched the dog vibrate like a statue in an earthquake.

"You're gonna kill him, May-May!"

A few more infinitely long seconds passed, and Bo had seen enough. He reared back and kicked the rigid dog hard in the chest, sending him rolling off the electric floor.

Judas rose, disoriented and unstable, and then slunk back into his cage as if stricken by some strange beast.

"You want to make them tough, not kill them, I thought," Bo said, himself shaking.

"See what I mean?" May-May said. "You're not tough enough. He'll be all right. And you can bet your ass he'll hold on tomorrow, long and tight." He laughed loudly and thumped his dismayed helper between the shoulder blades. "Thanks for the training tip, Lester. We'll put it to good use."

Bo glanced over toward Judas cowering in the back of his cage. His Adam's apple rose then fell. "I ain't sure you did him any good."

* * *

After the training lesson, Lester and May-May headed to the house to talk business. Bo went back to his chores.

Lester leaned against a post on the porch. He held the beer May-May offered but did not drink it. "Remember the business associate I mentioned to you before?"

May-May took a long swig of his. "The one that wants to throw some money into dogfighting?"

"Yes. Well, I was just talking to him. He's put a lot of pressure on us."

"How's that? He ain't backin' out, is he?"

"No. Not by any means. But he made it perfectly clear that he and his fellow investors will be watching the nationals closely. If he's happy with what he sees," Lester gave a thumbs-up gesture, "you and me are on easy street. If not, he's out."

May-May smiled broadly. "No problem from this end."

"Good. That's what I wanted to hear. We can't have any mess-ups."

"I know that."

"We have to keep security tight. There will be a lot of opportunity for leaks."

"I've got it covered."

"And you'll need to line up a really big arena. And safe. There'll be a big crowd."

"I'm working on that."

"It's very important. Don't cut any corners."

"I won't."

"Big and safe. And by that I mean secret."

Their conversation melted into a hideous discussion of recent victories in the underground world of pit bull fighting and other current events in the game.

Eventually, May-May found himself standing next to Lester's rented car as the Texan prepared to leave. "Can you imagine how the price of a good pup is gonna go up when pit fightin' gets big?"

Lester gave him a narrow-eyed grin. "Keep it in mind. You and me will be on easy street."

CHAPTER 21

KENT HUMMED "SINGIN' IN THE RAIN" AS HE headed his truck home from the Red Horse Inn. Dinner with Aubrey and Barry had been wonderful.

Misty rain made the leaves on the road as slippery as black ice, but he didn't care. He took his time, no hurry. The cool night air coming in his cracked window felt refreshing. He stroked Lucinda's head on his lap.

He did not notice a set of headlights behind him until they were within what seemed like inches of his rear bumper. He tapped his brakes and adjusted his mirror. In response, the lights burst to high beam, illuminating the interior of his truck like midday.

He slowed, opened his window to cut the wet glass glare, and turned to look behind. From the height of the lights and the rumble of the tires, the vehicle had to be a jacked-up pickup truck.

"May-May. Figures," he said to Lucinda. He waved the truck to pass.

The truck's engine roared, and as it came alongside, Kent heard a gravelly Indian war whoop. An electrical pulse rattled down his spine. He remembered what Tammy had said about May-May being out of control. She had been right too. He'd beaten her and probably killed her, and he'd raided Aubrey's hotel room. Kent didn't want to mess with him tonight.

He slowed to the shoulder, giving May-May a signal to pass and be gone, but the big truck slowed to stay abreast. Kent slammed his foot onto the accelerator, but his truck was no match for a high-performance 4x4. The big truck stayed just off his left rear quarter. For half a mile, the two vehicles raced along the country road, Kent's in front by a half-length. As they approached a tight curve ahead, he slowed. May-May pulled up even and released another war whoop. There was an explosion, then another.

Kent ducked as his rear window disintegrated into thousands of tiny glass diamonds. He felt the steering wheel spin in his hands and the tires catch on the berm. His truck careened into the ditch, bounced along like a hay wagon in a field full of woodchuck holes, then slammed to a stop against a roadside maple. He gripped the wheel, too dazed to move except to instinctively reach for Lucinda. She whined softly. A warm trickle of blood descended his forehead.

Beyond the wailing inside his head, he heard sodden footsteps approaching. Then, within inches, May-May's ground-glass voice and sour breath. "I warned you to stay out of this, Kent. I'm telling you for the last time, I'll kill you and your pretty lady if I have to. Stay out of my way!"

Lucinda growled. The footsteps faded away. Kent relaxed his head onto the steering wheel, and his mental screen faded to black.

● ● ●

"Jerry, give these boys another round," Bo said in a tone that was meant for everyone in Kolbie's Tavern to hear.

The old bartender moved slowly to his bank of taps and yanked the gaudy handles. He knew each patron's preference without asking. He could not remember the last time he'd mixed a cocktail.

Bo swaggered back and forth in the smoke behind a row of sullen customers perched precariously on bar stools. "We fixed 'em over at Copithorn, didn't we?"

Several nearby faces turned him a warning stare. Jerry concentrated on the glass he was filling.

Delighted to have caught their attention, Bo beamed to his audience. "Relax. Ain't no one going to figure it out. Especially after all this time. Shoot. Trail's too cold." He looked around the bar. "Hell. There ain't nobody here that wasn't here the night we planned it. We can talk about it."

A boar-shaped man who could have just gotten off a bulldozer slammed his bottle on the bar. "Shut up, Bo."

"Lighten up, Frank. You and Jim snatched that little white dog, right? And Robbie, you got him inside the plant. 'Robbie the janitor,' our man." Bo gave Robbie a joshing punch in the shoulder the way May-May would have done. It made a puff of dust. "All of us was involved one way or another. Like May-May said, if we want to get dogfights going around here, we have to get the US Animal Protection Council off our backs." Bo mocked the name of the humane group as he spoke it.

Someone made a pleading whisper loud enough to be heard throughout most of the room. "Shut your mouth, Bo. We agreed not to mention it again."

Bo continued to saunter around the bar. "Ah, so what? It's kinda fun being a fireman and getting to put out a fire you know you started yourself. Ain't it, boys?" He let out a squawking laugh that made his Adam's apple bounce like the head of a woodpecker.

"Won't be so funny if somebody gets arrested for arson," Robbie said.

Bo waved him off. "It'll never happen. Nobody's going to talk. We stick together against outsiders. Right?"

"You better sit down yourself and stop flapping your lip, or we might just let you hang out to dry."

Bo spread his hands in a gesture of disbelief. "I'm not talking. I mean, I'm not *talking* talking. I'm just visiting with my buddies." He took a long draught of beer. "I still don't think anybody's even figured out that there's been a lot of dog and cats stolen around town lately."

"Don't get started on that either," Robbie said.

Bo ignored the advice. "Too bad we had to waste one in the fire. Takes a lot of animals to keep a bunch of fightin' dogs goin'. Ya know? I fed out four of them today even. Man, those dogs are coming along good." He paused to drink again.

"Coming along good?" one of the other dog men asked.

This was the part that intrigued most of May-May's local followers. Fires and petnapping were too illegal, too sinister, but dogfighting was fun and harmlessly illegal.

May-May kept most of the information about his dogs and training progress secret, just releasing enough tidbits near meet dates to whet the other men's appetites and give them reasons to place their bets.

"Yeah," Bo said, "we got a black dog name of Scorpion. Remember Little Jake that just barely got beat out in Texas? I told you about that dog. Well, Scorpion is ten times as good."

"Good enough to win at the championships?"

"Me and May-May has seen fights across this whole country. We been to Virginia, Ohio, even Arizona. I tell you there ain't no better dog. Plus"—Bo took on an erudite tone—"we got some new training techniques and a new high-energy food that guarantees us a trophy."

"This Scorpion dog is worth a bet, then?"

"He's worth a big bet. May-May says Scorpion is the dog that's going to put the East Coast on the map for dogfighting. And I know May-May's going to lay some big money on him come fight night."

Bo's oration was cut short by his boss's loud entry. May-May strutted to the bar, pulled off his coat, and high-fived his adherents.

"Where the hell you been?" Bo asked with uncharacteristic boldness.

May-May slapped his helper hard between the shoulder blades, spilling his beer. "Sit down and shut up, you skinny son of a bitch, and I'll tell you." May-May released an earsplitting Indian war whoop.

Bo, realizing that the top dog had arrived, tucked his tail between his legs and retreated to a nearby table.

Jerry set a bottle in front of May-May.

May-May grabbed it. "Jerry, give me a shot of Jack too. I'm celebrating."

The crowd settled in for what promised to be an exciting update.

May-May threw the whiskey to the back of his throat, held it for a moment, and then swallowed like a child taking medicine. He turned and leaned his back on the bar. "Well, I did a little reminding tonight," he said slowly.

All listeners were confused. Finally Bo asked, "Reminding?"

"Yep. The good doctor." May-May kept them hanging.

"What are you talking about?"

"Bo, remember how we gave that dog, Judas, a little something to think about while he was dangling from the jaw rope?"

Bo's expression darkened. "That electric griddle, you mean?"

"Yep. Well, that's kinda what I done tonight for old Dr. Kent Stephenson."

"Just come right out and tell us what went on."

"Okay," May-May said amiably and took another sip of beer. "I got to thinking. With some new information Kent received from a person who shall remain unnamed, he could give us a little trouble."

"Tammy, you mean?" Bo said.

Quick as a snake, May-May grabbed the front of his assistant's shirt and half lifted him from his chair. "Shut up, you idiot. I said 'unnamed'!"

"Sorry," Bo said, as he wiggled loose and ducked away.

"Anyway," May-May went on, "I figured I ought to give him a little reminder that he's a local boy, born and raised, and that bad things can happen if a local boy takes up with outsiders against his own people."

The crowd looked disappointed. They'd heard May-May's small-town bluster before.

May-May sensed it. "So I shot him," he said.

Every man gasped. Jerry ceased his puttering behind the bar. May-May let the moment hold.

Suspense got the best of Bo first. "You what?"

"Well, I guess I didn't really shoot him, I mostly shot *at* him."

The crowd breathed again.

Bo swallowed, the protruding lump on his throat vibrated furiously. "Is he okay?"

"I suppose so." May-May shrugged and took another drink. "Depends on what you call okay. Once I got the idea what I wanted to do, I started driving around town hoping I'd find him in his truck. Sure enough, I pick him up pulling out of the Red Horse."

"You'd better watch it. I hear you ain't been too lucky at the inn lately," someone joked.

May-May rubbed his lower back, flexed his knee back and forth, and took the tease like a sport. "As long as I stay off the roof, I'm all right."

"And as long as Doc Stephenson leaves that hound of his at home," Bo said.

"Yeah. That too. I'm going to kill that son-of-a-bitchin' dog yet. But that's another story. So I follow along behind him at a safe distance until he turns out on the old state highway where the road gets a little tight." May-May's eyes glazed over, his voice rose and fell, and he began to gesture like the great storytellers. "I pulled up right behind him and flashed those big ol' high beams of mine right inside his cab. Lit her up like a propane lantern. I could tell he couldn't see too good 'cause he was fussin' with the mirror and all. Then he slowed right down, and I let out a war whoop. Scared the shit out of him."

May-May filled the barroom with a falsetto Indian cry. "He figured something wasn't right and took off. So I come right up beside him and let those big knobby treads on my truck tires roar in his ear for a minute, then I let out another war whoop to really shake him up."

"Did he know it was you?" one of the listeners asked.

"I didn't yell my name or nothin', but he knew. Anyway, after I figured he'd had enough of that, I took my twelve gauge and hung it out the passenger window." May-May's face took on a macho expression as he pointed an imaginary shotgun out an imaginary window. "And I gave him a couple loads of double-O buckshot. Blam! Blam!"

The crowd shifted nervously.

"You told us you didn't kill him," Bo said.

"No, I pumped one through the back window and another into his rear tire. Last I saw he was bouncing his way down through the ditch."

"Then you might have killed him."

May-May shrugged. "Maybe, but I doubt it," he hedged. He'd let them worry about it awhile. "Old Doc wasn't going too fast. But I sure as hell gave him a warning he won't forget real soon."

May-May finished his beer with dramatic flair and turned back to the bar. The crowd buzzed as it broke up into small groups discussing May-May's exploits like armchair quarterbacks.

When attention was off May-May, Jerry the bartender approached him quietly. "Got a phone call for you here a while ago. Man said to have you call him back." He slid a napkin with a number on it across the bar.

"He give a name?"

"No. Sounded pretty secret like, so I didn't ask."

May-May looked at the phone number and recognized an area code in Texas. "Give me another Jack, will you, Jerry?"

When it came, May-May finished it in one gulp, just like the first one, and headed to the pay phone in a secluded corner.

On the first ring a terse voice answered. "Hello."

"The New Yorker here. Someone called for me?"

"Hold on."

A moment later a different voice, more cordial, came on the line. "Everything is set. Last Saturday of this month."

May-May knew it was Lester but was careful not mention his name. "Finally," he said, feeling the excitement rising inside like the flush from the shots of Jack Daniels.

"You ready?" asked the voice.

"All set at this end."

"Good, 'cause I put the word out in the *Chronicle*. We've got a lot of people interested. Make sure you got plenty of places for people to stay. Motels that don't watch too close, places to park RVs, you know. Turns out a lot of folks never been to New York before. They're going to mix a little business with pleasure."

"We'll show 'em a good time."

"You got a place to hold the fight?"

"Yes sir. My wife—I mean my late wife—made a connection for us there. Couldn't be better."

"Your wife died?"

"It was sudden."

"Sorry to hear it. Now, I got your black dog. What's his name?"

"Scorpion."

"Right. I got Scorpion lined up to go against the top heavyweight from Ohio. You'll make sure it's a crowd pleaser?"

"It'll be a dandy. 'Specially if we win." May-May chuckled into the phone.

"Well, the best of luck to you. Watch the *Chronicle*. It will have a lot of details. Otherwise, it's all rolling."

"Not soon enough for me. This is what us folks in New York have been waiting for."

"I don't have to tell you, New Yorker—keep all this under your hat."

"No problem."

"Then we'll see you in a couple of weeks." The line went dead.

May-May's smug grin shone like a floodlight when he returned to the bar. "Well, boys, we got ourselves a fight."

A round of cheers and congratulations to May-May rolled through the crowd.

"Is that what the phone call was about?" Bo asked.

"Yeah. Just like I promised, we got the National Dogfighting Convention coming to little ol' Jefferson, New York."

Another loud cheer went up from the crowd.

"The top pit bulls in the country are coming here?" Robbie asked in disbelief.

"You got it." Excitement fueled more questions.

"When? Where we going to hold it?"

May-May loved the control. He held up his hand. "Now wait a minute. What do you think? Would it be very smart for me to answer questions?"

The listeners became quiet.

"Of course not," he said with parental certainty. "We've got to maintain absolute security on this. The less people who know, the less likely the wrong folks will find out. You get my drift?"

Heads nodded reluctantly.

"I probably told you more than I should already, but I'll say this—it's on for sometime real soon. And my dog Scorpion is scheduled for the championship fight against the best pit bull in Ohio. It's all out in the *Chronicle*, so when you get your copy, you can read about it. But make damn sure it don't fall into the wrong hands." He pumped his fist into the air and whooped loudly. "We'll show 'em that dogs from New York can fight!"

Bo smiled broadly until May-May reached over and grabbed his earlobe like a father would hold his disobedient son. "Now you listen good here, Bo Davis. I don't want any of this to get out. You keep your yap shut."

"You know I will, May-May," Bo said, through clenched teeth. "And you keep your eyes and ears open for infiltrators too."

CHAPTER 22

THE TEARAWAY SANITARY PAPER CRACKLED AS
Kent sat up on the exam table, blinked, felt a sting. He ran his fingertips along the bandage above his left eye.

"Except for the Joe Frasier–Thrilla-in-Manila look for a week
or so, you're going to be just fine," the doctor said.

When Kent laughed his head felt like it would explode.

"Just take it easy. Lots of ice on the lump. Aspirin. Stitches out
in a week to ten days."

"Thanks, Doc." Kent felt his forehead gingerly. "Taking it easy
will be no problem."

The doctor gave a few instructions about calling her if he felt
dizzy or had vision problems and then departed with a wave.

Kent turned to Aubrey, who had been observing from a chair
in the corner of the exam room. Her expression was a picture
of concern.

"How'd you know I was here?"

She pointed her thumb toward Merrill, who was leaning against
the wall. "He called me."

Merrill read his brother's face. "Don't look so surprised. Just
because Ms. FOAM and I don't see eye to eye on a few things doesn't
mean we can't at least be civil to each other. I figured you'd want
her here."

"Thanks. You were right."

Aubrey reached up and took Kent's hand. Merrill grunted at such sappiness.

"How's Lucinda?"

"She's fine. I had Sally look her over. Not a scratch on her."

"Where is she?"

The chief gave him a sheepish look. "I snuck her up to Barry's room at the inn. You're making a criminal out of me."

"Don't blame your devious nature on me, brother."

The chief stepped over and closed the exam room door. "Yeah. Well, speaking of devious nature, tell us what happened out there tonight."

Kent told them what he knew–– wet roads, bright lights, war whoops, and a big 4x4 truck. Two explosions, their half brother's warning, and then blackness.

When he was finished, Aubrey gave Merrill a pleading look, her palms up and extended. "Jesus, Chief."

"What?"

"Come on, Chief. You know damn well there's a bunch of crazy dogfighters out there. It was one of them, your half brother no less, who shot at Kent."

"I'll thank you not to tell me what I know, ma'am. I know nothing of the kind until I have proof. I'm a cop, remember? Kent could be mistaken. He just got a thump on the head. So far, all I have is a known radical animal rights activist"—he made a grand gesture back at her—"and a veterinarian turned amateur dick"—he pointed at Kent—"telling me they've seen dogfighting paraphernalia at a farm in the hills whose owner has an alibi corroborated seven ways to Sunday."

"Whose wife suddenly died after talking to the brother of the police chief," Aubrey said.

Merrill shrugged, held out his hands palms up. "In a farm accident."

"That was no accident! You know it. What about the break-in attempt at my hotel room?"

"No connection to anything yet."

Aubrey wove her fingers together across the back of her neck and groaned. "Can't you at least bring May-May in for questioning?"

"Again? Yeah, I could do that," Merrill said. "I'd get the same list of witnesses to his whereabouts as before."

"What about a tail? Some kind of surveillance?"

Merrill shook his head as much as to say even the suggestion was asinine. "This town is not LA. We don't have an army of under-cover agents poised and ready to set up a stakeout."

"Then what the hell can you do?"

"We're working on it!"

"Take it easy, you two," Kent said. He massaged the lidocaine tingle along his brow. "I keep thinking about what Tammy said about the dog men starting the fire at Copithorn because they wanted to distract another humane group that was pestering them."

"Yeah," Aubrey said, bringing that back into focus. "She couldn't remember the name of it."

"Right."

"But she said May-May had been reading a magazine about them."

"She said he wanted to know his enemy."

"Exactly!" Kent turned to his brother. "There you have it."

Merrill showed a blank look. "Have what?"

"A starting place. A direction. If we can find that magazine, we'll know who the other humane group is."

"Then we can see what they had on May-May." Aubrey said.

Kent slid off the exam table, stepped over to Merrill, and tapped him on the shoulder. "And do you want to know something else?"

"What?" Merrill said, knowing his brother would tell him anyway.

"I know right where that magazine is."

Aubrey snapped her fingers. "I do too!"

Her eyes met Kent's, and in unison they said, "On May-May's kitchen table."

● ● ●

The first hint of red was appearing in the eastern sky when Kent guided his truck between ruts along the driveway to May-May's farmhouse. The embarrassment of having to drive his truck around town with a dented grill and plastic duct-taped over his rear window was salt in his wounds.

He talked heatedly to Lucinda. "So I lied to Aubrey and Merrill! There was no other way. They weren't about to let me come up here alone. Not after what May-May pulled last night."

He touched two crisp white gauze pads that covered his sutured forehead. He felt a sharp pain when the stitches pulled and quickly took his hand away.

"Merrill can't come up here and get that magazine without a warrant. That would take forever and tip May-May off to boot. I'm at home resting like the doctor ordered, right? I'll tell them the truth later."

He pulled to a stop well away from the house and shut off his lights.

May-May's truck was parked with its front bumper within a few inches of the porch, eliminating every step possible between the cab and his bed. A light was on in the kitchen. Kent stepped onto the porch and peered in through the door as he and Aubrey had done. No one visible. Remembering the noisy door, he lifted it over the rough floor as he opened it. He listened again. All quiet. Three steps to the table, still covered with grimy magazines.

As quietly as he could, he began sifting through old issues of *Sports Afield*, *Ammo*, and *Penthouse*, taking unwanted periodicals off the pile and setting them in a chair. For close to ten minutes, he sorted and found no information to reveal the second humane group's identity.

He was down to the last third of the pile when he heard a double metallic click behind him and froze.

"You just don't know when to quit, do you, brother?" came May-May's voice from the doorway of the room where he and Aubrey had found Tammy a few days before. A lethal viciousness in his tone told Kent, without looking, that there was a gun trained on him. Cocked and safety off, it was ready to blow away the back of his head or rip through his midsection.

He turned slowly, raising his hands as he pivoted. "I'd say I deserve a little more than this," he pointed to his forehead, "and a death threat. If that's what you mean."

May-May eased himself farther into the kitchen, .357 Magnum first.

"You don't deserve shit. You come sneaking around here twice now like you own the place." His voice rose. "You don't, you know. I do!"

Kent did not move a muscle.

"And I'm getting sick and tired of your meddling. Dammit all! I tried to make that clear to you last night."

"What the hell are you going to do, May-May? Kill everybody who tries to stop you from fighting dogs again?" He didn't care if May-May had a gun. "You can't! There are just too many Tammys around. Even you ought to be able to see that."

May-May's expression froze for a second and then broke into an evil grin. "You must be confused. Tammy got run over by a tractor. Remember?"

"Bullshit."

"I'm willing to kill you or anyone else who gets in my way, Kent. You bet I am. You're so goddamn high and mighty, Mr. Animal Doctor. You don't know shit. I'm the one with the gun pointed at your belly. Don't forget that." May-May stepped closer, holding the giant revolver within six inches of Kent's navel. "I've got help this time. Powerful help. You can't stop me. Merrill can't. Even your FOAM chick— the one I still plan to fuck— can't stop me."

Kent exploded. He slammed his left fist into the back of May-May's wrist. The .357 discharged a round that grazed Kent's leather belt then flew from the big man's grip and across the table of magazines. In the split second May-May's glance followed it, Kent drove his fist into his larynx.

May-May grabbed his throat with one hand through his beard. He gasped. Stared wild-eyed at Kent. He teetered, flailing his other hand wildly toward his half brother.

Kent swung a right cross to May-May's jaw. "That's for last night!" The impact stopped May-May again, rocked him on his heels.

Kent felt himself releasing years of suppressed rage. He buried his fist in May-May's soft belly, and his brother retched. "That's for Tammy!"

May-May dropped to his knees. A kick to the side of his head rendered him unconscious and sprawled on the kitchen floor.

Kent towered over May-May. For a long moment, he stood trembling, silently staring at his motionless brother. Then, almost inaudibly, he said, "That last one was for Mom."

Kent renewed his search for the magazine that would reveal the identity of a second humane group, all the while glancing for movement from May-May. Minutes later, he uncovered a dog-eared periodical. Its cover was creased and warped by coffee-cup rings. Even so, Kent could make out the title: the *Councilman, US Animal Protection Council Quarterly*. Triumphantly, he thumped the nose of the sad-eyed dog pictured on the cover.

He heard a soft moan and looked over to see May-May rustling back to consciousness. Kent watched him, studied him, wondering what had caused this man with half the same blood as him and Merrill to take the low road. What factors in the man's life had twisted his interest in animals into a brutal disregard for them? He was pondering that thought when his eyes involuntarily shifted focus to a cracked brown leather satchel barely visible among an assortment of cooking pots on a low shelf just inches from May-May's head.

He snatched it up and read the brass nameplate to confirm what he already knew: *Aaron Whitmore.*

"May-May, you bastard."

He stepped over May-May's slowly writhing body, planning to kick him again. Why bother? He had what he came for, the name of the other humane agency and a bonus, physical evidence tying May-May to Aaron's death. He needed to find Merrill.

CHAPTER 23

AS USUAL, THE AIR IN MERRILL'S OFFICE
reminded Kent of an autoclave. "Can't you turn the heat down in
here?" He stepped to a window and tried to open it.

"It's jammed," Merrill said.

"And you complain about my clinic?"

He had already spent close to half an hour defending himself
against their onslaught for venturing back to May-May's farm.

"It was worth it. I was able to find the magazine! Now we know
who the other humane group is."

Aubrey fried him with her eyes. "Okay, let's forget what an
utterly stupid, dangerous thing you did. So you found the magazine.
Let's go with that."

"Wait a minute."

It was time for his ace in the hole. He reached down next to his
chair, lifted a Big-K bag onto his lap. Earlier, when they had gathered
for the meeting, he had brushed off their inquiries as to what was in
the bag. Now all eyes were drawn to it.

Slowly, with as much suspense as he could fold into his voice, he
said, "I forgot to tell you about one other thing I found at May-May's."

Aubrey and Merrill stared at the bag, brows furrowed, and
said nothing.

"You want to know what I've got in here?"

Both nodded.

Kent lifted Aaron's leather satchel from the bag.

Aubrey's expression remained blank, but Merrill's eyes widened with instant recognition. He reached across his desk and let his fingers play over the coarse cowhide of the ancient briefcase. Years of daily use had withered it to parchment, like Aaron's own skin. Only the brass nameplate still shone with its owner's name. The men at the police station had given it to Aaron when he got the chief slot back in the sixties. It became as much his trademark as his shield.

"Holy shit!"

"My sentiment, exactly!"

Aubrey flashed glances at both men and back to the satchel. "What's that?"

"Aaron Whitmore's briefcase."

"It was at May-May's farm?"

"Yep."

"Wow."

He let them stare at it, too dumbstruck to ask the obvious.

"Guess what's in it," he said at last.

Neither offered a suggestion.

He unfastened two buckles, folded back the flaps. He reached in and extracted a sheaf of typed pages. Held it up. "Aaron's upcoming article."

He slid off the paper clip that secured the pages and cleared his throat. He read aloud:

There Is an Arena in Our Woods
Aaron Whitmore, staff writer

This week I'm going to ask for indulgence on the part of my regular readers. I'm going to veer from my usual topics in this column...matters related to the proud traditions of hunting and fishing. I do not do this casually. However, we sportsmen have a problem that must be addressed. Only we can resolve it. It is outside the game commission's jurisdiction. The police can't stop it. I know—I was a policeman for three decades. Oh, they would try, and maybe they would score a few minor victories, but they would not win. This travesty will continue until you, the compassionate, animal-loving people of Jefferson, close ranks, leaving it no quarter. If you choose to look the other way, or God forbid, participate in it, the curse is here to stay.

Close to a year ago now, I was holed away in my cabin on Cuyler Lake staring at the frighteningly blank sheet in my typewriter and wringing my hands.

Like all good newshounds, I was monitoring the airwaves with my scanner. I listened impatiently, hoping for that elusive scintilla of an idea. Something I could mold into an article. Maybe a fisherman bragging about a near-record brown trout or a conservation officer calling in a poaching incident. Anything that would provide me with a few columns to flop on my editor's desk before Friday's noon deadline. But there was nothing that night, just the incessant drone of truckers up on the interstate two valleys over. Their voices bounced off low clouds and ricocheted down into my cabin like hail on a tin roof, abrasive and tedious, until a strange conversation faded in. A chill ran up my spine like a wet-footed spider. Broken fragments of male voices. Two at first, then several more, too garbled to recognize. "...dog meet tonight...usual place...convoy at nine thirty..."

For the longest time, that scrap of conversation played in my head, and I tried in earnest to convince myself that the speaker meant "dog meat," not "dog meet." Not that the former would have done much to relieve my consternation.

A few weeks after that, another incident occurred that removed all question.

It happened last spring—early May. I was hiking at dusk, owling as I went, trying to locate a flock of roosting turkeys to hunt the next morning. Before I realized it, I was clear around the lake from my cabin, and the last reds of sunset were fading to pewter. That didn't bother me. I know the area like the back of my hand. Half a mile, over two knolls, and I would break out of the woods onto a dirt road. From there I would have an easy hike and be at my cabin in an hour.

The first leg of my trek went as anticipated. Within a few minutes, I was walking briskly down the grassed-in, two-rut road, enjoying the darkness and misty-sweet smells of nature emerging from winter. Suddenly there were noises, distant at first, but louder as I approached.

I slowed and then stopped, cocked my head, and listened. They were crowd sounds—revving engines, rambunctious chatter, and laughter. Occasional cheers went up from what sounded like at least a hundred people.

A teenage drinking party, I thought with a nostalgic chuckle. Some things never change. I'd keep to the shadows until well past. They'd never know I'd found them out. There was a time—way back when—as a young cop, I might have shut them down, but that was then...not anymore. I am older now. And slower. And smarter.

I hadn't taken more than a dozen steps to circumvent the rowdies when my newsman curiosity grabbed me like a bear pulling salmon from shallow water. Against my better judgment, I crept toward a clearing where the revelry originated. I was in my stalking mode, crouched, soft silent footsteps, eyes and ears scanning. I ducked beneath a bush and beheld a sight that knocked the wind out of my lungs with as much force as the time I fell out of my tree stand. The moonlight played off a sea of four-wheel-drive vehicles—big mothers, little ones, jacked up, low-slung, beat-up, pristine—like the parking lot at the dirt track on a Saturday night. This was no high school beer party.

At that moment, a hideous sound that I had not heard in years turned my backbone into a ramrod. It was a mix of guttural gnashing noise, high-pitched whines, and shouts from the crowd, all coming from a long-forgotten barn fifty yards away.

I hunched there trembling as if I'd been standing through hours of sleet and wind on a deer stand. I stared at the decrepit building, hating it for what it concealed. Light slipped through cracks in its weathered board walls like a giant tin lantern. When people moved inside, the rays shifted. But the sounds, the horrid sounds, ripped at my ears until I thought my head would explode. A moan escaped my lips between clenched teeth. I took one last look at the parked vehicles, shook my head slowly, spit into the damp leaves.

I will never forget that makeshift arena, or how it blighted our community. I swore, then and there, I would do everything in my power to see that you do not forget it either.

Kent looked up from Aaron's pages at the pair of spellbound faces. " There's more. You can read the rest on your own. Pretty nasty stuff. Aaron had it all figured out. He was going to expose May-May and ruin his big-money connection's plan for a national championship."

"It got him killed," Merrill said.

"But what I can't figure out is how he let a guy like May-May lure him out to a place like the boat launch in the middle of the night. He was a cop. He knew May-May. He had to realize it was crazy dangerous."

Merrill nodded. "Why didn't he just go ahead and print his article and the hell with it?"

All three stared at the pages. No one answered.

Finally Aubrey asked, "What do we do now?"

Kent reached to the edge of Merrill's desk, picked up the USAPC magazine, and tossed it to lie directly in front of his brother.

"What about contacting them? See if they have anything."

Merrill leaned forward slowly, took up the periodical, and studied its cover. "What's the name of this watchdog group again?"

"The USAPC, United States Animal Protection Council," Aubrey said. "They are by far the largest and best funded of any group in the animal rights movement."

"Great! A *big* group of rich bleeding hearts."

"Actually, they're much more mainstream than most groups. They've been around since the fifties. It's a good bet they are the ones after May-May and company. FOAM has worked with them on a number of campaigns. Sometimes they try to steal the show a little too much, but…hey, they're all right."

Merrill leafed through a few pages.

"I can get you some names and numbers to start with," Aubrey said.

Merrill flipped a few more. "Says here they're headquartered in Washington, DC." Then he acknowledged her offer. "That would be helpful. You get me some names, and I'll follow up on them."

Aubrey made a call to FOAM's home office in LA, and by midafternoon the Jefferson Police Department fax machine was rattling away: names of USAPC officers with phone numbers, copies of several back issues of the USAPC quarterly bulletin, similar to the one from May-May's, and a summary of Aubrey's previous contacts at USAPC with opinions as to how helpful they might be.

Merrill took the packet into his office, perused it, and was pleasantly surprised by the amount of background material Aubrey's cronies had amassed. He took a few minutes figuring where to start and then decided the top seemed like the logical spot. He dialed the number for USAPC in Washington.

"This is Police Chief Merrill Stephenson in Jefferson, New York. I'd like to speak to whoever handles animal cruelty investigations, please."

"That would be our legal department. Hold, please."

On hold, Merrill listened to a message about clubbing baby seals in Alaska and one on the wanton destruction of the Everglades. A plug to spay and neuter one's pets was just coming on when the secretary cut in to tell Merrill she was connecting him with Al Kirms, USAPC's lawyer.

"Officer Stephenson, is it?" Kirms asked in a mellifluous voice that made Merrill suspect the guy was pretty high up the food chain.

"Yes. Chief of police, Jefferson, New York."

Before Merrill could state his business, Kirms took control. "I have an apology to make to you folks in Jefferson."

The lawyer's sudden admission of error caught Merrill off guard. "What?"

"I—we at USAPC—apologize."

Merrill envisioned Kirms smiling at the other end, enjoying the confusion he was creating. "For what?"

"For having you discover us on your own instead of us coming forward, of course."

"Well," Merrill said, trying to figure out what Kirms was pulling, "it is rather disconcerting."

"Actually it's a result of good police work on your part."

"Small town, undermanned, but we get the job done."

"It appears that way."

"So. What exactly is going on? Details, I mean."

"What do you know about our setup to this point?"

Merrill bluffed carefully. "In a nutshell, we have information that USAPC has been investigating a dogfighting ring that we are about to take down, and we don't want any screw-ups that could jeopardize a lot of work."

Merrill heard a soft laugh at the other end.

"No, chief. We at USAPC wouldn't want that either. Neither would the FBI."

The chief's eyebrows rose at the mention of the FBI. "What's the FBI got to do with anything?"

"They're one of the agencies involved in our investigation, which has come to overlap your investigation. Along with the US attorney general's Organized Crime Task Force, the US Department of Agriculture, and police forces in several states, including New York."

Merrill bristled. "All this shit is going on, and you're keeping us locals in the dark?"

"Let me explain," Kirms said.

Merrill was back in character, no longer walking softly. "Whatever happened to interagency communications?"

"I was getting to that, if you'll give me a chance."

"This kind of crap really pisses me off."

"Look, I said in the beginning we owed you an apology. Part of it is your own fault, though."

"Our fault!"

"Yes, for figuring us out too soon." The lawyer tried to make it sound like a backward compliment. "We were going to come to you. We always work through proper channels and jurisdictions, but you came to us first."

Merrill took a deep breath. Kirms was an experienced appeaser. "Okay then, Al," he honked the man's name. "Tell me what has been going on under my nose without my knowledge."

"With pleasure. Except, like you, I do not want to jeopardize our investigation. Suffice it to say for now that we have had a multiagency, interstate investigation in progress for many months, and it seems as though the whole thing is heading up in your back-yard. For details, though, which you are definitely entitled to, I am going to have one of our agents meet with you in person. He's in Jefferson as we speak, but it will take some time to contact him and make the arrangements. I'll have him fill you in completely, and you can ask whatever questions you want person to person. "You a hunter, Merrill?"

"What?"

"Do you hunt? For sport."

"Occasionally," the chief said, confused by the question.

"Ever hunt rabbits?"

"Yeah."

"Good. Tomorrow morning around eight o'clock, park your car where the old train track crosses West Hill Road and hunt the rail-road bed south. My man will meet you."

Merrill hesitated, impressed by Kirm's knowledge of Jefferson geography. "What's with all the cloak-and-dagger stuff? Can't we just meet and talk?"

In his imperturbable tone, Kirms said, "It's taken over a year to get this man placed where he is. Being seen with you could destroy all that work."

Merrill had been a cop long enough to be uncomfortable with one-on-one in the boondocks, but his curiosity would not allow him to back out. "All right. I'll play along, but I'm bringing another guy with me. He's a local veterinarian who has been involved with our investigation from the beginning."

"You vouch for him?"

"Like he was my brother."

"Okay. I'll tell my guy to expect two. Tomorrow morning at eight. He'll ask you what kind of ammo you're using. The answer is 'Federal.' Got it?"

"I got it. Federal. We'll be waiting."

CHAPTER 24

AT EXACTLY 7:55 A.M., MERRILL'S UNMARKED CAR pulled to a stop by the tracks on West Hill Road. Kent closed the door with Lucinda inside. She gave him a look of utter dismay. He was going hunting without her.

He stroked her gently through the cracked window. "You're all right, girl. This is all a fake."

Lucinda whined pitifully.

"You sure I can't bring Lucinda along?" Kent asked his brother over the roof of the car.

"Forget it!" Merrill said. "I don't want that dog treeing some USAPC agent and screwing up everything."

Each man took a side and headed south along the tracks, beating the bushes as they went.

"If I see a rabbit, am I allowed to shoot it?" Kent asked.

The tenseness of the situation had drained all of Merrill's humor. "Don't even put any shells in your gun, asshole. This is *not* a hunting trip."

"Touchy, touchy."

They went through the motions of hunting for a quarter of a mile before Kent noticed a patch of blaze orange against a tree up ahead.

"I see something," he said to Merrill in a low hunter's voice.

"Keep going steady," Merrill whispered back.

As they approached, the orange resolved into a man in hunting garb. He was long, thin, and walnut-colored, like the stock of the shotgun across his body. When they were a few feet away they stopped. Waited for the would-be hunter to speak.

"Morning, men. Any luck?" he asked in a voice that seemed to arise from a hollow log. His prominent Adam's apple jumped with each word.

"Haven't seen a thing," Merrill said.

"Me either."

"I think we need a dog," Kent said.

Merrill flashed him a *this-is-no-time-to-be-a-smartass* look.

The lean black man took the opening. "Maybe it's your ammo. What you using?"

Kent thought the question odd. If you hadn't seen a rabbit, it didn't make any difference what kind of shells were in your gun.

"Federal," Merrill said.

Kent stared at his brother, baffled.

"Good." The man smiled broadly and extended his hand, "I'm agent Dan Rodman.

Kent, realizing he had been duped by a code, rolled his eyes. He looked at the dark face with its rough scar on the right temple. "Jesus. You look familiar."

Rodman rocked his head back and released a low, resonant laugh. "You're pretty good. Think. Where'd you see me?"

Kent rolled through his mental file of acquaintances and clients, trying to place the man. "The animal shelter! I saw you get some pups and kittens at the shelter."

Rodman's physical features were the same, but the doltish look he displayed at the shelter was now replaced by keen-eyed savvy.

"You got it. And where else?"

"The day of the fire at Copithorn. You were out front in a truck."

"Right again."

Kent's recall was on target now. "Then you came into my office to buy some medicine one day."

"Perfect. To the dog men, I'm dimwitted Bo Davis, your brother's hired man." For just a second he dropped back into his Jim Crow act to demonstrate.

"Half brother," Kent said.

Merrill was eager for information. "So what's going on, Mr. Rodman?"

"Please. Call me Dan."

"Okay, Dan. Tell us about this investigation you guys have going."

The agent stepped over to an outcropping of limestone the size of a tabletop and sat. He gestured for his new companions to join him. Neither moved.

Rodman ignored the snub and began his story. "We've been after these bums for a couple of years. We got a tip there was a large-scale dogfighting ring operating out of Austin, Texas. So we started looking into it and were amazed at how big an operation it really was. Well, for years USAPC has wanted to nail some of these guys, but it's hard to get a case a DA can prosecute." He waved his hand in a gesture of frustration. "There's a lot of gray zone as to whose jurisdiction is whose. And even if you get a conviction, the sentences are light."

Kent nodded. "Bottom line, everybody realizes it's a problem, but nobody wants to waste their time if nothing is going to come of it."

"Yeah. That's what it boils down to." Rodman pulled his hat into his lap as if freeing his mind to work. "That was before these Texas players came along. The more we investigated, the bigger it got. These guys are definitely interstate, and probably international. Hopefully, we'll know that in a couple of weeks. They gamble serious money. They've got illegal firearms out the ying-yang, and at the fights, there are more drugs than in the Miami projects.

"Now we've got something we can really sink our teeth into. USAPC wants the animal abuse angle. But we were also able to convince some other agencies it was worth their effort. The FBI and ATF are in for the interstate transport of firearms and drugs. The attorney general's office in Washington has offered their Organized Crime Task Force because of the gambling, and the US Department of Agriculture is in because they need someone to string up as an example of how well they enforce the Animal Welfare Act."

"I can see the drugs and firearms thing, but if the penalties are so mild for dogfighting, why bother?" Kent asked.

Dan Rodman opened his mouth as if about to give a glib answer and then stopped. He studied his shotgun, slowly running his fingers up and down its smooth barrel. Then he turned to Kent. "Do you really want to know?"

There was a sinister tone in the man's voice that surprised Kent and told him that whatever the real answer was, it was not glib.

"Yes I do," Kent said, wondering what can of worms he was opening.

Rodman set his gun against a tree an arm's length away. "Okay, I'll give you the unabridged version, starting with my life history and"—he tapped the scar on his temple —"this little beauty mark of mine.

"I was born and raised in one of those shotgun shacks you used to see sitting in the middle of the cotton fields all over the Deep South. Ours was just outside a tiny crossroads called Wakefield in north Louisiana, about five miles from the Arkansas line. My mama and daddy were hardworking, church-going, scratch-out-a-living-for-the-family folks. I was the oldest of four kids. We never had nothing. Our idea of a good time was going fishing with Daddy on Sunday afternoon.

"Now don't get me wrong with what I'm about to say here, because my daddy was a good man. I loved and respected him till the day he died." Rodman hesitated, having second thoughts about telling his story. "Daddy had one fault. At the time I didn't even see it as a fault, since most the other men did the same thing. He used to raise a few pit bulls and do a little dogfighting."

Rodman shook his head at the irony of his memories.

"You know, it sounds weird, but he really liked his dogs and treated them well. Except for letting them get chewed up in a pit. If you can believe that.

"It was different then. Still wrong as hell, but different. The men weren't so nasty. They were all good Baptists. You wouldn't see a drop of liquor or hear a cussword through the whole night of fights. And they called the dogs off as soon as they could tell one had it over the other."

"Less bad is still terrible," Kent said.

Rodman nodded heartily. "I agree. It was still bad. And I hated watching the fights. I went along and helped my daddy whenever he'd let me, and I loved seeing all the people and the excitement. But I tried not to watch the actual fights if I could help it.

"Well, one time my daddy took me over into Dawson Grove, a little town just over the line in Arkansas, not much bigger than Wakefield. He told me this fight was going to be different. The crowd would be bigger, and they'd be mean, and there'd be a lot of drinking and swearing and more gambling than usual. He said not to tell Mama because she'd get mad if she found out he went, let alone took me too. He said the only reason he was doing it at all was because he had a dog he thought could win, and we'd have some extra money for Christmas."

Rodman paused, his face tightened. "We never should have gone. They were a bunch of white crackers, and I knew a couple of black folks had no place being there. Daddy was right. There was lots of cussing and drinking, and seemed like everybody had a gun or a big knife. More money than I'd ever seen was flying all over the place. Dead and maimed dogs started piling up like cordwood.

"Then, to make a long story short, Daddy's good dog got matched up with a real popular pit bull owned by a farmer named Milton Ross. Turns out Daddy's dog won, but ol' Milton had a snake-mean son named Lester who didn't like the outcome and accused my daddy of using a rub—cheating.

"They argued and things got nasty. I was scared to death. So Daddy takes me by the arm and backs out the door, figuring we better forget the money and get out while the getting was good."

Rodman's voice choked with bitterness. "They jumped us out by our truck. They pushed me around a little, but they really went after my daddy. They had him on the ground and just kept kicking him and hitting him with clubs. I thought they were going to kill him, so I jumped at Lester, and that's when he gave me this permanent reminder of that night." He tapped his scar with a finger.

"When I woke up, I found Daddy. He was breathing, but that was about all. They beat him up real bad. Somehow I got him loaded in the back of our old pickup and brought him home."

Rodman sighed deeply.

"In one short night, Daddy lost his money, the best dog he'd ever had, and his health. He lived, but he was never the same. After that night, he was kinda simple and moved real timidlike."

Kent remembered the loss of his own father. Rodman's story made his skin crawl. "Being in the South," he said, "nothing ever happened to the cracker's son who did it to your dad. Right?"

"Ol' Lester? No. Cops never arrested him. Hell, they probably never heard about that night. We didn't press charges. We were too scared. It was a secret, illegal gathering. There wasn't anything we could do."

Rodman's voice took on a faraway dreamy tone, yet at the same time it quivered with a vicious rancor. "No, ol' Lester hasn't paid for what he did—yet."

"Yet?"

Rodman nodded and let his face form a smile, but it held no humor. "The story's not over. A few years later, I went to Louisiana Tech and got a degree in law enforcement. I figured I'd become a cop. Except what I never realized was that ol' Lester gave me a partially detached retina in my right eye the same time he gave me the scar. So I couldn't pass the physical.

"One thing led to another, and eventually I ended up going to work for Alcohol, Tobacco, and Firearms, the ATF, out of Austin, Texas. Lo and behold, a couple years later I'm on an illegal firearms investigation, and whose name should come up?"

"Lester Ross," Kent said.

"Right. From then on I was a man possessed. Like a beagle on a rabbit, I wasn't stoppin' for nothin'. Not till I had him."

"Did you get him? Eventually?"

"Not yet."

"There's more?"

"Federal budget cuts being what they were, I eventually got 'severed' from ATF, before I had a chance to get Lester."

"But you weren't about to give up on him, so you joined USAPC."

"You got it. And I brought my pet case with me. Pardon the pun."

Neither of the brothers laughed.

"Tough break," Merrill said. It was obvious he considered moving from ATF to USAPC a demotion.

"Not really," Rodman said. "For me, the switch was easy. Like I said before, I loved and respected my daddy except for one thing—dogfighting. I hated everything about it back then, and I hate everything about it now. I'd rather chase bad guys abusing animals than gunrunners anytime."

Kent wasn't about to be left hanging. "So what happened to Lester Ross?"

For a moment, Rodman's eyes shifted back and forth from Kent to Merrill, dangling a secret before the brothers. "He's coming to Jefferson."

"No kidding!"

"Yep. He's into dogfighting in a much, much bigger way now. See, ol' Lester went on to get real rich with computers. But you can't change a leopard's spots, they say, and he still likes to fight those pit bulls."

Kent remembered what Tammy had told him about how May-May was in over his head with big-money types, possibly gangsters. "Lester Ross must be one of the backers for the national championship."

"That's right. He's behind it. And Lester's connected to some even bigger guys who are watching really close. They're using the nationals as a testing ground. It's downright scary, because if they like what they see, they're going to use syndicate connections to market dogfighting way beyond anything that ever went on in this country."

Merrill shook his head. "It's unbelievable."

Kent kicked at a decaying stump with the toe of his hunting boot. "Well, we'll just have to stop them."

"We'll get 'em. I haven't been tailing Lester and taking May-May's crap all this time just for the hell of it."

"How?"

"We'll catch them in the act."

"You are actually going to raid their meet?"

"That's the plan."

"Are you going to be there?"

Rodman smiled. "I sure as hell want to be."

"Won't Lester recognize you?"

"Not a chance. As a matter of fact, he and I crossed paths at May-May's just the other day."

"You're kidding me. Lester Ross was in Jefferson already?"

"Yep. He didn't know me from Adam. Arkansas was too long ago. The ATF protects the ID of its agents, so he never knew I was after him for guns. For all he knows, I'm dumb ol' Bo Davis." Rodman gave out a baritone laugh. "And maybe he ain't far off."

Kent knew there was nothing dumb about Dan Rodman. He was sure as hell glad he wasn't Lester Ross.

"And"—Rodman's voice became optimistic—"by some piece of luck these idiots decided to hold their national fighting convention in New York. It appears none of them bothered to find out that New York is on the forefront of animal welfare, and what they're doing is a felony with some good long prison terms and hefty fines."

Kent saw his brother puff up at the thought of New York being tough on crime.

"Like I said, they're well organized. They run it like prizefighting. They've got an official rulebook. They've got a very professional-looking trade journal called the *Chronicle* that talks about meets, spotlights breeders, runs ads for equipment dealers, the whole nine yards." He ticked each item off with his fingers as he said it. "There're guys out there making a living as professional trainers and handlers."

"What about the actual fights?" Kent asked.

"I've been at some where there's an auditorium full of people, young, old, blue-collar, white-collar. From all over. They'll wager a couple hundred grand on an average night."

Merrill let out a long whistle but said nothing.

"If that surprises you," Rodman continued, "what's about to happen will really floor you. This fight coming up in Jefferson is a whole 'nother ball of wax. It's for the national championship. It's guaranteed to be way bigger. More people, more money, more guns, more drugs."

"Jefferson, New York, dogfighting capital of the world," Kent said.

"As soon as we find out where and when it happens, we're going to drop on them like a big blob of birdshit and end this whole thing." There was a smug confidence in Rodman's voice.

Kent marveled at what was happening. All the plans and effort put into the investigation. And they had kept it secret! "How long have you been in Jefferson, anyway?"

"Bo Davis came to town about ten months ago, supposedly looking for farm work. Took me a while to make the connections, but I'm in now. Maylon Mays is the man here. I know he's your brother, but I've got to tell you, he's got a gold-plated line of bullshit."

Neither brother registered surprise.

"Somehow he sold the big boys in Texas that they ought to come east with their convention. Open up new territories, I guess. Then he got wind we were around, so he tried to take advantage of FOAM's presence to take USAPC heat off his crew. He's behind the Copithorn fire."

Merrill and Kent just nodded.

"I thought that would be a blockbuster," Rodman said obviously disappointed. "You guys already knew that, didn't you?"

"Uh-huh."

Rodman touched the brim of his hat in a salute to them. "I should have guessed."

"And we know about his bunch of dogs," Merrill said.

"Right."

Kent decided to bluff. "And his break-in at the hotel. And staging his wife's murder." He looked with satisfaction at the agent's expression of amazement. "And Aaron Whitmore's."

Rodman stopped bobbing his head. "How do you know that?"

"We recovered a series of articles Aaron wrote that condemned the movement of dogfights into Jefferson. He died in what was supposedly a suicide just before they were to be published. We put two and two together."

"I read about that, up on Cuyler Lake. A murder rap? It's too good to be true. If we can pin one on these guys, they're gone for good, and every agency will get a piece of the credit. It makes the stakes a lot higher. The attorney general is going to flip when he hears this stuff."

"What do we do from here out?" Merrill asked.

"We'll need you as part of the team, I'm sure, but beyond that, instructions will come down from the top."

"What about FOAM?" Kent asked. "Aubrey Fairbanks has been working with us on this from the beginning. We include her, right?"

Rodman shook his head slowly. "Probably not. The more people involved, the more chance for problems. I doubt they can contribute much more than they have already. Plus the FOAM people can get pretty emotional."

"I agree one hundred percent," said Merrill.

"Too dangerous," Rodman said. "I'm telling you, we're talking guns, drugs, and money. It's a very volatile combination. We don't want anyone hurt. See if you can keep Fairbanks and FOAM out of it for now."

"She isn't going to like it," said Kent.

"Do what you can." Rodman stood up and stretched. He picked up his shotgun and started away. Then he stopped and turned to face the brothers. For a long moment the three of them eyed one another in silence. Rodman's Adam's apple rose and fell. "I never thought to ask if either of you had a problem with me going after your brother."

"Half brother," they said in one voice.

Then Kent said, "And if he's a bad guy, he's a bad guy."

Rodman seemed satisfied. He turned and walked away. "We'll be talking."

CHAPTER 25

KENT AND AUBREY SIPPED NIGHTCAPS AND fumed at each other across a tiny table in a quiet corner of the Groggery. Dinner had been great, as usual, until Kent brought up the subject of his hunting venture along the railroad track earlier that day. He told her about Dan Rodman, the USAPC's reason for being in Jefferson, and the difficult part— that FOAM was not going to be included in further moves against the dog men. The evening went to hell in a hurry.

Aubrey used a tiny straw to poke at the muddled fruit in the bottom of her glass and bristled at the prospect of her exclusion. "I've been in this from the beginning. FOAM's been in this from the beginning. Where do they get off cutting us out? I told you. The problem with the USAPC is they always want to run the show."

Kent rattled his scotch and tried to keep the conversation at a slow enough pace that it might not be considered an argument. It didn't work. "Nobody's trying to take over the show, Aubrey. As a matter of fact, the show was already in progress a year before we came on the scene."

"Still, we are involved! Deeply involved. And we've made a huge contribution to the case."

"They don't deny that," Kent said, "but as I said, there are several other agencies involved in this too. Their concern is that too many more and the chance of something getting back to the dog men goes way up. It would jeopardize the entire investigation." He held up his glass, played with a trickle of condensation on it, and lied. "I have to agree with them."

Aubrey glared at him, furious at his betrayal. "That's a lot of crap. FOAM is less likely to leak information than any of those other agencies. I'd stake my worthless reputation on it. The problem is that the USAPC wants all the headlines."

Kent decided not to mention Rodman's concern about FOAM being emotion-driven. "Rodman said all orders come down from the top. That's the FBI and attorney general."

"That's a cop out!"

He took a different tack. "These dogfighters are dangerous. Very dangerous."

"I realize that."

"There is a lot of nasty stuff that goes along with dogfighting. Guns, drugs, gambling. This thing is much more volatile than your average rodeo protest or research lab picket."

Aubrey slammed her glass to the table and hurled her words at him. "Eat shit, Kent! I've been in tough spots before."

He looked around to see if anyone else had heard her. "Take it easy. I didn't mean it that way. I'm just relaying the information they gave me. And to tell the truth, I'm trying my best to persuade you not to get any closer to this thing for my own selfish reasons. It would kill me if anything bad happened to you. Remember, there have been two murders already."

"If you care about me, you'll let me do what I came here to do."

"Good." Kent made a grand gesture. "Go protest at Copithorn. I have no objection to that."

"No! I mean, work for animal rights. What these guys are doing makes all other acts against animals pale in comparison. And they are conspiring to make it grow and spread throughout our country. It is the ultimate abuse of animals. You said it yourself. I want to have a part in exposing these sons of bitches."

Kent stood slowly, deliberately, signaling that he was through arguing. "As I said, I don't call the shots."

"Yeah. Well, they'll let a burned-out veterinarian in, but not us. That's real fair."

Kent tossed some drink money on the table without counting it. "I'll call you."

"Don't bother."

Kent strode across the darkened barroom. As he pushed through the door into the lobby he ran head-on into a person coming his way. He caught his balance, cursed under his breath, and glared at the offender. He gasped, seeing the dead, as he stared into Tammy's Indian eyes. "Jesus Christ, Nathan. What are you doing here?"

Nathan's face was like stone. "Barry said you and his mom were here. I need to talk to you."

"Can it wait?"

"It's important. I got something to tell you."

Kent drew a calming breath and released it. "Okay. What's up?"

Nathan's eyes flashed defiance. He pointed in the direction from which Kent had come. "Maybe we better go back in and sit down, Doc." It was more of an order than a suggestion.

Kent gave him a long, appraising look. "Okay." He turned back into the darkness of the Groggery.

Nathan followed without a word.

Aubrey, once again, had her legs stretched the length of the booth, head back, deep in thought. She sensed more than heard their approach. When she saw who it was and their somber looks, she coiled her feet back under the table, and made room for them to sit. Her eyes flashed Kent. *Now what?* She said nothing.

"Nathan's got something he wants to say."

Nathan slid in across from the two adults. He did not hesitate. Kent guessed he'd put a lot of thought into his words. "My mom knew who killed Whitmore. She just didn't want to rat on him." He stopped, as if that said it all, and that everything else should fall log-ically into place.

Kent and Aubrey held, waiting for more.

"I should have seen it," he said. "Whitmore was trying to give him a break, but the jerk-off wouldn't take it."

"Who, Nathan?" Aubrey asked. Her voice held the tone of a mother consoling a suffering child.

"Hold on a second," Kent said, the anger gone now. "Nathan, maybe you should start from the beginning and tell us everything you know."

"Okay." He took a deep breath and released it slowly. "I overheard May-May talking to Bo. He's May-May's helper. Mostly screaming at him, really. He was all over him about killing my mom."

"Bo killed your mom?"

"No. May-May did, when she told him she figured he killed Whitmore and that if he didn't stop all the dogfighting shit, she was going to the police. I heard him yelling at Bo to keep his mouth shut about it."

"May-May killed Tammy? You know that for sure?"

Nathan's face went white. His eyes became puffy. "Yes! I heard him say it. My mother always stuck up for him. I never did anything bad to him either, but he still always hated me." Nathan turned them a proud look. "But I stuck up for him too. Just like Mom did. All the time. No matter what people said about May-May, he was my mom's husband and my stepfather, so I just told them to fuck off." His voice dropped to a whisper. "But not anymore. He killed my mother, and I want him dead."

Then Nathan looked straight into Kent's eyes. His voice rose, raspy with anger and determination. "I know nobody but me cared about my mom. I'm going to tell you just what happened so you can string the bastard up. For her."

Aubrey leaned toward him, "We cared about your mother, Nathan."

"Whatever. You let me do this while I got it in me."

Kent gently eased her back.

Nathan started again. "You remember the night we went coon hunting? You and Barry saw me climb out from under the cover in the back of May-May's truck?"

"Yes."

"Remember I told you I hitched rides from May-May like that all the time, and he never knew it?"

"Yeah."

"Well, the night Whitmore died, I did it—hitched in May-May's truck. May-May gets this phone call at our house while we're eating supper. After he hangs up, he's all nervous and mad, and says to Mom he is headed into town for a drink." Nathan twisted his mouth into a dubious expression. "Which is easy for us to believe. And then he leaves.

"Anyway, I am looking for a way to get into town to see this girl. So I slip into the truck bed. What he doesn't know is that when he's bouncing that big beast of his down our lane, I'm jiggling around in back. He hits the bars. Me and this girl sit under her umbrella smoking cigarettes and making out in the park where we can keep and eye on his truck. It's raining to beat hell. About ten he comes out, staggering, of course. I tell the girl goodbye and load up again. I figure we're headed home and good thing because I'm soaked and freezing to death. But next thing I know, he's pulling into the Cuyler Lake boat launch."

Kent could feel himself shaking, a mix of emotions—anger, frustration, and relief—jamming his sensory system. He reached over and took Aubrey's hand.

"I'm thinking, *What's May-May up to now?* He pulls in and shuts off the motor. I hear him get out and walk a few steps. I figure, oh, he's just taking a piss, but then he's talking to somebody. I pop a few snaps on the cover to get a better look. There's Aaron Whitmore in his Land Rover, nose to nose with May-May's truck. Rain beating down, May-May standing at the window next to Whitmore. Neither one sounds very happy to be there.

"I just keep low. I'm watching and listening. May-May has those big KC bar lights up on top of his truck. They're shining right inside Whitmore's cab.

"Whitmore is yelling, 'May-May, I know what you're planning.' He shows him this old leather book bag and says he's got all kinds of stuff in it that could land May-May back in jail. Now May-May's crazy mad. Mad about what Whitmore is telling him, and mad about standing in the rain probably, too. He pounds his fist on the Land Rover's roof a couple of times, real hard. I can see Aaron getting all scared-looking. I think he wants to say the hell with this and bolt, but his Land Rover is wedged in between that railing in back and May-May's truck in front. So anyway, he says he really doesn't want to rat out May-May because he figures it would break your mother's heart."

"What?" Kent said, startled at the mention of his mother in this mess.

"Well, Whitmore tells May-May it broke your mom's heart when he went to prison last time. It would probably kill her if he went again. Whitmore doesn't want to be responsible for that. So he says to May-May, 'I'll cut you a deal. Quit the shit you are doing, I'll tear up my story.'

"That makes May-May goes ballistic. He tells Whitmore he's known all along he's sweet on your mom. And he doesn't give a shit if she gets hurt. This thing he's doing is his ticket to the big time. Whitmore says something like, 'Okay, to hell with you. The story goes in tomorrow.' May-May totally loses it. He reaches in the window and grabs Whitmore by the throat. I swear he's going to pull old Whitmore right out. Whitmore is kicking and clawing and making all these gurgling sounds. Next thing I know, he's got a gun."

Nathan formed his hand into a gun and pointed it into Kent's face. "Pow! I figure that's it for my stepdad. But the bullet misses. Must have gone within an inch of his ear. May-May lets go of Whitmore's neck and grabs the gun. So now the two of them are wrestling for the gun in kind of a tug of war. And remember, it's raining like hell. Everything's like all slippery. They're yanking and swearing till, all of a sudden, May-May's grip gives, and Whitmore goes rolling back into the Land Rover with the gun. He's down below the dashboard, so I can't see him, but the gun goes off again. May-May hits the deck. He must have been figuring Whitmore was coming out shooting. But everything got dead quiet. Pretty soon I see May-May ease up real careful-like and peek in the Land Rover. Then he starts laughing. A big cheerful laugh. He just stands there half dancing and muttering to himself. Dancing real weird. He pulls a rag out of his pocket and wipes around the window where he's been touching. He goes around to the other door, reaches in, and picks up the gun. He wipes it real clean in the headlights, then he puts it back. He says something like, 'Looks like a suicide to me!' Then he grabs the book bag they argued over and gets back in the truck. Next thing I know, we're peeling out of the boat launch."

For a long time, Kent and Aubrey stared at Nathan, stunned by the pictures the boy had painted— the relief, the clarity, the anger wrought from each scene.

Kent asked him, "You want a soda or something?"

"No thanks."

Kent looked questioningly at Aubrey who signaled no by holding a palm over her highball glass. He waved for Tammy's replacement to bring him another Scotch.

"You are going to be in real danger if May-May finds out you talked to us."

"I don't give a shit. He killed my mom. I want to bring him down."

"Where are you staying tonight?" Aubrey asked. "How are you getting home?"

"I didn't give it much thought. I haven't been spending any time there anyway. May-May doesn't even notice I'm gone."

Aubrey made the expression women reserve for new babies and stray kittens. "Barry is upstairs."

"I know. I was watching the Knicks with him before I came down here."

"He's got an extra bed in his room. He'd love to have company." Nathan was silent.

"Come on," Aubrey said. "It's colder than cold outside. You don't want to be out there."

Nathan thought some more. He lifted his head, looked at Aubrey. "You're nice."

"Thank you."

"I'll stay."

"Great. Just head on up."

Nathan rose, turned to go, and then came back around. "Doc," he said. "Remember all the mean things I said about old Mr. Whitmore when we were coon hunting? Him being a control freak, and a jerk, and all?"

"Yeah."

"Well, I didn't really mean them. I wasn't thinking right. He was always good to me. I'm sorry. I know he was a good friend of yours."

"Thanks, Nathan. That means a lot to me."

When he was gone, Aubrey said, "Holy shit."

Kent lifted his glass in a melancholy toast. "That clears up a lot of stuff. Doesn't it?"

"It sure does. But it leaves one big question."

"Which is?"

"Now what?"

"Right. I'm thinking we play him out a little more rope."

"What does that mean?"

"It means that if we have Merrill arrest him now, we have no proof that he was organizing the dogfighting syndicate. And even if we did manage to get May-May, we'd scare off his big-money backers. They'd get away and find another little guy to take the fall next time.

"Figures. Doesn't it?"

"Definitely."

"And it brings us back to our original problem."

"Which is?"

Aubrey cast him a fiery look. "Why does the USAPC have the right to cut FOAM out of the action?"

Kent held up both hands. "I'm not going there again."

"Then you might as well head home."

No arm-in-arm stroll back to her room. No kiss goodnight. He trudged slowly back to his truck. He needed to talk to Lucinda.

CHAPTER 26

AT ELEVEN THIRTY THE NEXT MORNING, AUBREY was still in bed. Her head throbbed with a headache aspirin wouldn't touch. Twisted in sweaty sheets, staring blurry-eyed at the ceiling, she sifted through the ashes of her relationship with Kent.

"Shit," she said, rolled over. Focused as best she could on the clock next to her bed and calculated the three-hour time difference on her fingers. She picked up the telephone and dialed a Los Angeles number.

"Raul Pentes, please. Tell him Aubrey Fairbanks is calling."

Immediately an effeminate Latino voice came over the phone. "Aubrey? I figured you'd dropped off the face of the earth."

"Almost. I'm outside of Syracuse, New York, in a little place called Jefferson, hanging on by my fingernails."

"I'm so worried. What are you doing there?"

"Sometime when we're by the pool with tall, cold umbrella drinks and lots of time on our hands I'll give you the whole story. But in a nutshell, I'm about to do some undercover work for FOAM, and I need your help, Raul."

Aubrey heard a long sigh at the other end.

"You still doing the animal rights thing?" Disappointment was heavy in Raul's tone.

"You didn't figure I'd quit, did you?"

"What a waste! You should be out here flashing your face on the silver screen."

"Forget it, Raul. I had enough of that con."

"My bad luck. What can I do for you?"

"You're still doing makeup, aren't you?"

"All day, every day. They all love me, and why not? I am the best." Raul let his voice drop into a whisper. "You wouldn't believe who's sitting in my chair as we speak."

"Big star?"

He kept his secretive tone. "I'm not at liberty to give out names, but I'll tell you she's the lead in the new Stephen King movie."

"No kidding!" The one thing Aubrey did miss about Hollywood's acting scene was being an insider, getting the facts behind the images so carefully fabricated for the public. Of course, she reminded herself, it was that very mentality that had driven her away from Hollywood. "I'll have to check out the face you give her."

"Do that, please. And let me know what you think. Only if you like it."

She let him hear her laugh. "Okay, Raul. Anyway, I was hoping I could get some makeup from you, and maybe a blond wig. Something trashy. I need to become a biker's moll. You know what I mean?"

"I can do bikers, male or female, in my sleep."

"Great. You still have my sizes on file, right?"

"They're still the same?"

"Close enough."

"Thatta girl. You are so beautiful."

Aubrey ignored Raul's flattery. "How about a Harley jacket, boots, old jeans?"

"Can do."

She gave Raul her hotel address and thanked him. When she hung up the phone, she felt a strange exhilaration as she kindled her tiny ember of a plan. She dialed another California number.

"Fallon Camera," came a sleepy voice on the other end.

"Joe? This is Aubrey Fairbanks."

"Ah, the princess who fled."

"Escaped is more like it. How are you, Joe?"

"Overworked, underpaid, stressed-out, horny. Shall I go on? Can you help?"

"No, but it's good to know you haven't changed." Aubrey pictured the ponytailed, goateed, reclusive photography wizard in his studio amid his pother of cameras, lights, tripods, umbrellas, cables, and backdrops. Eight-thirty—he'd be alone. Slumped in a chair sipping morning coffee. She got right to business. "I could use a favor."

"Now there's something different."

"Hey," Aubrey said. "Seems to me I helped you along the road to success a time or two. Way back when."

"Shooting glamours of you bumped me from the depths of the unknown to the pinnacle of photographic acclaim on which I now perch," Fallon said with a sarcasm that mocked himself while adulating Aubrey. "I concede, dearie, I owe you. So what do you need?"

"I need a camera. A video camera."

"No K-Mart near by?"

"It's got to be hidden in a purse or something so I can carry it and use it without it being seen."

"I've been working with celebs long enough to know when not to ask why."

"Thanks."

"Disguised video camera. No problem."

"The smaller the better. And the bag or whatever has to be appropriate for a tough, biker-type woman."

"Kinky."

She gave Fallon her address.

"Aubrey," Fallon said, "this clandestine stuff can get people riled. I don't want to read in the paper about anything bad happening to you."

Fallon's words buzzed in her head all afternoon, but she kept working her plan. "I'll be goddamned if I'm going to sit on the sidelines for this game."

●　●　●

Kent waited for Rodman. He paced like a chained-up dog, ran his finger along a windowsill in his animal hospital reception room, rolled the dust between his fingertips, then flipped it off. He studied a faded pen and ink reprint of a famous animal scene one of his veterinary suppliers had sent him years ago. Waiting was the worst. Now cats—*they* were waiters. They had patience, sublime self-control. He looked over at Aubrey and Stef sitting along one wall, conversing in low tones. They were cats.

He hated the quarrel that raged between Aubrey and him. He could tell it made her uncomfortable too. She sneaked sidelong glances at him and forced her conversation with Stef to fill any awkward silence. Not that she'd admit it.

Only Merrill seemed to be himself. Like Kent, he was a dog. A bulldog. He paced back and forth across the room, stopping occasionally to criticize the stuffiness or to complain about barking on the other side of the thin wall. "I feel like we're a bunch of illegals huddled in some truck, trying to dodge the border patrol."

"Sit down, Merrill. You're making everyone else nervous," Stef said.

"Not a chance. Every time I sit in one of those chairs I get covered in animal hair."

"It's not that bad."

"It is too. He bent over and snatched a tumbleweed of fur off the floor as it rolled by. "Look at this stuff."

"Sit down!" Stef said more forcefully. "Your squirming won't get Rodman here any faster. It just makes everyone else more edgy."

Merrill made a big production of beating the hair off a chair with his handkerchief, and sitting.

Kent was too distracted by Aubrey's shunning to care about Merrill. The closest thing to communicating with her had been through Stef, but Aubrey had reluctantly accepted a backstage role during the raid. He was thankful for that.

Merrill's irritability surfaced again. "You two have become quite cozy, haven't you? It wasn't that long ago you'd have torn out each other's throats. One trying to demolish the other's business, and all."

Stef wasn't about to take the bait. "Merrill, you've got to be one of the most hardheaded people I've ever met. Aubrey and I have agreed to disagree on one issue. That doesn't mean we can't have a civil conversation. For Pete's sake, ease up."

"I won't ease up till this whole thing is over."

Everyone breathed a sigh of relief when the door pushed open and Dan Rodman ducked through it. "Thanks for parking out back, everybody. And you, Merrill, for not bringing a squad car. I'd hate to have my cover blown at this late date. Some pit man could be cruising by, see my truck mixed up with a police car and a bunch of do-gooders, and"—he snapped his fingers—"we're screwed. Just like that. It can happen in a small town."

"We know. We live in a small town," Merrill said with an edge on his voice.

"Anyway," Rodman said, "we got the news we've all been waiting for. It's going down tonight."

Kent thumped a cardboard cutout of a horrified flea that was screaming the name of some pet shampoo. "They don't give much notice."

"That's how they do it," Rodman said. "The organizers know the exact time. Everybody else just gets some general idea of when to be ready. Then, they're told to hang tight."

"I know, I know," Kent said. "It still burns me."

"So where is it?" Merrill asked.

They all stiffened as Rodman's Adam's apple rose and fell. "That's part of the problem."

"There's a problem. Why am I not surprised?" Merrill said.

"Well, kind of. Turns out ol' May-May is a little smarter than we gave him credit for."

"I find that hard to believe," Kent said.

Rodman took a seat without looking for dog hair. "Last night I was at Kolbie's Tavern. May-May spread the word; the fight is to be on the Indian reservation." He paused to let them mull that over.

It took a second for the four listeners to comprehend.

"Oh, man. Good move, May-May," Kent said with genuine admiration.

Aubrey forgot their stalemate. "What's the big deal?"

"The reservation is off limits to all law enforcement except tribal police. Technically, it's not even part of the United States," Kent said.

Rodman nodded. "You got it."

"That sneaky son of a bitch," Aubrey said. "That *sneaky* son of a bitch."

Merrill moved into his policeman mode. "Where on the reservation? It's a big place."

"That's the second problem. We don't know just where. Yet. But as we speak, there's a pile of state troopers checking out likely places. Over the years, they've gotten a pretty good idea what's what on the reservation."

"I thought our police couldn't go on the reservation," Aubrey said.

"They can't *officially*. But—just by coincidence, you understand—a lot of policemen decided to go rabbit hunting today…on the reservation." Rodman hunched his shoulders feigning innocence. Another pause. "With radios and stuff."

"The official line," Kent said, "is the agencies involved are working like hell to get permission from the tribal council to enter."

"That's right. And they better get it before time for the raid."

"What do we do in the meantime?" Stef asked.

"For your part, Stef, I'd suggest you post a lot of extra guards at your plant tonight. They may try to create another diversion."

The muscles in her jaw knotted. "I'll walk the place myself."

Rodman turned to Aubrey. "Thank you and the others at FOAM for all the help you've given us to this point. We could not have done it without you. If you stay close to a phone, I'll see that you are informed every step of the way. That's a personal promise."

Aubrey returned an unreadable look.

"Kent. You are the official veterinarian. We'll want you to confirm the condition of the dogs and, if any need to be treated, do that. Merrill, you are the local police agency…which leads me to problem number three."

"Just how many problems have you got?" Merrill said.

"The FBI is getting cold feet. Turns out they don't have a cooperative agreement with the USDA, so their lawyers tell them they may be on shaky ground."

"Meaning what?"

"Meaning technically the USDA is the agency responsible for enforcement of the Animal Welfare Act—which is what animal cruelty cases fall under. They are the lead agency. If USDA and the FBI don't have an official agreement to work together, defense lawyers will have a heyday with FBI involvement."

"Great time to find out there's no such agreement."

"Hey, Merrill. How long have you worked in law enforcement? You know how it goes."

"True."

Rodman pointed a finger at him. "So, it's your boys, the county and state police, and us USAPC agents. All told that makes about fifty units to hit the scene. Plus any tribal help."

"Fifty units!" Stef shook her head. "Amazing."

"If you can find the spot," Merrill said.

"We'll find it, all right. The hard part is going to be getting permission to run all those cops onto the reservation."

Suddenly, Kent agreed with Merrill's assessment of the stuffy room. He loosened his collar. "What's the actual plan for the raid?"

"That will depend on the site, but basically we will try to surround it then hit it hard and fast."

"SWAT team stuff?"

Rodman nodded. "Full gear. Body armor and all. Kent, you probably don't have any."

"I can fix him up," Merrill said before Kent could answer.

"Good," Rodman said. "Remember, I'll be on the inside, hopefully. So watch where you are shooting if it comes to that. I'm skinny, but I'm still a pretty big target."

Nobody laughed.

As Rodman pulled on his cap, indicating that the meeting was over, Kent asked, "What time of day do the fights start?"

"They won't announce that till a few hours beforehand. Usually it all begins in the evening, around dusk. We just want things to get underway enough that we have definite proof that they gathered to fight pit bulls. The longer it goes, the more dangerous it gets because of the booze and drugs. You guys stay at the police station, and I'll get word to you as soon as they give a time." He turned to Aubrey again. "When the place is secure, I'll give you a call. I'll make sure you and FOAM get a good head start on the press. So be ready."

Stef gave Aubrey a there-that-should-work-out smile.

Rodman looked around the room. "Any more questions?" No one spoke. He turned to Kent. "Then I'll need another bottle of penicillin before I go. Just to make it look good."

CHAPTER 27

AUBREY TWISTED HER BLACK MANE INTO A TIGHT
knot on the back of her head and covered it with the blond wig that
had arrived via Federal Express from Raul Pentes. She studied her
reflection in the hotel mirror. Her eyes widened at the transforma-
tion. Even back when she was acting, it had amazed her how wigs
changed a person's appearance.

No way would May-May recognize her. He'd only seen her up
close one time. That was in the darkness of the Groggery, and he had
been cockeyed drunk, to boot.

She shook the golden tresses onto her shoulders, slid on a pair
of rose-lensed glasses, and then turned slowly. She felt the motorcycle jacket's oiled hide and shuddered. She was actually wearing the
skin of an animal. This once. The outfit was perfect.

She lifted the crumpled drawstring purse from the bed and
admired it again. Alternate smooth leather and suede patches covered its black surface. Fallon was a genius. Even looking closely, she
could not tell which patch hid the video camera lens.

She took the nickel-size electronic wafer that was the remote
control, reviewed the location of its various function buttons, and
slipped it into her jacket pocket. She took a deep breath, released it
slowly, and reminded herself that the whole hideous affair would be
history in a few hours.

● ● ●

Testosterone gushed like toilets flushing, pouring into the bloodstream of every man in the place, when Aubrey stepped into Kolbie's Tavern. Two dozen pairs of eyes reflected all nature of lewd thought as they stared at the sleek motorcycle mama. She maneuvered to the bar like a Harley through heavy traffic. Instantly, Jerry was across from her.

"I'll have a Southern Comf—" She caught herself midsentence. "Gimme a Coors."

Disappointed, Jerry's expression sank to its usual blandness.

"I've got that one, Jerry."

Aubrey turned toward the voice and found herself staring dead-on at May-May's bearded hulk near the end of the bar. It was like a kick in the stomach. She stifled a grunt and gave him a flat biker smile— tight lipped, no teeth. He returned a schoolboy grin and for a second her fear turned to nausea. As casually as she could, she scanned the room, searching the blue haze for Rodman. No luck. She turned back to May-May.

"What's your name?"

"Maylon. Folks call me May-May." He seemed grateful for a distraction. The interminable wait for the go-ahead call, Aubrey guessed.

"Thanks for the beer, May-May," she said, toasting him with it.

"You're welcome, ma'am."

"Ma'am? That would be my mother. I'm Tina."

"Okay, Tina," May-May said. He stared at her openly, his dark eyes drifting slowly from her face down to her motorcycle boots. "You from around here?"

"Nope."

He tugged at his beard. "You work around here?"

"Not yet."

"Where you from?"

She shrugged. "A lot of places. Albany last."

May-May cocked his head, continued to study Aubrey-cum-Tina. "You sorta look familiar."

Aubrey's heart beat like it would fracture her ribs. She pushed out a weak laugh and shook her head so that the bangs of her wig fell to conceal more. She braced her elbow on the bar and distorted her face with the heel of her hand. "I don't know how I would be." A rough woman peeved at such a callus inspection.

Within minutes, several other men found excuses to congregate at the bar. May-May shifted, keeping himself between Aubrey and the newcomers. A bantam guarding his new hen.

"What you boys up to tonight?" she asked. "Just gonna hang around and make Mr. Kolbie rich?"

May-May said, "Hell. Any other night we might think about doing just that, but not tonight."

"Oh, yeah? What's so special about tonight?"

"We're gonna make *ourselves* rich, not Kolbie."

Aubrey looked unimpressed. "Really? How's that?"

"Gambling."

"Shit. Nobody gets rich gambling."

May-May set his bottle down hard on the bar. "They do if they got the inside track on what dog's gonna win."

"What's dogs got to do with anything?"

"That's what we bet on."

Aubrey gave him a confused look. "Dogs? Like racing?"

"No, not racing," May-May said. "Fighting."

"I don't get it."

"We bet on dogfights. Pit bulls. To see which one can take the other."

"Sounds kinda weird to me."

"It's exciting, watching them go at it, and all. Man, how they do chew each other up. Especially when you train them yourself." May-May paused, relishing the thought. "It's a good feeling watching them fight till they can't go no more, just because they got loyalty to you. Makes a fella feel like he's right out there fightin' with his dog."

Aubrey reeled with revulsion but willed herself to stay in character. "You mean you guys train dogs to fight each other?"

"Not just any dogs. Pit bulls. They're the best fighters, and we fight ours against ones from all over the US."

"Well, that I'd have to see to believe."

"Matter of fact, we got a really big fight going tonight."

At that moment, the pay phone rang, and all conversation ceased as Jerry picked up the receiver.

"May-May, it's for you."

"Excuse me, Tina. This may be the call we've been waitin' for." May-May radiated self-importance as he swaggered to the phone and turned to the wall, guarding his privacy.

The crowd waited, anxiously staring at May-May's meaty shoulders and listening to his mumbling. After a brief conversation, he carefully replaced the phone on its hook, turned back to the crowd, and beamed a triumphant smile.

Preserving the moment, May-May offered no explanation of the call. He stepped back to the bar and downed half a beer.

"Come on, May-May," someone in the crowd prodded. "Was that the word?"

May-May let silence hold the room for a few seconds more and then said, "It was the call we've been waiting for, all right."

"What did the guy say?"

"Said I could tell you the plan me and him set up if I wanted to."

The crowd began firing questions like duck hunters opening up on a flock. Aubrey displayed a half-interested gaze.

"Is the fight on?" a ruddy-faced man in back asked.

"Yep."

"When?"

"When we all get there."

"Did he tell you where?"

May-May scowled. "I picked where!"

A version of "Then let's get going!" came from several spots in the crowd at once.

"Just hold on a minute." May-May held up his hands. "We gotta make sure nobody follows us."

"How do we do that?"

Like a kindergarten teacher, May-May said to his class, "We're gonna have a convoy. Make sure you take your gambling money and load up."

A cheer rose.

"Get your CBs turned on too." He yelled a frequency to the dispersing crowd. "I'll lead!"

Aubrey put on the face of a little girl who had just been left out of a game of jump rope. She sat quietly against the bar as if expecting the crowd to leave without her.

May-May cleared his throat to get her attention. Stuck out his chest. The bantam rooster again.

She turned sad eyes toward him.

"You want to ride along with me?"

Aubrey fluttered her lashes. "With you? To the dogfight? I'd love to." She grabbed her crumpled leather bag and headed from the bar with the top cock in the barnyard.

May-May's jacked-up pickup was polished so deep she could see her reflection even by the sparse light of Kolbie's parking lot. The mammoth truck must have sucked May-May dry of every penny he didn't spend on dogs and drugs.

She reached up to open the door. It swung almost waist high. If it had not been for the chrome running board, she would have needed a ladder. She pulled herself up onto the seat and felt May-May's clothes-stripping stare appraising her tight jeans.

"I swear I've seen you before." May-May searched for the connection that eluded him.

"Oh, Jesus. We going through that again?"

She sat close to May-May, hoping the tight angle would make it harder for him to study her, as the convoy snaked through the night. She felt his arm brush against her each time he reached for controls. She wanted to scream.

She noticed another pickup to the right, where the highway teed with a dirt road. As they approached, May-May reached down and blinked his lights off then back on. The other truck reciprocated.

"He's one of us," May-May said. "We got a few spotters out just to make sure there's no tagalongs. This fight tonight is for the national championship. First time it's ever been held in the east. We don't want any mess-ups."

"National championship? Must be some important people coming."

May-May gave a grunt to indicate that was an understatement. "Some real big guys. Office types who run their own businesses and stuff. I'll tell you, just 'cause you ain't never heard of dogfightin' don't mean it ain't happenin'. I've gone to some huge fights out west and down south. A lot of rich guys are into it. You'll see tonight."

A voice crackled over the CB. May-May took his mike and signaled back that all was well.

"I'll be damned," he said, dropping the mike into Aubrey's lap. "We just went by another spotter, and I didn't even see him."

On country roads lit only by headlights, it was impossible for Aubrey to tell where they were going. May-May led the convoy onto progressively narrower, more primitive roads.

They passed another spotter, and May-May said, "I guess I better give him a call on the CB." His tone was almost a warning.

Keeping his eyes on the road, he slid his hand off the wheel and into Aubrey's lap, where he had dropped the mike. He groped between her thighs.

Aubrey stiffened, but willed herself not to move.

May-May's hand slid along her upper legs, ignored the tangle of spiraled cord, and came to rest flat and firm on the zipper of her jeans.

She tightened her throat to stifle the scream. Shut her eyes. Her lack of resistance was tantamount to permission as far as May-May was concerned. "Maybe we should pull over for a little while. Let these others go ahead."

Aubrey grabbed his wrist and wedged his hand back up onto the wheel. "There'll be time for that later. Right now you're in charge. You got to get everybody to the fight."

As she repelled May-May's exploring hand, her elbow struck a metallic bulge high on the man's right hip. The shock of being so close to a gun drained her of blood.

The truck continued deeper into the solitude of the rural night until finally May-May turned it onto a rutty dirt road. They lurched and pitched for half a mile back into the forest and pulled to a halt in front of a gigantic pole barn.

"We're here."

Aubrey squinted into the dark. "Where's here?"

"This is the lumber storage building for a sawmill." He pointed into the woods. "Back down along the creek is the mill where they do the sawing. You can't see it from here. The Indians don't use it much anymore."

"Indians?"

"Yeah. We're on the reservation."

"Big building."

"We're going to need it for the crowd tonight."

Other vehicles from the convoy began sliding into a hastily arranged parking area. As occupants disembarked, they joked raucously. Some began removing pit bulls from crates. Some began assembling portable washstands and stacking plastic barrels of water. All was done with the methodical efficiency of an experienced team.

As they worked, a second convoy arrived. This group included more women and children than the first.

Aubrey was genuinely impressed. "Wow! I guess there are lots of people."

"And there's a couple more groups to come. There'll be a record crowd. See all the campers and RVs? Those folks've come a long way."

She pulled the strap of her handbag onto her shoulder, aimed the patchwork at a mammoth motor home, and touched the remote in her pocket. She felt a tiny whir as she panned the vehicle's length to include its California license plate.

People with expensive rigs and wearing upscale apparel mixed boisterously with people in tired-looking pickups and tattered work clothes. She surveyed the burgeoning crowd for Dan Rodman without finding him and was soon distracted by the strange activities around her.

A middle-aged man and two children bolted together a washstand. "What are they doing?"

"Getting ready to wash their dogs."

"Kinda late for grooming, isn't it?"

"Not grooming," May-May said, amused by her ignorance. "It's part of the rules. All dogs get a bath in skim milk before they fight."

"Skim milk?"

"Yep. It keeps anybody from cheating."

"How's that?"

"Some handlers try to put poison on their dog's skin. Then when the other dog bites him, he gets paralyzed."

Aubrey grimaced. "You're kidding."

"No, I'm not. Dogfighters call it a 'rub.' Usually it's nicotine. And if you get caught using one, you're in sorry shape."

"So why milk?"

"Milk neutralizes it," May-May said authoritatively. "And each handler gets the right to smell the other dog's skin just to be sure."

"Imagine that." She touched the remote control again. "What some people won't do to win."

"Money talks. Come on. I'll take you inside?"

She let May-May lead the way into the pole barn. It had been cleared of lumber. The entire floor was covered with a thick layer of sawdust that damped the noise and freshened the air. The room was cavernous. A row of incandescent bulbs shed sparse yellow light around the perimeter behind professional-looking bleachers. High on the center rafters was a bank of fluorescent lights casting a painfully white glow onto a twelve-foot-square fighting pit. An ethereal greenish cast reflected from the carpet that lined it and boiled up over its two-foot walls.

"Looks like somebody did a lot of work to get ready."

May-May scanned the full 360 degrees and got misty. "Yeah. Nothin' good in life comes easy."

The room stirred with activity. A heavyset fellow in bib overalls and a snow-white beard manned a tote board and barked orders to a crew that was taking bets at a furious pace. High school boys wearing T-shirts boasting cynical slogans flirted with girls in tattered jeans while they set up grills for hot dogs and hamburgers. Two men arranged taps in front of a pyramid of silver kegs.

At a long ringside table, a group of dogfighting aficionados sat in earnest discussion. A two-foot-tall bronze statue of a pair of pit bulls locked in mortal combat stood in the middle of the table.

May-May saw Aubrey staring at it. "That's the National Dogfight Championship trophy. Goes to the owner of the top dog."

Aubrey guessed the men were judges and that the statue weighed close to fifty pounds. She had it on tape along with May-May's candid description. "It's ugly, but it's beautiful."

"To a dogfighter, there's nothing ugly about it."

May-May was distracted by the approach of a stocky man with an expensive suit and rabid eyes. He gave Aubrey a smile that made her recoil and then stuck out a hand to May-May. "Well, Mr. New York," he said, "looks like we finally made it."

May-May beamed and pumped the hand. "Sure does. It sure does, Mr. Ross."

"All is going well at your end, I take it."

"Not a hitch. I guess we can finally relax."

"A little, but don't let your guard down."

May-May pointed to the judge's table. "How are things going over there?"

"Just a little hassle about the scratch line. One of them went and measured it. Five foot ten instead of six feet. Big deal." He rolled his eyes, indicating he'd been through such matters before. "You know these judges. A bunch of prima donnas. Always have to find something wrong to make themselves important." He glanced at the tough blond girl with May-May. "Who's your friend?"

May-May remembered his woman and slid his arm around her, pulling her in. "This here is Tina," he said. "Tina, meet Mr. Lester Ross." He made a sweeping gesture. "Mr. Ross is the one that mostly made this happen." He winked at Ross. "With the help of a few of his friends."

Ross reached up and patted May-May's shoulder like a good dog. "That's right, May-May. I owe you a lot." He turned back to Aubrey and slowly ran his eyes over her.

"She's a pretty thing, May-May." As if it was good-natured teasing, he said, "When you're done with her, I'll take her."

"No, I think I'll keep her."

Aubrey's heart was pumping glue. She managed to mix a coy, flattered look with her biker smile and tried to think of a way to veer the conversation. To her utmost relief, a voice from the direction of the judge's table beckoned Ross.

"Gotta run," he said. He wheeled around and headed for the table.

"Who was that guy, again?" Aubrey asked, able to breathe and delighted she had tape rolling.

"He's the main organizer. Lester Ross is his name. Came all the way from Austin, Texas."

"Seems pretty high and mighty to me."

May-May snorted a laugh. "Lester may be a pain sometimes, but we're sure glad he's here. As a matter of fact, he's working to see that dogfighting becomes a big sport in America."

As they walked away from the ring, she asked, "What's a scratch line?"

"It's where the dogs have to cross to know if they're still game. You see, when one dog is wore out, the ref calls time. Then the handler has three minutes to work on his dog and get him ready to go back in. When they put him back in, if he doesn't charge at least to the scratch line, he's out."

"A few inches make a difference?"

"Rules is rules."

The bleachers were starting to fill up. Beer was flowing, and the crowd sounded more and more eager to get things underway.

"I'm going to have to leave you for a while, Tina," May-May said. "The fights are about ready to start, and I'm the official referee."

Aubrey tried to look impressed.

With a hand in the small of her back, he guided her to a front-row seat. "Now, from here you'll get a good view of everything. Believe me, it'll be a night to remember."

Aubrey nodded weakly and took her seat.

"Don't worry," May-May said. "When the fight's all done, you and me can go out and celebrate. Just the two of us."

May-May strutted away. Aubrey scanned the crowd for Rodman.

CHAPTER 28

A WOMAN WITH A SKELETAL FACE, SPANISH-moss hair, and a witless southern drawl bounced excitedly in her seat next to Aubrey. "Looky there. They's gettin' ready to start!"

Aubrey felt her intestines knot as it dawned on her that even if Kent and Merrill showed up and stopped the fight once it started, she was about to witness one of the ultimate manifestations of man's brutality to animals.

The crowd hushed as Lester Ross stepped to the center of the ring, hands held high.

Aubrey positioned her purse in her lap and touched the remote.

Ross's tone was jubilant, pitched to work his audience into a frenzy. "Welcome, everybody, to Jefferson, New York, and the National Dogfighting Convention!"

The crowd roared.

"Most of you know me. My name is Lester Ross, and as commissioner of this crazy mob, I'm your emcee for tonight."

More cheers.

"At this time, I would like you all to direct your attention to the table on my right. Sitting there are our five esteemed judges. Take a bow, boys."

A murmur of appreciation buzzed through the crowd, and Ross let it hold. After a moment, and with a booming voice, he said, "And on that table you can see for yourself the championship trophy our winner will be taking home. Ain't it a beauty?"

The noise forced Ross to use hand-signals to beckon May-May, who was in ringside darkness, but stepped proudly to center ring. They let the din continue. When it finally began to ebb, Ross silenced it with lifted hands.

"With me here is Maylon Mays, our host in New York and referee for tonight. At this time, I'd like to turn the show over to him. Let's hear it for all his efforts!"

May-May did his bantam-in-a-barnyard thing again. "We New Yorkers are real proud to be the hosts this year, and we think we put together a real exciting bunch of fights for you tonight." He held up a single sheet of paper. "Everybody got a card?"

Spectators waved their programs.

"Then let's get on with it! Tonight's first match is Mike Fink, a thirty-eight-pound black owned and handled by Bucky Reynolds from Columbus, Ohio, against a thirty-six-pound brindle called Heaven Help Ya from Little Rock, Arkansas. He's owned by Maurice Jenkins and trained by Skip Taylor. Both are two-year-olds and undefeated champions in their regions." May-May spoke into the dim light just outside the ring. "Boys, bring out the scale."

Two men pushed into view a wooden device that resembled a miniature gallows.

Aubrey swooned with the relief of a mother who just located her missing child when she recognized one of the men as Rodman. She reminded herself that he did not expect her to be there. He would not recognize her in her makeup and wig.

May-May instructed the handlers in a voice that rang throughout the building. "Okay, men. Hang your dogs."

Each contestant was suspended by a strap at the end of the steelyard. All five judges took a perfunctory glance at it to verify the animal's weight.

"You guys can check for a rub." May-May said to each handler.

A mocking voice in the crowd shouted, "No sniffing under his tail, Skip."

Skip Taylor was a sixty-year-old woodchuck with weathered skin and crisp blue bib overalls, new for the occasion. His eyes flashed back and forth from May-May to Maurice Jenkins, his dog's owner. He vibrated with nervous energy just at the prospect of being at the nationals. The crowd laughed and jeered. He waved off his right to check the black dog's skin.

The opposing handler was Bucky Reynolds. Midtwenties urbanite. Sleeveless sweatshirt, fingerless gloves. Tattoos of barbed wire surrounded his melon-size biceps. He had metallic-red hair and dead eyes. He sneered back at the crowd, bent down, and buried his face into Heaven Help Ya's coat. He stroked the dog from ears to tail, his fingers deep in the fur, then touched his fingertips to his tongue. He worked the taste around in his mouth. Nodded approval to May-May. "Nothing on him but milk."

"All right, then. Let's roll 'em out!" May-May said.

The crowd went into hysterics. Aubrey went into tetany.

The handlers grabbed their dogs by the scruff using both hands. Each gladiator's muzzle was directed into his corner so that the dog could not see his opponent.

"Face your dogs!" May-May said.

Both men spun their dogs to the center. The dogs instantly fixed on each other. Their conditioned response to annihilate any other animal in the ring forced all else from their minds. They strained forward with such strength the men could barely hold them.

"Release your dogs!"

Aubrey was paralyzed by the scene that unfolded a few feet in front of her. The dogs did not growl or bark. Like silent missiles of flesh and blood, each rushed at his adversary and simultaneously leaped high. Their chests collided. Gnashing wildly in the air, they scrambled for a bite hold, clawing with their front feet to offset their opponent.

The black dog managed a grip on the brindle's ear and, clamping his teeth like a steel-jawed trap, shook it violently. The brindle whined almost inaudibly while his ear tore away from his head, leaving a bloody pulp. He spun under the black dog, took a mouthful of soft underbelly, and held. Blood oozed from between his lips. The black twisted, got a hind leg, and sank enamel spikes to bone. The scraping sound sent moans throughout the crowd.

Skip Taylor knelt inches from his dog, ignoring the blood splattering his new overalls. "Shake his guts out."

"Attaboy, Mike," Bucky said, pounding a clenched fist onto the mat. "You're hurtin' him bad."

The stalemate ran for ten minutes before the crowd grew bored.

"Parting stick!" someone shouted.

"Start 'em over!" another person said.

May-May recognized the crowd's dissatisfaction and reached for the canoe paddle that served as a parting stick. He drove it between the dogs and levered hard.

"Corner your dogs, men!" he said. "Three minutes."

Each man corralled his dog against the plywood wall and sponged cold water, frantically trying to revive his contestant. In exactly three minutes, they were released into battle again.

Aubrey's insides burned. Acid rose to the back of her throat as the fight waxed and waned. One dog dominated, then the other, for almost half an hour.

Where was Kent? What was keeping them?

She distracted herself by watching Rodman stare at the spectacle. Disdain blanketed his face. Suddenly, for no apparent reason, he looked up. His eyes caught hers before she could turn away. A flicker of recognition flashed across his face, then surprise, then a mix of fear and anger.

She stared back at him, not knowing what else to do.

His face twisted into a question and he mouthed, "What the...?" Then dropped it abruptly as May-May slogged around the ring now drenched with blood, urine, and saliva, too close for them to signal. Rodman cut his eyes back and forth from Aubrey to May-May, weighing his options.

The black dog had his opponent's throat in a crushing grip. The blood poured around his mouth and the brindle's breathing turned to bubbles. In agony, the courageous warrior looked at his handler, struggled vainly a moment more, then rolled back his eyes and slowly collapsed into the slime.

"That's a turn!" Bucky shouted, pointing with a bare finger extended from his glove. "He turned."

Bettors backing Mike Fink cheered. Those with bets on Heaven Help Ya snarled oaths of disgust. May-May held back the black dog with his stick.

"Okay," May-May said to Skip Taylor, "you've got three minutes. If he don't scratch, he's out."

Bucky dragged Mike Fink back to his corner and watched with confidence as old Skip, wild-eyed and sputtering incoherently, struggled to revive his dog.

Heaven Help Ya was still gasping for breath when May-May said, "Three minutes. Face your dogs!" The dog's eyes were glazed. He needed assistance from Skip just to stand.

Bucky was all smiles.

"Let him go!" May-May said.

By sheer instinct, Heaven Help Ya made one last, powerful lunge toward Mike Fink and landed unconscious.

"He's out!" May-May said.

Skip kicked his lifeless dog hard, skidding him through the muck. "You worthless son of a bitch!" He lifted him by a fold of skin and, grunting loudly, hurled him over the plywood, out of the ring.

Heaven Help Ya landed with a nauseating thud at Aubrey's feet. She retched hard and covered her mouth. She tried to stand, but her knees buckled. She sank back into her seat with a nasally moan. She cast her eyes around the arena, searching for Rodman. At that second, she saw something a thousand times more horrifying than the dead dog at her feet— May-May was glaring at her. His eyes flashed a furious, terrifying glint of recognition.

Aubrey willed her legs to carry her. Edged her way along the bleachers. When she looked back, May-May was gone. She allowed herself to breathe again, ducked around behind the seats, and headed for the door. She was reaching for the latch when a grasp on her arm, as firm as any pit bull's jaw, stopped her. She whirled and found herself looking at Rodman's angry face. Keeping a tight grip, he reached over and lifted her wig just enough to confirm his suspicions.

"What the hell are you doing here?" he asked, his face just inches from hers.

Aubrey struggled to free herself.

Rodman shook her hard enough that her teeth snapped together. "Lady, you are in deep shit!"

A voice came from behind them. "Who you got there, Bo?"

It was May-May, and his sarcastic sneer made it perfectly clear he knew the answer to his own question.

Rodman spun Aubrey around to give May-May a better look. "Why, I done caught me one of them infiltrators you was warning me about."

May-May stepped close, eyeing Aubrey. "You know who she is?"

"This is the FOAM woman! Can't you tell?"

"By Jesus, I think you're right, Mr. Bo-Bo."

May-May's hand darted toward Aubrey's head. He grabbed a handful of blond hair and yanked hard enough that real hair would have come out. The wig flew, and Aubrey's black hair fell loose.

She twisted hard to break away, but Rodman's grip held. She swung a blow toward May-May's bearded face, but he stopped it midflight, like catching a baseball.

"Pretty feisty, ain't you, *Tina*," he said. "Yep, Bo. You're right. Good thing you was payin' attention. You saved me from looking real stupid, boy."

He grabbed Aubrey by the collar of her leather jacket and wrenched her out of Rodman's grip. He shook her harder than Rodman had.

"So, what are we gonna do with you?"

"I'll get rid of her for you, May-May," Rodman said.

May-May laughed. "I bet you'd like that. No. I brought her. I'll take care of her myself."

Rodman fought to keep himself in his role. He sent up a quick prayer that Aubrey would have the presence of mind to keep his identity secret.

"What you gonna do with her?"

With one hand, May-May lifted Aubrey the way he'd lift his pit bull pups. With his other, he grabbed her shirt at the throat and yanked it, sending buttons flying. He leered at her chest and laughed as she clutched the jacket's lapels together with her fists.

"First, I'm going to take her out back and have some fun. Then I'm going to kill her."

Before May-May could react, Aubrey's right hand came off her jacket and shot to the big man's face, nails extended. Quick as a cat, she ripped four long gouges across his eyes and nose.

May-May cursed loudly, covered his burning skin with his free hand. But he did not let go of her. "A *lot* of fun!"

"You'll have to kill me before you do!"

May-May gave a short laugh, reared back, and slapped Aubrey hard across the face. Her knees buckled. "We'll see."

Rodman sucked in a deep breath, harnessed every repressed ounce of hatred he held for May-May into his balled fist, and braced to swing at the center of his former boss's face.

CHAPTER 29

MERRILL'S UNIT WAS THIRD IN THE QUEUE OF headlights that slinked down the tree-hung road through the Indian reservation like a snake into a rat hole. Kent was in the passenger seat, Lucinda bolt upright in back. All eyes were fixed on the taillights that jostled in front. All pupils were dilated to the max.

With a move concealed from his brother, Kent slipped his hand into his coat pocket. His fingers touched the silky fibers of Aubrey's scarf. He had found it tied to the steering wheel of his truck earlier that afternoon, sometime between their meeting at his clinic and when he joined Merrill at the police station to await Rodman's call. She obviously wanted him to find it. He caressed it the way he'd done a dozen times already. He envisioned its colors without removing it from his pocket—maroon and green paisley, the one she wore the night they had dined at Stef's. The one he had longed for that night. It still held her scent. He wanted to hold it to his face, breathe her in again. He cut his eyes to his brother. Merrill wouldn't understand. Instead, he rolled it gently in his fingers.

He pushed his hand deeper into his pocket until he touched the tiny medallion that was attached to the scarf. It was the sort of tag any dog might have dangling from its collar, only gold. He envisioned its inscription:

My name is
KENT
I belong to
AUBREY FAIRBANKS
555–3409

"You keep your wits about you out there, Kent," Merrill said.

"Is that my brother worrying about me?"

"Damn right. This could get dangerous. Remember, our unit hits from the front. Straight up the road. Their spotters will be inside watching the fight by now, so they shouldn't be a problem. We go in after we get radio confirmation that the other units have the place surrounded, bust down the front door, and arrest the whole shittery."

Kent felt the stiff body armor under his jacket. "Is this bullet-proof stuff really necessary?"

"Goddamn right it's necessary!"

"Seems like a little overkill."

"*Kill* being the operative word there, brother."

Kent reached over the seat and stroked Lucinda. "You're going to have to guard the car, girl."

"I guess it's appropriate we have a dog accompanying us on a dogfight raid."

"Kinda like having a UN observer."

"Just make sure she stays in the car."

"She will."

Merrill brought the black-and-white to a halt behind the others. An officer emerged from the lead car and signaled for silence. Kent gave Lucinda a pat that signaled pleading would not win her the right to accompany her master this time. She sat quietly as the men emptied from their cars, closing doors softly.

The officer in charge pointed at a thick stand of pines and whispered tersely, "They're just on the other side of those trees. Stay down." He tapped his radio. "When the place is surrounded, I'll give the word, and we go in fast."

There was a burst of metallic clatter as agents racked shells into their weapons. Kent clutched the black bag of emergency medical supplies he and Sally had thrown together. The strike force ducked off the road into the protection of the pines.

Kent crouched in the dark, trying to convince himself that the danger was minimal. Dogfighters were mainly a bunch of scofflaws with no real intention of doing anyone harm. The body armor was just an extra precaution, the weapons for show. But dog men were gun nuts, and they'd be drunk by now. May-May had already killed Aaron and Tammy and torched Copithorn. His mouth felt like the pads of a dog's feet. He swallowed loud enough that Merrill heard.

"Take it easy there, brother. You let us bust through the door first. You'll be okay."

Kent was at the same time insulted and relieved at his brother's implication. He was deciding what reply would be appropriate when the radio chirped.

"There's our signal," Merrill said.

Instantly the others charged toward the pole barn at a dead run. Kent pushed through the underbrush with all his might to regain his position but was still behind. He could see other agents closing in from both sides and the back. A man washing his pit bull was swarmed by agents before he could utter a sound. Moonlit agents pointing shotguns skyward leaped from vehicle to vehicle in the parking lot looking for stragglers. A drunk who stood lilting back and forth, urinating against a massive maple, cursed irritably as he was smothered in bodies. Other agents crashed the door and flooded toward the arena.

"Police! You are all under arrest!" the lead officer barked through a bullhorn. "If you are seated, remain seated. If you are standing, lie face down on the floor. Put your hands on your head and do not move!"

Kent heard a dull, thudding rumble as dozens of guns and knives rained onto the floor, shed by owners trying to avoid weapons violations. People screamed. Others clambered over each other rushing for an exit.

He scanned the arena for Rodman. Saw nothing of the agent. Then he noticed panicked spectators tripping over a body as they stampeded. Rodman's lean frame was lying face down in the sawdust. His arms and legs were twisted the way limbs fall when there is no life. Kent pushed through the melee. He knelt over Rodman, braced his arms to shield against the churning crowd.

"Rodman!" he said, feeling the man's throat with his fingertips.

There was a low groan. Rodman drew his arms and legs in, raised himself to a sitting position, and shook his head to clear it. His eyes were glazed, a deep red bruise was forming on his cheek, and blood trickled from one nostril.

"Where are you hurt? Can you stand up?"

Rodman sat still, trying to fathom the chaos around him. He rubbed his cheek. In a fuzzy, drifting voice, he said, "I took a swing at May-May. Then a couple of guys jumped me."

Kent helped him to his feet. "We've got to get you out of here."

Rodman grabbed Kent's arm. "Aubrey is here."

"No. She's waiting at her hotel for your phone call. Remember? You need a doctor."

"No. She's not! She's here. I saw her. I *talked* to her." Rodman pushed up on his toes, using his height to search the crowd.

Kent scanned too. Rodman's tone sounded too sure to be the disoriented babble of a concussion victim. "Then where is she now?"

"May-May has her," Rodman said, still looking. "She had on a disguise. Blond hair, tough-girl clothes. He recognized her and grabbed her. That's why I had to hit him. The last thing I remember is May-May dragging Aubrey toward that door." He pointed to an inconspicuous walk-through door. Both men headed for it.

They pushed through into the dampness and dark outside. Before their eyes could adjust, a beam of light as bright as Kent's coon-hunting lantern blasted into their faces. Both men bridled back, squinting and shading their eyes with their hands.

"Stop where you are!" came a command voice. "Put your hands on your head." For the second time, Kent heard the slide action of a shotgun rack ominously. This time from behind the light.

"We're after one of the guys who may have escaped," Kent said and stepped toward the voice.

"Don't move a muscle!" came out of the darkness.

"We're with you!" Kent said. He wanted to be looking for Aubrey, not standing with his hands on his head.

Three men in midnight-blue SWAT team uniforms emerged into view. On their vests, in iridescent block letters, was the word POLICE. They kept their guns pointed at Kent and Rodman.

Rodman spoke for the first time. Slowly. Controlled. "I'm USAPC undercover agent Dan Rodman. This is Dr. Kent Stephenson, veterinarian assigned to this operation."

One officer extended his hand. "Show me some ID."

"I just told you, I'm undercover. I don't have any ID on me."

"Well, I do." Kent brought his hand down toward his wallet pocket but stopped abruptly as the officers ducked. Their guns took a more accurate bead on his chest.

"I said don't move!" the officer warned him again.

Another of the policemen spoke. "Sergeant, sir, that *is* Dr. Stephenson. I know him. He takes care of my father's cows."

The sergeant hesitated. "Are you sure?"

"Positive."

"Take a good look, and tell me again."

The baby-faced policeman stepped to within three feet of Kent. "Yes, sir, that's Dr. Stephenson."

"Put down your weapons, men," the sergeant said in an apologetic voice. "We had to be sure."

"Of course," Rodman said. "Did you see a big guy, heavyset with a beard, come through here? May have been holding onto a woman."

"No, you're the first ones we've seen."

"How far out are your perimeter people?"

"We *are* the perimeter people. "Our orders were to close in."

"May-May slipped through?" Kent asked.

Rodman gave the sergeant a questioning look.

"We sure didn't see him."

The sergeant and his men were instantly out of Kent's mind. He turned to Rodman. "Where is his truck?"

Rodman pointed toward one area of the parking lot. "Out there."

Kent took off in that direction at a dead run, Rodman followed.

Within minutes they located May-May's truck, popped the hood, and disabled it by yanking several ignition wires.

"Okay." Kent said. "We know he didn't take his truck, and he isn't going to take his truck. Where can he be?"

Rodman turned a 360, peering off into the darkness. "It's a big reservation."

"He's got Aubrey."

"There's woods in every direction. We don't have time to search the whole place!"

Frustrated, Kent jammed his hands into his pockets. One of his fingertips brushed against the metal collar tag with his name on it. He longed to tell Aubrey he loved her, that he was sorry he ever doubted her. He pulled her scarf from his pocket and held it to his face, drawing in her scent. He paused and then inhaled against the cloth again. The next second he was headed toward the hidden police cars at a dead run.

"Where are you going?" Rodman asked, chasing after him.

"Lucinda. We need Lucinda!"

By the time they reached the cruiser, Rodman's longer stride had brought the two men abreast.

"I knew there was a reason to bring her along." Kent waved the scarf for Rodman to see. "This is Aubrey's. She gave it to me. Lucinda can get her scent from it. She'll take us to Aubrey, I guarantee."

Agent Rodman accepted it as gospel since he could offer nothing better.

Kent opened the door, and Lucinda sprang out then circled happily around his legs. He thumped his chest with the flat of his hand. Immediately the big coonhound rose on her haunches and placed both front feet squarely on his chest. Kent held the scarf for her to smell. "Where's Aubrey? Where is she?"

Lucinda's eyes sparkled, her tail wagged furiously at her master's game.

"Go find Aubrey!"

Lucinda dropped to all fours and stared directly at Kent as her canine cognizance registered his alarm. She raised her muzzle and began casting in each direction. She drew the breeze across her sensitive olfactory lobes, and then began working her way toward the pole barn.

"She thinks Aubrey is inside," Rodman said.

Kent raised a hand to quiet him. "Let her work."

When Lucinda reached the parking area she dropped her nose to the pine-needle-covered ground and froze. For an instant she was a statue. Then like a released spring she shot into the woods singing her trailing bark.

Kent felt a mix of amazement, admiration, and hope. "She's got the trail!"

Both men tore after Lucinda, following her path along the mill creek. Branches, invisible in the darkness, clawed at their faces. Wet leaves on muddy banks forced their feet from under them. Kent cursed the heavy body armor strapped to his torso but struggled after Lucinda with the strength of a man afraid for someone he loved.

"There's the sawmill up ahead. I see a light," Rodman said.

Kent squinted into the dark and saw a single bare bulb sending pale-yellow rays through a window. He caught movement silhouetted by the light. With renewed strength he charged toward the sawmill.

"That's got to be them."

He saw the flash of a gun muzzle in the window before its report shattered the night sounds.

"My God! May-May shot Aubrey!"

He ran toward the light like a man possessed, screaming as he charged. When he was within a few feet of the door, it opened, and May-May's dark shadow filled it. Kent dug in his heels, but his momentum carried him forward until he was point blank in front of the same huge pistol May-May had aimed at him back at the farmhouse.

May-May's left eye was badly swollen and his nose deviated to the side. Kent remembered what Rodman had said about throwing a punch. There were four nasty, linear gouges running across May-May's eyes and nose.

May-May's voice sounded strangely sad, defeated. "Didn't I warn you I'd kill you if you got in my way?"

Kent held up his hands. "May-May, this is me, Kent, your brother."

"*Half* brother. As you and Merrill like to remind everybody."

"May-May, don't make a bad problem worse. If you kill me, you still won't get away. Put down the gun."

"It's too late. I ain't gonna go back to jail."

May-May raised the gun. The muscles in his forearm rippled when his finger tightened on the trigger. The muzzle flashed. The air went out of Kent's lungs as if a horse had kicked him in the chest. The impact drove him backward and onto the ground. He wanted desperately to renew the attack, but his limbs would not respond.

There was another gunshot. It came from behind him. Through blurred eyes, he saw May-May double over, curse, and then fall with a deadened thud. Kent lapsed into a surreal state of half consciousness.

He felt strangely detached yet numbingly afraid. He wanted to smile and cry, run and rest. He felt Rodman's arms sliding under him and carrying him into the mill house. He could hear the man's bass voice, now pitched with excitement.

"Hang on, partner. I gotcha."

Rodman set him in the light. He heard Aubrey crying—crying for him. Like music, it stirred him back to reality. He lifted his head while Rodman searched him for bullet wounds.

"My chest," Kent said through clenched teeth. But his attention was on Aubrey, tied, like Joan of Arc, to a support post in the middle of the room. He reached out for her. Her eyes were rimmed in white. Half cries, half screams poured from her throat, muffled by duct tape across her mouth. She thrashed her shoulders, trying to free her hands.

"It's a damn good thing you had that vest on, Kent. You'd be dead for sure," Rodman said.

"I told you my chest hurts!"

"That's what I'm telling you. It's bruised. The vest stopped the bullet. See?" Rodman held out a gray lead mushroom picked from Kent's shirt.

Aubrey struggled hard again.

"Untie her."

Rodman worked at the ropes. As she shook free, Aubrey ripped the gag from her mouth and pointed.

"Kent! Lucinda is over there in the corner. May-May shot her!"

How could he have forgotten Lucinda? That must have been May-May's first shot, the one he had thought was aimed at Aubrey. He dragged himself toward the blackness of the corner.

"She saved my life!" Aubrey said. "May-May had a knife right in my face. He said he was going to cut me. Lucinda came through the door and charged him. She knocked him down, but he pulled his gun and shot her!" Aubrey moved her lips as if speaking, but no more words came.

Kent found Lucinda lying on her side. She didn't move when he stroked her face. A dark pool of blood enlarged on the floor next to her chest. He could not tell if she was breathing. Frantically, he pulled her into the light. Frothy red bubbles oozed from in front of her shoulder.

"She's got an open chest wound! Her lungs are collapsed." He shoved Aubrey's scarf at Rodman. "Hold this over the wound. Push hard with the flat of your hand."

While Rodman plugged the wound, Aubrey stroked the lifeless hound and whispered words of encouragement.

Kent felt the dog's neck. "She's still got a pulse." He held her mouth shut and began blowing slow rhythmic breaths into Lucinda's nose. Each time they watched her chest inflate then deflate. After several breaths, he paused, hoping to see her chest rise on its own.

"Come on, Lucinda, honey. Breathe!" Aubrey said. "Take a breath."

Kent put his hand on Lucinda's ribs. He could barely feel a heartbeat. He lifted her lip— blue-gray membranes. The same terrifying pallor he'd seen so many times before, when an animal was about to die.

For several more minutes, he agonized over his best friend, wishing with all his heart that he could give her some of the life he had wasted. At the next pause, there was a minute movement of her diaphragm.

"That was a breath!" He resuscitated with renewed vigor. Another pause, another breath, until finally she was breathing on her own.

Aubrey started laughing while tears ran down her face.

Kent ripped off his coat, bulletproof vest, shirt, and T-shirt. "I'll make a better bandage with this shirt, and we can carry her to the car."

While Kent fashioned a pressure bandage, Aubrey knelt next to Lucinda, leaning over so that her cheek was pressed against Lucinda's velvet jowl. "How could I ever have been so wrong, girl?" Gently, she kissed her. "You've taught me more about animals than I ever thought possible. Stay with us. We need you."

Kent glanced up from his task, their eyes met. They did not need to speak.

Rodman used the jackets to make a stretcher, and within minutes they were racing to the car.

"What about him?" Aubrey asked as she stepped over May-May's body in the doorway.

"We'll send someone back for him," Rodman said. He nodded toward Lucinda. "She is more important."

By the time they reached the parking lot, the assault team was shoving the last of the dog men into paddy wagons.

Merrill commandeered an ambulance and helped load Lucinda. Kent called the dispatcher on Merrill's radio and gave instructions to alert the veterinary college.

"Have the emergency crew ready to receive a gunshot patient. An approximately ninety-pound coonhound with an open chest wound."

Rodman reached to close the ambulance's rear doors with Kent and Aubrey inside next to Lucinda.

"You're welcome to ride along with us," Kent said.

"Thanks," Rodman said, but shook his head.

"No," he said, savoring a thought. He rubbed the scar on the side of his face that had become so much a part of him that Kent no longer noticed. "I think I'm going to look up ol' Lester Ross and have a talk about old times. You know what I mean?"

Kent gave him a thumbs-up.

"You look after that dog!" Rodman said as he slammed the doors.

CHAPTER 30

KENT AND SALLY LIMITED MORNING APPOINT-
ments to must-sees only so they could get on the road in time for
eleven o'clock visiting hours at the veterinary college. The whole crew
came along. Kent, Aubrey, Barry, and Nathan took off in the lead car.
Merrill tailgated them with Rodman, Stef, and Sally. They all bubbled with the lighthearted camaraderie of those who had endured
battle and won.

Kent rubbed his chest gingerly, daydreamed out the windshield. The bruise on his sternum still hurt right down to the bone.
Aubrey had been horrified by the dinner plate–size patch of purple that emerged exactly over his heart. She'd been too put off by it
to make love. But desperation breeds ingenuity, and Kent wearing a
T-shirt had proved to be the solution.

Today the bruise felt better, especially after news from the vet
college that Lucinda was finally stable. It had been one hell of a week.

They entered the veterinary college hospital through double-
wide glass doors, paraded across a sky-lit expanse of polished ter-
razzo floor with stylized park benches along the walls. Most of them
were occupied by anxious clients. Some guarded pet carriers harbor-
ing feline loved ones. Others struggled to control dogs on leashes.

At a bustling reception desk, Kent gave his name to a young
woman who greeted him with a smile, hands poised on a keyboard,
ready to take admissions information. When she caught his name,

however, her hands withdrew from the keys. Her smile widened as she stood and nodded greetings to their group.

"You're here," she said, skirting her way around to their side of the counter. She let her eyes roll skyward and pointed in the same direction. "The higher-ups told us you'd be coming. I'm supposed to take you right on back. If you'll all follow me."

Kent smiled and nudged Sally, pointing out Merrill's obviously pleased reaction to VIP service.

The receptionist guided them into the intensive care unit. It smelled of cleanliness and glistened with state-of-the-art electronics. There was stainless steel everywhere.

A veterinary student looked up from the patient whose catheter she was adjusting. "Wow! Big group of visitors. You are all here to see Lucinda Stephenson, I take it?"

"That's right. I'm Kent Stephenson, her owner."

"Dr. Stephenson, right? They told us you are a veterinarian."

It was the first time in years that Kent felt proud to be a veterinarian. "That's right. I graduated from here before you were born." He waved at all of the hi-tech equipment. "Things certainly have changed."

"Techniques and equipment have changed, for sure, but that's all. We're still here trying to help the animals, just like you guys." Out of the corner of his eye, Kent saw Barry straighten, square his shoulders.

The young woman was polite and confident. He focused on her name tag. "You are...Marlene?"

"Yes. Sorry." She held out her hand and shook Kent's with a firm grip. "I'm a senior, on my ICU rotation." She scanned the group again. "Lucinda must be some special dog." There was genuine amazement in her voice.

"Why is that?"

"First she arrives in an ambulance, sirens blaring, in the middle of the night. The chief of surgery *and* the head of anesthesiology, not some lowly residents, are ready and waiting to handle her when she arrives. Now they're breaking the rules for visitors?"

Kent's eyebrows went up. "We're breaking the rules?"

"Usually it's a max of two people in ICU. No exceptions. Till now."

"I hope it's not a problem."

"Oh, it's no problem," Marlene said. "The dean called down a while ago, said you were coming. Some special dog, I'd say."

She led them to a strange contraption that looked like an oversized stainless steel cabinet with a glass front door. A green label cautioned OXYGEN. Crystalline tubing snaked from a suspended plastic bag through a port in the top, carrying fluids to the patient within. A perfect chorus of *ahhhhs* began as everyone recognized Lucinda.

She was on her side, mostly covered in blankets and bandages. She looked like she had lost twenty pounds. Her skin hung. The luster was gone from her coat.

They studied her, each entertaining thoughts of how near death she seemed. Then, from nowhere, a twinkle came into the hound's eyes, and as if to prove them all wrong, she began to wag just the tip of her tail.

Kent slipped one arm around Aubrey's waist and the other over Barry's shoulder.

"God, I love that dog!" Aubrey said, unabashed at her own revelation.

Marlene opened the glass panel. "You can pet her for a minute or two, that might cheer her up. Then she'll need her oxygen again."

"We've got to get you feeling better, girl," Barry told her as he fondled her ears. "Doc and I need our coon-hunting partner."

The whole group laughed at one another, embarrassed to be misty-eyed for a dog.

"Sweet Jesus!" Sally said. "Even Merrill's crying."

Merrill smeared his eyes with the back of his hand. "I always figured her to be something special."

They stood for a long time simply enjoying being in Lucinda's presence.

Eventually, Barry and Nathan became distracted. They wandered around the room eyeing all the medical paraphernalia. "Look at all this stuff!"

Kent glanced around. He did not know what a lot of it was for, let alone how to use it. He had let himself go to seed. He had quit trying, isolated himself from this wonderful profession. So many people would give anything to be a veterinarian, and he had forsaken his privilege as one.

"You know, Barry, if you go to veterinary school, this is what it will be like. No doubt even more, by then."

"Mom always said she didn't want me to be around animals."

"I changed my mind. You'd make a great vet," Aubrey said.

Stef stepped up from behind and gave Kent a pat on the back. "That's the Kent I grew up with."

"As a matter of fact," Kent said, "I've decided I'm going to use the money you're paying me as Copithorn's animal-care supervisor to build a new veterinary hospital in Jefferson." He turned to his brother. "That sound like a good idea to you?"

"Amen to that."

"I'm not going to let you in the new one," Sally said to the chief.

Kent drew a deep breath and released it as he appraised all that surrounded him. "I guess I needed a real jolt to get me fired up again." He looked at Barry. "And I'm going to need some help, you know."

"You mean to take care of Lucinda when she comes home?" Barry said.

"Yes. And to help me in my new hospital after that."

Nathan leaned an elbow onto Barry's shoulder. They bent to where they had a better view of Lucinda. "We're your men."

Kent turned to Marlene. "When do you figure she'll be able to come home?"

"Actually, I don't make that decision. The chiefs will call it. But I know they're concerned that she hasn't eaten anything. No matter what we offer her, she says, *Forget it*. She belongs to a vet and all, so my guess would be they'll discharge her as soon as she starts eating."

"I'll be right back," Barry said and left the room.

Stef spoke to Rodman, who had been keeping his usual low profile while he observed the reunion. "I just can't believe you were able to get Armani back for me. I'm in your debt forever."

"Yeah," Aubrey said, her voice reverberating out of the oxygen cage as she pressed her cheek to Lucinda's. " How amazing is that? You actually smuggled him away from the dogfighters."

Rodman gave them a sheepish look. "Smuggled is too glamorous a way of putting it. The first time I was at Kent's clinic buying medicine—I'm sure you don't remember me being there, but—you came in panicked because Armani was missing. I recognized you as the Copithorn lady. I figured you had suffered enough with the fire and all, but I couldn't very well say, 'Hey, ma'am, I know where your cat is,' so I just made a mental note of his description and left. Next day I was out at May-May's and there he was, scared stiff but otherwise okay. I convinced May-May that even though I was a hard-ass, I liked the looks of that cat and wanted him for my own. He didn't think anything of it. So I took him to my trailer up along the edge of May-May's farm, and he's been hiding out there with me ever since. He's been right in the thick of things the whole time."

"I'll thank you every time I see him curled up on his rug by the fireplace."

"He's a good cat. I think he kind of liked slumming around with me after living in the lap of luxury with you. I just wish I could have saved the rest of them."

"What's going to happen to those SOBs anyway?"

Rodman leaned back against a counter. "Well, the way those boys have turned over to save their own asses, and knowing how bad the attorney general and the USDA want to show that the Animal

Welfare Act has some teeth, I'd say just about all the high rollers will get the maximum."

"Especially since there are Aaron and Tammy's murders with nobody alive to pin them on," Merrill said.

"Don't forget arson," Stef said.

"Right. They'll be looking to string up someone there too. Plus you can throw in a few weapons violations, interstate transport, that sort of thing, and lots of marijuana and coke." He took on a whimsical tone. "Yep. My ol' buddy Lester Ross is going to be cooling his heels for a long while."

The whole group muttered words of satisfaction at that news.

Rodman said, "I had a nice long talk with him. He knows just who dogged him to the bitter end. He can stew on that in jail."

"What about all the videos Aubrey got?" Stef asked.

"They'll have a heyday with that." He gave Aubrey an approving look. "She got everything. No doubt any judge who sees it will be in a hanging mood." Rodman's tone held the contentment of one who had finally received reparation. "I don't care if their lawyers go to Mars for a jury, they'll be cooked when those tapes are shown. I can see the headlines now: Attorney General's Office Takes the Bite Out of Dogfighting."

They turned as Barry burst back into the ICU waving a white paper bag. "I've got what Lucinda needs!"

Aubrey and Stef backed out of the cage. "What is it?"

"Is it okay if I try my secret weapon?" Barry asked Marlene.

"That depends on what your secret weapon *is*."

Barry extracted a foil-covered mass from his bag. "She'll eat a hamburger, if she'll eat anything."

"Ah, kid. I taught you well," Kent said.

Marlene shrugged. "Looks safe enough to me." She held the glass door as Barry leaned in and unwrapped his delicacy.

Instantly, the greasy odor of fast food filled the room. All eyes were on Lucinda as Barry pushed the foil with its juicy contents towards her nose.

No reaction. Barry slid the food closer. For another moment still nothing, then the familiar sparkle appeared in her eyes, and her nostrils began to twitch. Slowly, she lifted her head, rolled upright, and sniffed the burger. She looked out at Barry then back to the burger. She reached down and nibbled it, licked her lips appraisingly then took a good bite.

Barry shook a fist victoriously. "Yes!"

"You're a natural veterinarian," Kent said.

They watched with silent smiles as Lucinda finished her first meal in days.

Marlene eased the door closed. "That's it for now," she said. "A little at a time, but it's a great sign. I'd bet they'll release her in no time if she keeps eating like that."

Aubrey patted her purse. "I'll leave you some burger money."

Barry reached into the bag again and pulled out more hamburgers. "I figured it's after noon, and we haven't eaten since breakfast, so I got some for the rest of us."

Everyone but Aubrey accepted a burger eagerly. Barry handed one to his mother. "Here, Mom, try this. I think you forgot how good they taste."

In the excitement of the moment, Aubrey took the offering. Glancing from her son to the burger, she slowly unwrapped it and cautiously lifted the top roll. A brown disk of beef loomed at her.

Kent, Barry, and the others watched in amazement as she exhaled loudly and with great resolve raised the hamburger to her mouth. Her lips parted. She moved it closer. Then she froze. She set the burger on the counter. "Sorry, guys. This is where I draw the line."

ABOUT THE AUTHOR

Frank Martorana grew up working with animals on several farms around Schenectady, New York, and at the veterinary hospital of Dr. Stanley E. Garrison in nearby Burnt Hills. In 1976, he graduated from the College of Veterinary Medicine at Cornell University. Since then he has been the "family doctor" for countless horses, cows, dogs, cats, and many other creatures around Cazenovia and Hamilton, New York. When he is not treating animals, he is hard at work readying the second and third books of the Kent Stephenson series for publication.

Please visit his website at www.frankmartorana.com

Don't miss the next thriller in the Kent Stephenson Series.

Simpatico's Gift

*It's the middle of the breeding season, and the top stallions
in Kent's practice are being systematically eliminated by
sudden death, rare disease, and mysterious disappearance.
Kent, his teenage daughter, Emily, and his hound, Lucinda,
put their lives on the line to find out who is behind it and
why. What they discover rocks the horse industry.
And it will rock the very soul of any lover of these great beasts.*

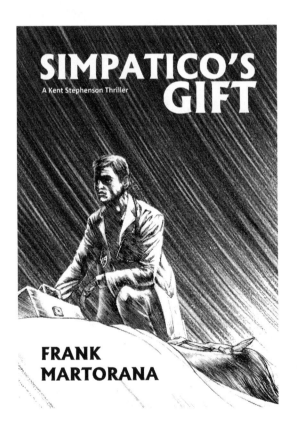

Visit www.frankmartorana.com for updates